Greyl

BRIGHOUSE HOTEL

Susan Pleydell was the *nom de plume* of Isabel Senior, née Syme. She was born in 1907 into a well-to-do farming family at Milnathort, near Kinross. They moved to Dollar when she was in her teens, and later to another farm near Rumbling Bridge. She had great musical ability, inherited from her mother, and after a local education was sent to the Royal College of Music to study the piano. Later she taught at a girls' school in Bexhill at which time she was introduced to Murray Senior, then head of History at Shrewsbury School. They married in 1935. He had two headmasterships in the 1950s, one of a grammar school near Manchester until 1956, the other in South Wales. She taught the piano at Shrewsbury and for some years afterwards.

She had always been well read and having long had an urge to write began in earnest in the mid 1950s. It took a lot of effort to reach publication, but the first novel, *Summer Term,* eventually appeared in 1959. It makes full use of her experience in schools, as does its sequel, *A Young Man's Fancy* (1962). Her other eight novels, the last published in 1977, benefit from her experience in music, her Scottish background – and, of course her own imagination, sympathy and powers of observation.

She died in 1986.

BRIGHOUSE HOTEL

SUSAN PLEYDELL

Greyladies

Published by
Greyladies
an imprint of The Old Children's Bookshelf
175 Canongate, Edinburgh EH8 8BN

© Susan Pleydell 1977

This edition first published 2014
Design and layout © Shirley Neilson 2014

ISBN   978-1-907503-35-1

Set in Sylfaen / Perpetua
Printed and bound by Berforts Information Press Ltd.

BRIGHOUSE HOTEL

ACKNOWLEDGEMENTS

Though the hills of Scotland are in my blood I have never been a climber and therefore I needed a lot of help in writing a story about climbing and the Mountain Rescue Service. For this, and great enjoyment, I am indebted to a few people and many books.

First I want to thank my nephew, T. Murray Syme, without whose knowledge and enthusiasm the story could not even have been begun. My gratitude is also due to Mark Greenstock, leader of the Harrow School "Marmots" Club and to the manager of Kingshouse Hotel, Glencoe, which is the Rescue Centre for that area. The books are too numerous to mention individually, but though they have all contributed something the two which stand out as most valuable are *Call Out* by Hamish McInnes and *One Man's Mountains* by the late Dr Tom Patey.

Brighouse Hotel has a very close, though not exact, resemblance to Kingshouse for which I have a great affection, but it is set in an imaginary glen in Wester Ross. All the characters are fictitious.

S.P.

PROLOGUE

QUITE A NUMBER of people in the restaurant recognized Keith Finlay. They had seen him on television and he had impact. Hirsute and goggled in the Himalayas, clean-shaven in "live" climbs at home, tidily dressed in studios, there was always the unmistakable star quality which outshone everybody else in the picture and lingered in the memory. Not that he could be accused or deliberately stealing the show: though he was one of the greats, possibly the greatest mountaineer of his generation and certainly the most publicized, he made light of his achievements, speaking of them with deprecating amusement. He had simply been endowed by Providence with charm and an extra allowance of vitality—or bounce —which brought him very near flamboyance. And the fact that his father was Sir James Finlay, head of the great building and contracting empire, was no handicap.

Nobody k new the girl with him. She was a tall girl, nearly as tall as Keith who, though well built, was smallish for a man; she had a lovely figure and she walked in with easy, unselfconscious grace. Though she was not a beauty her colouring was nondescript and her features irregular and not strikingly glamorous, she had fine eyes of dark grey and she had style; a rather quiet distinction in marked contrast to Keith's star quality. On the whole, the restaurant considered that if she was Finlay's girl she was not unworthy. But was she? They were clearly on very

5

easy terms but neither showed any sign of emotion.

Clunie Ritchie was not Finlay's girl. She had known the Finlays for as long as she could remember and in Glen Torran, where Sir James owned most of the land and the Ritchies had owned a holiday cottage, she had been Keith's girl for one delirious summer four years ago when she was eighteen. The affair had not survived the winter. The following summer he had roared about with a deb called Diana, a guest at one of the neighbouring shooting lodges, and had apparently forgotten that he had ever singled her, Clunie, out. Since then they had met now and again and a curious relationship had grown up between them. There were long periods when they neither saw nor heard of each other and no reference was ever made to the delirious summer but they had been very much in love. It had left a particular intimacy of a limited kind and under the surface the attraction each had for the other was still there.

It showed briefly in Keith's eyes when they were seated at their table and, so to speak, taking stock. "You're looking good," he remarked. "Marvellous in fact." His frank stare appreciated her dress, her hairdo, her whole style and he grinned at her. "Sophisticated too. What would Kintorran think? It would hardly recognize wee Clunie Ritchie."

She bowed ironic acknowledgment. "Thank you—if it was a compliment."

"Of course it was. I'm all admiration. I'm impressed. Why's it so long since we met?"

"Different orbits," said Clunie. "You're always in distant

6

lands scaling inaccessible peaks, which is something I never do."

"Don't tell me you've given up climbing?" he began and became aware of a waiter at his elbow. "Oh—what'll you drink? Champagne cocktail?"

"Lovely," she said and looked at him with laughing eyes. "Wee Clunie's quite up to it. Debauched by certain standards. How did you get my address, by the way?"

He searched his memory and then said, "Alan. I ran into him in Princes Street last week—or it might have been the week before."

"I'm surprised he remembered it."

"Oh, he didn't remember it. He said I'd find it in the phone book."

"Ah. Quite a feat on your part remembering that. And how was Alan?"

"Seemed much as usual, but I only saw him for a minute. He was off to Patagonia or—no it was Ecuador. He's mad—if you don't mind my saying so."

Clunie didn't mind at all. She had long thought her brother mad. "He's a maniac! Which makes two of you."

"What? I'm not a maniac. I'd say I'm uncommonly sane."

"Of course you're a maniac. But don't imagine I hold it against you. I wouldn't mind being one myself—of the harmless kind like you and Alan. You're never troubled by doubts."

"Are you troubled by doubts?"

"Frequently."

"Well, I'm sorry to hear it," said Keith, "but I don't

admit I'm a maniac. I'm just doing my own thing."

"And with outstanding success," she said cordially. "Alan's just doing his own thing too but his doesn't hit the headlines. Nobody's interested except a few other ethnologists. Perhaps he lacks the necessary flair."

He eyed her suspiciously. "What flair?"

"Oh—showmanship—panache . . . Mind, I don't think he cares a damn whether people are interested or not, but getting on the telly would do him good financially."

"Are you accusing me of exhibitionism?" Keith demanded. "If you want to know it's a damned nuisance, but how far would I get without publicity? It's all very well for Alan. All he does is pack a few spare socks and push off. A climbing expedition's different. It can't be done without money—a lot of money. How are you going to get it? Through publicity. And months of organizing. Backing—personnel—permits—equipment. Equipment! God, it's a nightmare! Lists, lists, lists—I do lists in my sleep."

Manners, said Clunie's conscience. The temptation to needle Keith in his Public Figure mood was almost irresistible but she was his guest. Biting back a reminder to take a tin-opener, she said quite truthfully that the mere thought of the effort involved made her blench and allowed him to choose their dinner from the enormous menu cards presented to them.

When the waiter had gone she raised her glass, saying with a warm and lovely smile, "To the Expedition! It's the Hindu Kush this time, isn't it? I don't know anything about it except that it's in Afghanistan. Alan's been there but he's only interested in the people. Who's going? Anybody I know?"

Keith's slight huffiness cleared. Clunie's smile would have dispelled worse sulks than he indulged in and he was pleased that she knew about the Hindu Kush. The party was to be small, he said. The current trend favoured small manoeuvrable groups. Clunie intelligently suggested a comparison with commandoes and he approved. "That sort of thing. Only four lead climbers and a few extras. Three or four vehicles will take the lot. Oh, this'll interest you. Your boyfriend's coming. Malcolm Graham."

"Malcolm?" She was surprised. "My poor Keith, you're sadly behind the times. I haven't seen or heard of Malcolm since we sold the cottage three years ago."

"Haven't you? I gather he's remained faithful to your memory, however," said Keith amused but alert.

"Well, I suppose that's flattering," she said. "If it's true. But how would you know? He's probably got a dozen girls in Glasgow—if that's where he is."

He laughed. "Not him. Yes, he's in Glasgow when he's not at home in Kintorran, and if he'd even taken a girl to the pictures the whole glen would know about it."

This was not so exaggerated as it sounded. As Clunie well knew, Kintorran gossiped as much as small towns normally do and the grapevine was wonderfully efficient. The Grahams, too, were a united family who had no secrets from each other. "Are they still as 'Scots wha hae' and mistrustful of foreign parts?" she asked.

"Oh, more so. The doctor never goes farther than Inverness now. Once Malcolm came to Switzerland with

9

me for some climbing and you'd have thought he was going to the moon. Or the dogs."

"You must have been very persuasive to make them let him venture to the Hindu Kush," said Clunie. "Was it worth it? I'd have thought you'd want someone with wider experience, especially in a small party. More like Andy McKillop."

"Well, Malcolm won't grow any less green if he stays where he is," Keith pointed out. "He's a very good climber—there aren't many better—and he's wasted teaching general subjects to the lower third and hauling novices up the Torrans."

"Is that what he's doing?"

"That's his life. I thought about Andy of course, but he's getting on and he's very busy running the glen: rescue service, mountaineering school, training courses—the lot. Besides, though Malcolm's experience is limited he's had plenty of it and I like climbing with him. We're a good team."

And he's docile, thought Clunie. More experienced men might argue with the leader but it would never occur to Malcolm to question Keith's judgment. She made no further comment, however, and Keith talked on about the planning of his expedition. Clearly he badly wanted to talk, preferably to someone who knew enough about climbing to understand the language and necessarily to one who was safe. It poured out like a torrent, neither very comprehensible nor very interesting, but there was no need to listen very closely.

The soup came, chilled and delicious, and Keith broke

off to choose the wine. The soup was followed by whitebait, the whitebait by slices of succulent sirloin and then a perfect sorbet. Clunie ate and drank with the enjoyment of a healthy girl who normally makes extensive use of convenience foods and recalled other meals with Keith: hunks of pork pie on hilltops, substantial Scottish teas at the Grahams' house or their own cottage, and her first grown-up dinner at Kintorran Lodge, a grand baronial mansion in the style of Balmoral, where Sir James was jocular, Lady Finlay awe-inspiring and the food moderate. They had had wonderful holidays in Glen Torran when they were children and young teenagers but it wasn't the kind of thing that lasts. Alan grew tired of it, seized by the wanderlust that still held him, and her parents neither shared D and Mrs Graham's exclusive devotion to Scotland nor their belief that families should cling together. It was time, they thought, that Clunie widened her horizons and they themselves would welcome variety. For Clunie the end of the Kintorran cottage was an escape. She had never gone back to the glen.

Enjoying the whitebait while Keith compared the merits of various makes of equipment she reflected on the mysteriousness of love. She had never really liked Keith above half: she saw his faults with merciless clarity; he was selfish, insensitive and often surprisingly dense, but it made no difference. And green as she was that awful summer when Malcolm Graham saved her face, she knew that Keith was not only hurting her, he was hurting—damaging—himself. He didn't care a rap for the gorgeous

Diana. He was using her as a way out of something that threatened to involve him and for the first time Clunie wondered if he had hurt Diana too. She looked hardened but looks can be deceptive.

With the sirloin he passed from equipment to financial backing and negotiations with the Press and television, and this was Keith at his most likeable. His descriptions of people and interviews were graphic and he looked at her with a disarming sort of giggle, inviting her to laugh with him at his cleverness, his act.

Clunie did laugh but she was a good deal shaken up. Keith in this mood, honest and comradely, his best self, brought back the past too vividly. And brought back the past in another way. Seeing him, listening to climbers' talk, climbers' jargon, she saw the Torrans, her own mountains, the hills of home. She smelt the fresh highland smells, felt the exaltation of boots and hands on rocks . . .

"Oh!" she cried. "How homesick I am for the glen—the hills!"

Keith looked mildly interrupted. "Well go," he said. "There's nothing to stop you. I'll be there from about the middle of August. I want to get the team together for two or three weeks of hard training before Malcolm goes back to his stupid school."

"I'm so—I've completely lost touch."

"You wouldn't feel that when you got there. Everybody's exactly the same, only more so."

"And where would I stay? I can't rise to the Brig or—" she made a face, "—the Bethune Arms."

"The Grahams?"

12

"Oh . . . no."

"No," he agreed. "They're a hell of a strain. Well, come to the Lodge."

She laughed. "That would surprise your mother."

His mother wouldn't be there, he said. "Hasn't been for years. Spends most of her time in the south of France." He grinned suddenly. "But it would be perfectly respectable. Gavin and Moira will he there. You know Gavin's married?"

Clunie had heard about the marriage of the elder Finlay son. "It sounded very suitable," she said. "Is she nice?"

"No," was the reply. "Worthy. So's Gavin of course."

"Oh. But what a comfort for Sir James to have one steady son worthily married."

"Comfort!" Keith jeered. "They bore the old man to death. Gavin was always the dullest of God's creatures and Moira's worse. You'd detest her. But why not come, Clunie? You wouldn't have to see much of Moira. I don't."

She shook her head. 'No. I don't think so. Probably not at all. Certainly not to the Lodge. *Think* of the talk."

"Oh the hell with that. Who cares?" he said airily. You do, thought Clunie, when you remember about it. "We could do some climbs," he was going on. "I won't be busy all the time."

"Thank you," she said. "What could be more delightful? Flapping about on the end of a rope with the famous Finlay's curses blistering my ears."

He laughed at her. 'All the same you shouldn't give up climbing. You looked like being quite good."

She thanked him again. "Praise indeed," she said

13

politely.

They spent a long time over their dinner and the talk never flagged but as he drove her home Keith fell silent and at the door of her flat he took her hand and said, "You wouldn't ask me in, I suppose?"

"Why certainly," said Clunie. "Come in and meet Tina."

His look was eloquent. "That Presbyterian conscience."

"Two Presbyterian consciences, Keith."

"I suppose so. One's manageable, I find. Just. If I overstep the mark Grandpa Walter gives me hell."

"Is he the one who glowers down from over the dining-room fireplace?"

"That's him. I never knew him, I'm glad to say. The portrait's bad enough. The reason Gavin's so virtuous is that he sat facing the thing every mealtime. I had my back to it."

Clunie laughed and he smiled and put his arm round her. For a moment they looked at each other and then he was holding her closely. Though he was not a big man he was very strong. If she had wanted to break away it would have been difficult but she didn't want to.

Presently he let her go. There was a pause and then he gave her a little shake and said, "Well . . . see you some time," and went running down the stairs. The house door banged. Clunie heard his car start and roar away.

She turned to the door of the flat. "Oh damn!" she said. "Damn, damn, damn . . ."

CHAPTER ONE

A SMALL ROWAN TREE, wizened and dejected but making a brave show of red berries, gave the sodden landscape its only touch of colour and Pat McKechnie looked at it kindly. He admired its determination to survive. Solitary, exposed, growing out of a cracked boulder, it must have sent roots a long way down to reach any sort of soil and it wouldn't find much nourishment when it got there. The only thing it did have in plenty was water.

Pat was sitting becalmed in his car with the window down, adding cigarette smoke to the smells of wet highlands and overheated metal and listening without much hope for the sound of some other vehicle. Except for himself and the rowan tree the glen seemed to be empty. The only sounds were the hissings and creaks from his suffering engine, steady rain and the water gurgling in the swollen river and pouring in torrents off the mountains. He was annoyed but not unduly. His was a philosophical temperament and the car might have sat down in many a worse place—in fact if she had managed to stagger on for two more miles he would have been home and dry though not precisely where he intended to be.

The clouds were right down, no sign of a break anywhere. The Torrans were big mountains but for all that could be seen they might not be there and even at

15

road level visibility was almost nil, though officially it would be daylight for hours yet. Pat sighed and threw away the end of his cigarette. Nothing for it but to start walking. From the litter of gear in the back of the car he brought out his fishing hat, a battered felt garnished with flies, and buttoning his oilskin up to his chin set out—forward since there was nothing behind him but miles of empty glen.

He was a big man, six feet three in his socks and power-fully though not heavily built, with sandy hair and small, genial, blue eyes. Like many very big men he gave an impression of unruffleable good-humour, but the eyes were shrewd as well as genial and it was well known that there were no flies on Pat McKechnie, which was one reason why, though still under thirty, he was responsible for the management of Sir James Finlay's Scottish estates and enterprises. It was one of the enterprises he was heading for now: the Brighouse Hotel.

Two miles beyond the bridge which gave the hotel its name the glen came to an end with the little one street town of Kintorran on the shore of a sea loch. It was a holiday resort of a modest kind, particularly suitable for families with growing children for it had a safe beach, a couple of hard tennis courts and an almost perpendicular golf course. The families stayed in rooms, rented a house or in some cases bought one. Older holidaymakers, mostly fishermen with their wives, stayed in the Bethune Arms. Pleasure steamers called regularly in the season bringing tourists who wandered about for an hour or so and turned over the stock in Aggie Todd's Gift Shop. On a hump a little way out of the town on the northern, Glen Torran side, Castle Tornay, mostly ruined but still inhabited, stared glumly at the loch; on the southern side there was Kintorran Lodge, nineteenth-century baronial, but neither was a tourist attraction and Kintorran was in fact an uneventful little town, very much what it had been fifty years ago.

In the last ten years, however, a great deal had happened in the glen. For this there were two reasons. The first was the immense growth of interest in climbing and the consequent opening up of new mountaineering grounds. Glen Torran in Wester Ross was more remote than the Cairngorms, Glencoe or Ben Nevis, but motor transport made it accessible and it had some good publicity. Andrew McKillop, a climber of international fame and author of several books, lived in the glen and was, so to speak, the spearhead of the development, gathering around him a team of good instructors and guides; and Keith Finlay, a hero worshipped by young climbers, made it his base.

Sir James Finlay was the second reason for the rise in Glen Torran's status. Much that had been happening to his native land in the last decades infuriated Sir James and though even he was powerless against most of it there were some matters in which he could act. Conservation was one, the tourist industry was another. Though he had nothing against tourism, which was legitimate business and highly profitable, certain aspects of it disgusted him. The spurious Bonny Scotland—vulgar kiltie dolls and sprigs of white plastic heather; hotels upholstered in tartan with kilted landlords, endless piped reels and strathspeys and strange dishes that honest Scots had never heard of—these, he said, were a desecration of his country's heritage and he began buying land and hotels with the right potential.

Glen Torran was the starting point. When taxation and death duties forced the Bethune family to sell he bought the estate and made Kintorran Lodge his country home. And the Brighouse Hotel, a modest old inn modernized and extended, was perhaps the brightest gem of his collection.

Pat McKechnie marched steadily towards it. For so big a man who had already spent a long day on the hills with shepherds and foresters his step was surprisingly light and he was too well accustomed to being out in all weathers to bother about wet clothes. Indeed he was reflecting that it was almost worth the two-mile trudge for the enhanced pleasure of arriving. A few days before he had heard someone talking about the Brighouse Hotel, a stranger who had no idea of his, Pat's, connection with it. The man was one of a party of climbers and he was describing Glen Torran from the climber's angle. The Torrans, he said, not only offered a variety of good climbs, some of them first class, they were virtually unknown outside Scotland and the more dedicated members of the climbing fraternity. And there was this hotel. The Brig, they called it. The speaker had been quite lyrical about the hotel. "Nothing fancy," he had assured his listeners earnestly, "but it's got all you want. Good food, good beds; it's warm and there's lashings of hot water . . . And—" he grinned suddenly—

"damn good company."

Coming round a bend in the road Pat crossed the bridge, the peaty water of the Torran surging and creaming under it, passed a low white building, rather complex in shape, which was the hotel and went on to the last of a cluster of small satellites on which a board said MACKINTOSH. Built on to a cottage which bore a strong family resemblance to the old inn, it had been designed as a byre or stable, probably a combination of both, with a cart shed. It was still a multiple purpose building; part garage, part forge with a bit of carpentry and a quantity of climbing equipment. As the proprietor said, anybody like himself who wanted to live in the glen and be his own boss had to be a Johnnie-a'-things, picking up a bit here and a bit there. It was an untidy-looking place, but though his system might be obscure it was a highly efficient workshop for a highly efficient man. As Pat entered he came forward from a well-lit workbench, smallish and broad-shouldered with oily overalls and a cloth cap worn well back.

"It's you," he said and looked amiably at the sodden figure dripping on to his floor. "Ye're a wee thing damp, I doubt."

"It's raining," said Pat economically. "I need a tow, Tosh."

"Oh aye? What seems to be the trouble?"

"Fuel pump. I hoped she'd just get me here but she packed up two miles short."

Even as he spoke the rescue operation was under way. Mackintosh slung a stout sack round his shoulders and fastened it with a safety pin as he went towards an elderly and very dirty Land Rover.

"We'll get her in the dry," he said, "and then see can we sort it. I'm no very hopeful. I doubt I'll no lay my hands on a pump the night and it's no a thing ye can improvise. You bide here. I'll no be long."

This order was addressed to a large powerful collie which had got to its feet but sat down again obediently as the two men climbed into the car. It was characteristic of Tosh that he didn't bother to check his equipment. Among the mass of objects in the back of the Land Rover everything he needed would be ready to his hand.

"She might easy have set ye down in a worse place," he remarked as he drove past the hotel. "What about the timing? Are ye in a hurry?"

He was on his way to Edinburgh, Pat said, but there was no emergency. "Think you can get it done tomorrow?"

"Oh aye," said Tosh. "It's no a long job once I get the pump. I'll phone through and it'll be here in the forenoon."

Pat didn't ask where the pump would come from or how. Tosh had his methods and at this stage he wouldn't know himself which of his contacts would supply the pump, what car, van or lorry would be coming down the glen anyway and drop it off. Instead he said that if he got to Edinburgh tomorrow afternoon it would do. "I had a date tonight but nothing that can't be put off and it's nice to have an excuse to stay where I am."

"Aye, it's no the day for a pleasure trip," said Tosh

peering into the murk ahead. He cursed the weather which had, he said, been bluidy awful for the last four days. "It looked a wee thing more hopeful early the day but no for long. There's a lot o' wearied folk wondering should they go or stay." The weather was a matter of close concern. Though he was not in the great McKillop's class he was a well-known and highly experienced professional climber and what he earned as a guide and instructor was an important part of his income. But he was philosophical. "Ah weel, ye jist have to take what comes," he concluded and changed the subject. "Did ye hear about Morag? She's in the hospital."

"Dear me,' said Pat. 'Nothing serious, I hope?"

"Och no. Appendix jist. They reckon she'll be back in about a month."

"Poor Morag, though—and poor Harry. How's he managing?" Harry Craig was the manager of the hotel and Morag, the receptionist, was a foundation member of the staff and one of its mainstays. It was difficult to imagine the place without her but Tosh, with a gleam of amusement, said Harry had been lucky.

"Ye'll mind the Ritchies that had a house in Kintorran? They sold it two-three years back; like enough they fancied a change and Alan was aye a wanderer. No telling where he might be but Clunie, the lassie, took a fancy to come back and wrote asking Harry if he'd got a job for her. So Harry got his stand-in wi' nae bother." Tosh gave a brief chuckle. "I wouldnae say but what Malcolm Graham might have something to do wi't, or it could be Keith Finlay. The both o' them were boyfriends o' Clunie's at one time or another. Aye, she's a great lass and a bonny one to my mind—no jist ordinary. Seemingly she's been working down in London."

He remembered Clunie well, Pat said. "I haven't seen her for years but we saw a lot of the Ritchies at one time." Tosh remarked respectfully that it was likely they would, Dr Ritchie and Dr McKechnie both being professors, but Pat was still thinking about Clunie. "She hated my guts when she was little," he said as if the memory was highly diverting.

"I wouldnae wonder but ye asked for it," said Tosh.

"Quite likely," Pat admitted. "She was a little devil though. I hear Keith's mounting another expedition. The Hindu Kush this time, isn't it? Is he here?"

"No, but he's got the go-ahead and from what I heard he'll be back any day and a couple o' lads he's trying out for the team."

"Is Andy going?"

"No him," said Tosh. "Andy says in this team the emphasis is on youth and," he added dryly, "on Keith. He's no that keen on youth, Andy. Malcolm Graham's going though. This'll be your vehicle . . ."

Half an hour later Pat, carrying his suitcase, stepped thankfully into the hotel porch. Two pairs of wet climbing boots with socks stuffed into them stood on the stone floor, reminding him to wipe his feet. Harry Craig didn't mind people dripping on to his hall carpet which was designed to take it, but he was bitter about muddy footprints. He opened the inner door and in the receptionist's office a girl turned from a filing cabinet and

22

removed a pencil from her mouth as she came forward to the desk.

For a moment she and Pat looked at each other in surprised silence and then her eyes lit with laughter. "Have you wiped your feet?' she demanded.

"Thoroughly," said Pat.

"Well, what about shutting the door?" He obeyed and she surveyed him calmly. "Did you fall in the river?"

In a very patient tone he explained that it was raining and his car had died on him two miles up the road. He then greeted her. "Hallo, Clunie. Maybe ye dinna mind o' me?"

"Oh aye, I mind ye fine," was the response. "Hallo, Pat." He put his case on the floor and his sodden hat on top of it. "You've worn well," he remarked. "It's years since I saw you."

She agreed, adding cordially that it hadn't seemed a day too long. "Do you still think 'womans is a nuisance'?"

"What? Me? I never—"

"Certainly you did. At least that's what Alan said when he came swaggering back after being let play in your lot."

"Oh. Well, my views have changed. Or moderated. I'm in favour of women—in their place."

"What's that?"

He shook his head. "We'll leave that for another time. But you're wrong, you know. It was your youth not your sex that was against you. You were very small."

"Dah!" said Clunie. "Blatant discrimination. I suppose you want a room." She reached for the register. "And you'd better get out of those wet clothes before you catch

23

your death. Have a bath. Do you prefer a small room with a view of Torran Mhor or a more spacious apartment overlooking the car park?"

"I'll have Torran Mhor," said Pat. "And I'm touched by your concern. Big of you, I suppose, considering the way you harbour grudges."

It was her duty, she replied, to look after the welfare of guests, and the last thing the hotel wanted was guests with streaming colds. As she turned to get the key to his room the manager appeared from his office behind the reception area.

"Losh, man, you're drookit," he said. "I heard you had a spot of trouble. Got his room fixed, Clunie? Oh—you do know each other, don't you?"

"We do," said Pat. "Ancient foes. I thought it was just elephants that never forget but they're not alone. Thanks," he added with a grin at Clunie as she handed him the key.

Harry Craig's eyebrows rose but he wasted no time. They could carry on their war later, he said, but what Pat wanted now was a bath. "And a drink. I'll send it to your room. You go on."

Pat went, giving Clunie a vulgar wink and feeling remarkably cheerful. The lyrical man hadn't said a word too much. The Brig had indeed got all you want. He made his way along a passage which led from the old inn to the extension behind it; a low narrow passage with doors on each side and short passages going off at right angles. There were glimpses of a lounge with picture windows and an equally modern dining-room, and among others a cheerful sign pointed to BAR. There was no display of luxury but solid unpretentious comfort and efficiency. Sir James Finlay and Harry Craig had done a good job and the architect had shared Sir James's dislike of "anything fancy".

Presently as he relaxed in hot water, peaty brown in colour and soft as silk, he mused drowsily about chance and silver linings. Take that pump. An unmitigated nuisance it had seemed at the time but if it hadn't gone when it did he would have driven straight through and might not have been in Glen Torran again for weeks. In that case he would very likely have missed Clunie. Little devil though she was he had always liked her. She had spirit. A grin appeared in Pat's eyes as he recalled instances of Clunie's spirit. The difference in their fighting weight never deterred her: when her dander was up she bored in regardless and many a painful hack his shins had suffered.

Tosh had the idea that either Malcolm Graham or Keith Finlay might have something to do with her return to the glen. Pat reached for a towel, dried his hands and lit a cigarette. Then he drank some whisky and lay back to think about it. He, Pat, thought the glen itself was reason enough, but if Tosh was right Keith seemed the more likely. Malcolm, though a good-looking chap, a first class climber and as nice a guy as you could meet, was dull. Worthy was the adjective which came to mind. Nobody could accuse Keith of worthiness; his brilliance as a climber—and he was brilliant—was matched by his showmanship and a strong business sense inherited from his father and he exploited it without scruple. Clunie would be safer with Malcolm but how bored she would be! With all his faults Keith was not boring and Pat was far from disliking him but he wouldn't suit Clunie. Nor, when he came to think about it, would Clunie suit Keith. She had no capacity for hero-worship.

Greatly diverted Pat tossed off the whisky and surged out of the bath. He would watch the progress of events with interest—or would he? He paused for thought, water streaming down him on to the bath mat. Yes he would. One of the many advantages of his job was that he largely made his own timetable. When he got back to Edinburgh he would see if a holiday which was overdue because he hadn't known what to do with it could be taken now and combined with Glen Torran estates business.

Clunie would have been pleased to hear of this plan. It was a long time since she had thought about Pat McKechnie but she was really very glad to see him again and regretted that he was merely passing through.

The week since she had arrived at the Brig had been depressing. She had forgotten how foul the weather could be: the mountains, the hills of home, for which her nostalgia had grown into an almost physical hunger, had been hidden by mist and driving rain. And she had forgotten too how long her old friends' memories were and how limited their interests. Nobody wanted to hear what she had been doing, what she had seen in the years since she had last been in the glen. They couldn't wait to find out whether the magnet that had drawn her back was Keith Finlay or Malcolm Graham. There had been moments when she felt that returning to places and people that belong to the past was not a good idea.

But the sight of her old enemy, so vast, cheerful and uncomplicated, had cheered her up. Though she had hated him with her whole heart when she was small the antagonism had lingered only as the Pat-Clunie relationship. It was the form. When they met they fought and the fights, on the whole, were highly enjoyable. And she could see now that Pat had done her a good turn when she was five years old. The Ritchies and the McKechnies had spent that summer together while the two learned fathers collaborated in writing a book, and her rigorous exclusion from the big boys' games taught her a valuable lesson. There was no future in trotting about at Alan's heels. Indeed it is a mistake to trot after anybody.

The bar at the Brig was a convivial place in the evenings. It was a large pleasantly decorated apartment which contained a hard-bitten piano and could easily be cleared for dancing or a ceilidh. Though the hotel was geared for climbers and hill walkers, with fishermen recognized as fellow creatures, there were guests who were interested in none of these pursuits. Some of these spent their evenings in the lounge with books or knitting, others ventured into the bar as spectators. Harry had once remarked that they reminded him of visitors to the zoo, or, when he was feeling gloomy, of those who in bygone times went along to have a good laugh at the inmates of Bedlam. Not, he said, that he blamed the onlookers in his bar: climbers were all more or less mad and when Andy McKillop and Tosh and a few others got going there was plenty of entertainment.

It was always easy to tell the sheep from the goats. The sheep, openly listening or pretending not to, sat at tables remote from the bar itself. The goats congregated near it in voluble groups. They were the Glen Torran climbers, ranging from Andy McKillop, the doyen, and Keith Finlay, the star, to the boys and girls from bothies and tents and those members of the hotel staff who combined earning with climbing. One of these was the barman, a big blond young man with a beard and longish hair which made him look like a Viking, and an air of unassuming good-humour.

"I hear you got stuck," he said when Pat went in after dinner.

"So I did, Tom," said Pat, "but it would be kinder not to mention it."

Tom smiled. "Oh, you're sensitive. I'm used to it myself."

"I dare say. We all know your van—tied together with string and kept going by will-power."

"And Tosh."

"And, of course, Tosh," Pat agreed. "Well, I had its brother in my time but I'm past it now. At my age a man likes to be reasonably sure of getting to where he's going in comfort." He looked round, exchanging nods with acquaintances. "Everybody's very subdued. Weather getting you down?"

Tom said it had been terrible. "We've had about a week of it and nothing to do but hang about or get soaked going for dreich walks."

28

"It'll clear eventually. But somebody's been climbing. I saw a couple of pairs of very wet boots in the porch. Hardly worth it, I'd have thought: neither pleasant nor safe."

"No," said Tom, "but you can't wonder. If you've come a long way and your time and maybe your money's running out it takes a lot to stop you."

Andy McKillop appeared beside them. "And that's one of the things that makes jobs for the rescue boys," he said. "Aye then, Pat. You got stuck they tell me."

With a speaking glance at Tom, Pat returned the greeting. "Aye, ye auld so-and-so. What'll you have?" Andy said he would just have his usual. "And have something yourself, Tom," said Pat.

Where, Andy asked, had he come from today and Pat described his day which had been spent going round hill farms and plantations. "Damned wet," he said, "but a bit more visibility than here. The shepherds say it'll clear tomorrow. Any news in this neck o' the woods?"

"Well, you'll have heard about Morag," said Andy. "Clunie Ritchie's doing the job." A faint amusement appeared on his face, a reflection of Tosh's "Malcolm Graham or Keith Finlay?" expression, but Tom was unaware of such undercurrents.

"Poor Clunie," he said. "She can't wait to get her boots on and she's never even got a sight of the hills. She was asking today if they're still here."

"She's a climber, is she?" said Pat. "I'd forgotten that. Or maybe I never knew. I remember Alan climbing but Clunie might have been a bit too young."

Andy said that Clunie had done quite a lot. More than her brother whose heart was never in it. "She was good, no bad at all, but seemingly she didn't keep it up after they left here."

As he spoke Clunie herself came into the bar with Malcolm Graham, an exceptionally handsome young man whose regular features and splendid athletic body reminded those who thought in such terms of a Greek god. His normal expression which never varied much was one of simple kindliness, but it delighted observers by becoming worshipful when he looked at Clunie and he smiled very pleasantly at the sight of a friend.

"Hallo, Pat," he said. "I hear you got stuck. Bad luck."

"Oh, I wouldn't say that," said Pat. "If I hadn't I might not have seen Clunie for another fifty years and what a loss that would have been." He beamed benevolently at Clunie and Malcolm looked surprised.

"I thought you and Clunie always fought."

Pat shook his head. "Not me. I'm a man of peace myself, but with Clunie a grudge, imaginary in the first place, rankles for life. Still, she's welcome to lash out if it makes her happy. She's lost a bit of her edge among these London smoothies but she does her best."

"You haven't felt my edge," said Clunie. "It's my duty to be courteous to guests. I never even hinted that you just staged this breakdown so's you could get in out of the rain."

"What? Two miles up the glen in this weather?" cried Pat. "I've more nous."

"Nous?" said Malcolm.

"Just a swank word for sense," she told him and Pat kindly explained that he had missed out on his father's brains but he thought nous was really more useful.

"I never heard that Clunie takes after her father either," he added. "About her nous I don't know, but I'm sure she has many excellent qualities."

"Well, we've only your word for your nous," Clunie retorted. *"And* that you stuck two miles up the glen. You were wet before you started."

"I'm sorry, Clunie lass," Tosh put in from the background, "but I canna support ye. I'm a witness and it was a good two miles."

"Oh Tosh!" cried Clunie.

"Have a drink, Tosh," said Pat. "Have two drinks."

Tosh said, "One'll do for the now." He nodded at Tom who needed no further instruction and told Pat he had been on the blower. "The pump'll be here first thing the morn wi' the fish van. Ye'll be in Edinburgh—" He broke off as Harry Craig came in through a door behind the bar. "Ah, ah! Wait for it, boys."

CHAPTER TWO

"OCH NO HARRY, don't say it," begged Andy McKillop. "No the nicht, m'n."

"I'm not going to say it—not yet," said Harry. "Clunie, Miss Glover and her friend didn't check out, did they?"

"Miss Glover?" Clunie thought back. "No. They booked for three nights. Why? Aren't they in?"

"No. Where were they going? You asked, I suppose?"

Though the hotel had, of course, no authority, it was the custom to find out tactfully where guests proposed to walk or climb, particularly in bad weather and more particularly if the guests were not known. Miss Glover and Miss Thompson who had arrived the night before were strangers.

Under cover of friendly interest Clunie had discovered that they were going to do the Ridge Walk which involved sixteen miles of hard walking with a little scrambling thrown in.

"Och hail!" Andy exclaimed disgustedly. "You should have stopped them."

"I tried. I told them it wasn't a good day for it but all I got was a snub. Miss Glover said, 'Thanks, my dear, but we're not novices, you know.' And of course it didn't look so bad in the morning."

"What time did they leave?"

"It would be about half past nine. They were annoyed because they had to wait for their lunch packets while somebody checked out. One of them was saying why the heck couldn't they get them from the kitchen, but Harry's orders were that all lunches were to come to the office. Pity he wasn't at the desk."

Andy said it wouldn't have made any difference. "Some folk just won't be told," and Pat asked if their car was in the park.

"It's there. I looked," said Harry gloomily. It was impossible to tell whether he would prefer the ladies to have departed without paying or be lost on the Ridge.

"What's the time now?" Andy looked at the clock. "Ten to nine. We'll give them a wee while yet."

"I think I'll awa' to my bed," said Tosh. "I've Pat's car to sort the morn's mornin' and I'm no as young as I was."

They had kept their voices low but the slight air of tension round the bar had begun to interest the more observant spectators and Harry, looking a little annoyed, turned his back. "Who's here?" he asked. A rapid glance counted heads and he looked at Andy. "It's bloody dark already."

"It'll not get much darker though," Andy said deliberately. "And they should be safe enough if they've got any sense." It could be, he went on, that when they actually saw the clouds right down on the Ridge they changed their plans and went elsewhere.

"In fact they could be anywhere," said Harry. "Going round in circles as like as not."

"Well, if they're as expert as they made out they'll have a compass, but they could easy miscalculate distance and it'd be terrible slow going."

33

"I wonder did anybody see them?" said Tosh. "But I doubt nobody would be on the hills and visibility was about zero."

Pat remembered the two pairs of wet boots in the porch. "Whose were those?"

Clunie frowned, searching her memory. "Nobody said they were going climbing, but two men checked in just before you came. They had rucksacks." She looked round the room and indicated two men reading at a distant table. "That's them. Mr Pope and I forget the other one's name."

The men, approached by Harry, proved to be strangers to the glen and not at all communicative. One of them revealed reluctantly that they were on a walking holiday, collecting climbs, so to speak, as they went. Anxious to add at least one Torrans ascent to their bag they had, in view of the conditions, chosen an easy way up Torran Beag—the Small Torran.

"We had no difficulty," said the spokesman, "but it wasn't a lot of fun. And no view of course. We—or I— did see a couple of people on the hill. Not at all clearly and I wasn't all that interested." No, it was impossible to tell if they were men or women.

Could he, Harry asked patiently, show them on the map exactly where they were when he saw them? "If they are the people we think they are they're very much overdue."

"Well, I don't know that I can be very exact," said Mr Pope. He got up, keeping his place in his book with a finger, and followed Harry across to a large wall map while his silent friend returned to his reading. Andy joined them.

"This is Andrew McKillop," said Harry. "Our Rescue leader."

The introduction was acknowledged with a nod. "Ah. How d'do," and the map was scrutinized. Around the bar delighted glances were exchanged.

"I'd say it was about here," the pronouncement came at last. "Yes, just about here." The pointing finger moved. "We'd be about there. Quite a way off, you see." Mr Pope stared at the map for a moment longer. "I don't think you have anything to worry about you know," he said. "They seemed to be plodding along all right and there's nothing they could fall off, is there? Not at the height they were." He gave a collective nod and went back to his friend.

"Nothing like being cut down to size once in a while for the good of the soul," said Tosh gleefully.

Andy McKillop raised his eyebrows. "Meaning me? There are an awful lot of ignorant folk in the world and you know the way I shun publicity. I'm a modest man."

"I suppose you are really, considering you're the man that invented mountains," said Harry.

Pat had never seen the Glen Torran Rescue Service in action but he knew better than to offer his services. Whether you were a candidate for the regular team or merely happened to be present as he was now you waited to be invited, however experienced you might be, and Andy would know he was ready if wanted. He stayed silent, watching and listening while the operation was prepared.

Harry, who liked to be beforehand with events, went to organize flasks of hot coffee and check equipment from

35

the store—torches, headlights, R/T . . . Andy recruited his team.

"We'll no need many," he said. "No yet, any road." His eyes went round collecting Malcolm, Tom and two husky undergraduates from the bothy who were regular Glen Torran climbers. They stopped at Tosh, taking him for granted. "We'll take the dogs, Tosh," he said and as if at a signal both the big Alsatian which was his own and Tosh's collie got up from the corner where they had been snoozing, stretched luxuriously and stood with pricked ears. "Now, Clunie," said Andy.

"Yes," said Clunie. It sounded a little thick and she cleared her throat.

"You've got the list?" She nodded and he told her very precisely what he wanted her to do and then gave her a friendly grin. "You'll manage fine," he said. "It's not a major operation this. Just a nice wee practice for you."

Tosh had already disappeared and Tom, whose place behind the bar had been taken by a young waiter. Malcolm said, "Well, cheerio, Clunie. Maybe see you later," and followed.

"Can I give you a hand?" Pat asked as she turned to the door.

She paused. "Do you know anything about R/T?"

"Och aye," said Pat. "I was in the signal section at school. Nothing to it."

"Come on then," she said.

She was nervous. It was, as Andy had said, not a major operation, just what Harry called a mug-hunt and very different from a callout when a serious, perhaps fatal

36

accident was reported or suspected, or, most nightmarish of all, an avalanche. But this was the job at which Morag excelled. Morag knew the drill so well that she hardly needed briefing. She could assess the urgency of a call and the scale of operation required and it was not unknown for her to have appropriate forces mobilized before the leader had time to act. Calls went out, messages were relayed correctly and at top speed, vital contacts were maintained. Clunie had been shown how the R/T worked, she had studied the full callout list and, so to speak, learned the language, and the list Andy had given her was short, but she was going to be slow. Having to read every name and number was very different from knowing them all by heart, having the whole process at your finger-ends.

The manager's office, which was communications HQ, was just behind and opening out of the receptionist's office with another door giving access to the kitchen, dining-room and bar. Clunie, taking station as instructed, looked with dislike at the R/T but that horror would come later. Telephoning was the first job.

"If you give me the list I'll read out the numbers as you want them," said Pat. She handed it over and he began, "Jimsie Black, 623."

Clunie dialled the number. "Mountain Rescue," she said clearly.

Four men who lived in the vicinity, two shepherds, a gamekeeper and a forester, were instructed to stand by and on receipt of a further call go up to the Ridge at the points nearest their homes. They were told the approximate place and time the missing women were thought to have been seen and each was given the direction his search was to follow. Those who had trained dogs were to take them.

"Good," said Pat when this stage was completed. "Now all we have to do is tell the police the search is on and alert Dr Graham, or failing him the next medico. Police number . . ."

The police, like the four team members, listened and responded briefly. The next and final call brought the first waste of time.

"Mountain Rescue," said Clunie. "Is Dr Graham available?"

"He's out at the moment," was the reply. "Is that you, Clunie?"

Clunie said, "Hallo, Jean," and repeated, "is your father available to stand by? There's a callout."

"Oh, is there? Well, I should think he'll be in at any minute, but hang on and I'll ask Mother." Pause. "Yes, she says he'll be here. What's the callout for? Anything serious?"

"Not too serious, I hope. Two women not returned from the Ridge."

"Good lord! The *Ridge* on a day like this! What fools some people are. Malcolm's gone out, I suppose? Look, Clunie, would you like me to come up? I mean you're new to it and two heads are better than one."

When communicating with Jean Graham by telephone it was advisable to hold the receiver at some distance from the ear. Clunie caught Pat's eye and a snort of laughter escaped her. Jean was her oldest friend and she was fond of her—most of the time—but her eager desire to help was often a trial. "No, dear," she said. "Pat's assisting. He was in the signal section at school and he's got nous."

"He's got what?"

"Nous. Oh, never mind. Tell your father we'll call him if he's needed. 'Bye, Jean."

"Just as well that was the last call," Pat remarked dispassionately. "A nice smooth performance otherwise. What do we do now? May as well get the set warmed up."

Clunie gave the R/T another suspicious glance. "I hope your nous is reliable. I've forgotten all Harry told me about the thing and your school experience must be dated."

"No need to panic," said Pat. "You've only got to bend your mind to it as my pop says. It's perfectly simple."

It was quite simple when she looked at it properly. The door opened and Harry came in. "Okay?" he asked and looked at the set and then at his watch. "You can send out the tuning signal now. Remember what to do?" It was nervous work with two pairs of eyes watching her but it was successfully accomplished and Harry nodded. "Nothing to do now but wait," he said. "I'll be in the bar."

He hurried away to help the inexperienced young waiter and Clunie sighed.

"What's the matter now?" asked Pat.

"I've just thought how horrible to be lost on the Ridge on a night like this. Poor things! It's such a big area if they got off the track—and terribly rough." To "do the Ridge" involved crossing a shoulder of Torran Mhor, going to the top of Torran Beag by the walkers' route and stretches of high moors which were jumbles of heather, rocks and bog. "The men could easily be quite close and miss them."

"The dogs wouldn't miss them," Pat pointed out and added that unless both women were unconscious, which was highly unlikely, they would hear the men shouting and see their lights. He sat down in the manager's chair. "Haven't you got your knitting? It's very soothing to the nerves, I understand. Morag knits."

Clunie said she hadn't got any knitting, it wasn't a thing she did, but she agreed that it might be useful in filling up moments like this. Morag, she remembered, was an indefatigable knitter and she laughed suddenly. "What memories her jumpers must hold," she said. "I was doing this neck when the man from Wigan broke his leg and finished it just before they got him down."

"Cast something on," Pat advised. "It might encourage the softer, more womanly side of your nature."

"Not worth it. I won't be here long enough to get the hang of it and I'm not eager to be any softer than I am."

"You're just here till Morag comes back, I suppose. What are you going to do after that? London again?"

She shook her head. "Not London, but I haven't really thought about it. I'm sort of waiting on events."

"What events?"

"Oh—any. A lead. I'd like to get a job in Edinburgh, I think. For a while anyway."

Pat said he couldn't stand London himself. "But Jo likes it. He says if you live there you get your own howfs and it feels quite cosy. You remember Jo Carey?"

"Of course I do." Clunie smiled. She remembered his

friend Jo well. "He was much nicer than you. Good-looking too. I was in love with him when I was about fourteen but I never saw him again, alas. He's in London, is he? What does he do?"

"Barrister," said Pat and added gloomily, "Got married in June. A sad occasion."

"Why? Isn't she nice?"

"Oh yes, she's all right. Nothing against her at all if she'd married somebody else. But it was the end of an era. Nearly everyone I know is married. I felt like the last rose of summer, left blooming alone."

"Heart-rending," said Clunie. "Why don't you get married yourself?"

"Nothing I'd like better, provided I got the right girl."

"Well, it's no good being too choosey," she said. "Not at your age. But if you persevere you'll probably find some nice willing girl on some dusty shelf."

Pat gave her a dignified glance and said, "Reverting to your career. The last I heard about you—from your mum via my mum—was that you'd been globetrotting but seemed settled in London. Didn't you enjoy it?"

He was smoking his pipe and contrived to look so comfortable in Harry's chair with his feet on the desk that Clunie found herself talking freely. She was surprised when she thought about it afterwards but it seemed natural at the time. He was a good listener.

She said she had enjoyed it very much. Her father believed in young people seeing the world and standing on their own feet so she had moved around for nearly two years. "Not travelling in Alan's sense of the word, of

41

course."

"Alan's kind needs a pretty strong stomach, I imagine," Pat put in and she agreed, laughing.

"Which he has. Smells, dirt, flies, fleas just don't affect Alan and he eats *anything*. I asked him once if he'd ever eaten sheep's eyes but he said he'd never risen high enough: they're a delicacy."

"So you stuck to civilization?"

"Never off the beaten track. Europe—mostly on holidays—and I had spells working in America and South Africa. Then I came back and landed a nice job in London." She had had a lovely time, she said, and Jo was right about the howfs. "But it—well, it came to an end."

Pat nodded. "Things do. They go in phases and you know—quite suddenly sometimes—that it's time to move on."

"That's it.' She smiled at him gratefully. It was so nice to come across somebody who didn't have to have things explained. Since he did not she went on to do it. "It wasn't just one thing. Tina, the friend I lived with, got married and it seemed a kind of—what's the thing that starts other things off?"

"Catalyst?"

"Yes. Well that was the catalyst. Other friends moved on or married and my job went slightly sour, then Keith Finlay turned up when he was organizing this Hindu Kush expedition and I wondered why the hell I'd stayed away from the hills so long. I couldn't wait to get on a rope." She glanced significantly at the window. "I'm still waiting, of course."

42

"I don't remember you as a climber," said Pat. "You may have been too young—or we just didn't coincide."

"I'm quite sure," she said, "that climbing's one of the spheres in which you regard womans as a nuisance."

"Oh no—not *necessarily*. But—"

"All right. You needn't go on. We—Jean and I—started when Alan and Malcolm got keen and I did a lot here but I've hardly been anywhere else. Now I'm so rusty I'm almost scared to start again."

"We'll have to get you moving. It'll soon come back. Alan didn't go on long, did he?"

"Not really. Keith sort of adopted them as followers and Alan isn't a follower by nature. He's not a leader either, as a matter of fact."

Pat remembered that even as a small boy Alan Ritchie was not a docile follower. Not that he rebelled against leadership. He merely disappeared when he got tired of it and in the years since he had disappeared regularly for longer and longer periods. Now as an ethnologist he disappeared officially and had an income, though probably not a large one, but it had puzzled a good many people how a schoolboy and undergraduate got as far as Alan did in the holidays. "What did he use for money?" he asked Clunie.

"Blood," she said. She looked at him and laughed. "Did you know that in a lot of countries you sell blood instead of donating it? If he got stuck he just trotted along and hocked a pint—or litre."

Pat remarked that you couldn't be much more self-supporting than that and they both jumped as the R/T came to life. It was time, said Andy, to call out the chaps farther along the Ridge.

As Clunie was making the last call Alice Craig came in carrying a tray with sandwiches and a flask of coffee. The manager's wife was a large, rather beautiful woman in the early forties who took no official part in the running of the hotel but contributed a good deal to its success. Since her boys were largely off her hands she might have found the remoteness of Glen Torran boring, but Alice was never bored. She was very good-natured and keenly interested in the affairs of all the people around her, especially, as Clunie had reason to know, in affairs of the heart.

"No sign of them yet?" she asked as Clunie put the phone down. "What a nuisance. A hundred to one they're safe enough but you can't help worrying. What are these women like, Clunie? Sensible?"

"That I wouldn't care to say," said Clunie. "They're tough—at least Miss Glover is. I didn't really notice Miss Thompson."

Alice sat down rather wearily. "It's not the same thing," she agreed. "Poor Harry! He's been on his feet since six o'clock this morning and this could go on all night. He's tidying up the bar now." She looked at Pat. "He said to tell you to go along for a drink if you want one."

"I'll do that," said Pat, tilting his chair forward and getting to his feet. "Would you like a wee dram, Clunie?"

"On the house," said Alice.

In that case, Clunie said, she wouldn't hesitate. Pat departed and Alice eyed her amiably.

44

"You two seem quite harmonious," she observed. "I thought you couldn't stand each other."

Her round blue eyes were mild but Clunie was not deceived. Alice's eyes saw everything there was to see and not infrequently more.

"Oh, I used to hate him like poison," she said, "but I've grown out of such violent emotions. He's nicer than he was. Or I am."

"Both, I dare say," said Alice. "Age is mellowing up to a point." She hoisted herself to her feet as Pat came in with the drinks. "Well, I'm going to bed. If I don't sleep I'll at least be horizontal." The door closed behind her and then opened again. "You could play dominoes if you're bored," she said. "Goodnight."

Later, when his hotel was settled for the night, Harry came in saying that he would take over. "You can get off to bed, Clunie."

"I'm not tired," she said, surprised to see that it was nearly midnight. "I wouldn't sleep anyway, not knowing if they're safe."

"It could go on till daylight, you know."

"I'd really like to see it through."

Harry glanced at her. "All right, if that's the way you feel. I'm just plain bored myself. All I want is to get my head down and my feet up. What about you, Pat?"

He would stick it out, Pat said and added, "You don't seem very worried about the poor ladies."

"I'm not," said Harry. "It'll be a relief to see them back but you get a kind of instinct." He explained that from all accounts Miss Glover and her friend belonged to the pig

45

headed class, silly but not rash. "Evidently they're lost, but they won't have fallen off anything and if they have heavy colds they've asked for it." He yawned cavernously. "There are more sandwiches and coffee in the kitchen, if you want them, Clunie."

"I'll fetch them if we do," she said. "Why don't you go and put your feet up? We'll call you when there's a message."

He hesitated. It had been a long day and quite likely he wouldn't get to bed at all tonight. Clunie couldn't have been left alone, but if Pat was with her . . . "What about this business of ancient foes?" he asked. "Have you buried the hatchet?"

"Temporarily," Clunie replied. "Not very deep and the spot is clearly marked but I'll promise not to dig it up till the ladies are safe. I can't answer for Pat, of course."

Pat met the gleam in Harry's eyes blandly. "It's not me that uses a hatchet," he said. "I'm a peace-loving type and always was. It's a pity Clunie hasn't got a bit of knitting but you can drop off with an easy mind. We'll avoid controversial subjects."

"I'll be in the lounge—" said Harry and as he went out added, "You could play dominoes."

Clunie laughed aloud and Pat's slow grin appeared. "What do you suppose is the special virtue of dominoes in the eyes of the Craig family?" he asked.

"The most boring pastime next to knitting, I should think," said Clunie. "Perhaps it kept the boys quiet when they were small."

Though nearly two more hours elapsed before the

ladies were reported found there was no need to play dominoes and the lack of knitting was not felt. Pat had driven and trudged many wet miles in the course of the day and was extremely relaxed but he showed no tendency to fall asleep. Clunie had never been wider awake.

To her the very words Mountain Rescue Service had a ring of excitement; of the romance which belongs to high courage, endurance and disciplined training. It was something to be part, even a humble and inactive part, of the rescue team and she was thankful that this first callout was no more than a mug-hunt, hardly more than a rehearsal. For her part, after all, was not so humble. Though nothing urgent was required of her tonight the time might come when lives depended on her quickness and efficiency.

So she sat up straight in her chair feeling talkative and Pat with his feet on Harry's desk responded. There was plenty to talk about. Like Keith Finlay and the Grahams he belonged not only to her Glen Torran world but to her whole background. His people and hers were the same kind and had been so for generations. And he was better than Keith or Malcolm or even Jean in one respect: communication. Apart from Alan in the right mood—and Alan didn't hesitate to make it plain when he wasn't— she had never talked more easily with anyone.

They were still talking, a slow comfortable natter, when the mission-completed call came through. The ladies, said Andy, were cold, wet and exhausted but undamaged. He wanted the Land Rover brought to the point at which

47

they would reach the road.

"Well," said Pat, rather stiffly lowering his feet from the desk, "I regard this as something of a triumph."

"It isn't really difficult at all," said Clunie, giving the R/T an experienced glance.

"Oh that." Pat dismissed communications. "I told you there's nothing to it. But you realize we've been together for—what? Five hours—and never a harsh word or a blow. That *is* something, I reckon. A landmark, you might say.'

"Are you taking credit for tact and diplomacy?" Clunie demanded.

He held up a large hand. "Now don't start anything at this time of night," he begged and went to drive rescued and rescuers back to warmth and hot soup.

CHAPTER THREE

PAT'S SHEPHERDS were right. Early in the morning the weather began to clear and before noon it was a fine sunny day. Clunie's wide-awake alertness was still with her when she got up and she was glad she had not accepted Harry's offer of a long lie. Everyone else was going on as if they had had the usual night's sleep. The fish van brought the pump for Pat's car, Tosh sorted it and Pat drove off to Edinburgh. Andy and Malcolm were out early instructing a party of Rescue Service trainees. Miss Glover and Miss Thompson appeared for breakfast, vaguely huffy and inclined to sneeze.

They had decided to go and have their colds at home but they handed Harry quite a handsome cheque for the Rescue Service funds with grateful thanks. Harry later expressed the pious hope that the cheque wouldn't bounce.

Clunie was quite shocked. "Surely it wouldn't!"

"It's been known to happen," he said. "But I don't think this one will and it's a sign of grace that they thought of it. Some people don't even bother to say thank you. They think rescues come under social security." He looked at her. "Is the night catching up on you? Take the rest of the day off. You were good, you and Pat. Better go to bed."

By now Clunie was feeling rather frail and a free afternoon and evening were welcome, but she didn't want to go to bed. Along with the frailty she felt restless and she had a faint unaccountable sense of bereavement. And the sun had come out at last. She would borrow a bike and ride down to Kintorran, do a little shopping, look at the loch and drop in on the Grahams at teatime.

She was just going out when Alice appeared. "You're going to the town, are you?" she said. "Well, good. Clunie, you'll never credit it: Miss Bethune's got a young relative staying at the castle."

Clunie exclaimed. "No! Miss Bethune hasn't got a young relative. We'd have known."

"So you'd think," said Alice, her tone suggesting that in this matter Miss Bethune had not been quite open. Miss Bethune, sister of the late Sir Alistair and the only surviving member of her generation, lived with her friend Miss Tullis in the habitable part of Castle Tornay and maintained the dignity of the Family. She had very little money and by no means held herself aloof from her neighbours, but even Lady Finlay with the empire behind her never challenged her status. It was significant that though Miss Tullis was commonly referred to—but not addressed—as Molly, nobody spoke of Charlotte Bethune.

Alice had heard the news of the visitor from Mrs McAdam on the phone, she said, and it was quite true because Wattie told her and he had been working at the castle yesterday. Wattie was the jobbing gardener. "But he didn't know much," said Alice regretfully. "It's a girl— from London, Wattie thinks—and she hasn't been out yet. She's been ill. If you're going to the Grahams they'll probably know all about her."

"Probably," Clunie agreed and promised to find out as

much as she could.

She grinned a little as she mounted the borrowed bicycle. In the anonymity of London she had forgotten how gripping local news can be and a young Bethune was an event. Her shopping was very leisurely. In Kintorran's one street she met many old friends who wanted to hear about her family and tell her about theirs and they all told her about the girl who had come to bide at the castle. Though she had been there for several days she had not been seen and nobody knew any more than Alice, but tomorrow was Mrs Kidd's lady for the castle and working indoors she was better placed than Wattie for gathering information. One lady remarked hopefully that Clunie herself might know the lassie. "They say she's from London."

"It's a big place though," said Clunie.

Mounting the bike again she rode out of the town on the other side along the shore of Loch Torran to the beach where she used to build sand castles. There she sat on a well-remembered rock and settled down for a good stare. It was a mild, smiling day with an air of slightly unconvincing innocence as though dissociating itself from the dismal days just past. The loch was tranquil and colourful, the sand almost white. All round the hills were blue or purple or the grey of rock and the smell was heavenly.

Clunie gazed and breathed. How right she had been to come back. She had no illusions about Kintorran and the glen: however inviting on a day like this, life in a tiny remote community had its own problems. It was not for her. But the hills of Scotland were in her blood and she

51

wondered how she could have stayed away so long. She knew the answer, of course. However fond you are of a place and however much it hurts to leave home, new places and new interests heal the hurt and dim the memory. In the years of her absence it had sometimes happened that something would bring sudden vivid recollection and acute homesickness for the hills, but it soon passed and already she could foresee moments of nostalgia for London: her London where she had friends and, as Pat put it, howfs and felt herself at the centre of the universe and, moreover, quite at home.

In any case there was no doubt that it was a good thing to get around when you were young and vigorous and when, if you took a wrong turning, there was plenty of time to get back—provided you hadn't gone too far. She was very glad she had got around. But at this point a chilly little breeze ruffled the clear water of the loch and a somewhat similar breeze ruffled Clunie's self-congratulatory mood.

It was not the spirit of enterprise that had got her moving, or not entirely. Though it was true that she wanted to travel, to see new places and meet new people, she did not, like Alan, have the irresistible urge, and she might have stayed quite contentedly in her rut, shuttling between Edinburgh and Glen Torran if it had not been for Keith Finlay. She had run away from Keith and it was largely because of him that she had come back.

Clunie scowled at the loch. She wished Keith didn't come into it, that he was in the Hindu Kush now and Malcolm with him. She just wanted to be here: climbing with Tom and other friendly boys; perhaps Andy if he felt kindly disposed. And Pat. She had been busy when Pat left but he had said something about seeing her soon and fixing up a climb. Then there was Jean to argue with and Alice's gossip to laugh at . . . What she didn't want was emotion and awkward situations and both, she feared, were in store. Hard decisions too perhaps, but she was finished with running away.

She got up from the rock which was getting very hard anyway and walked back to the road. It was time to drop in at the Grahams' for tea.

Cycling from the Brig to Kintorran was fine, downhill all the way. The thought of the return journey made Clunie, a reluctant cyclist, wish she could ditch the bike. Even before the end of the street the climb began and she was at the slightly wobbly stage, wondering whether to get off now or press on a little farther when the question was settled for her. A girl came blundering out of the post office, head down, and walked straight in front of her.

"Hey! Look where you're going!" she shouted, dismounting with an undignified scramble.

"Oh—sorry." The apology was minimal and the girl was walking on when Clunie exclaimed again.

"Good gracious! *Davina Clare!* What in all the world are you doing here?"

Davina Clare stopped and stared at her. "Who—oh, it's you . . ."

For a moment they stood still in sheer astonishment and then walked slowly on up the hill, but it was another moment before anything more was said. Davina didn't seem to feel that speech was called for. Clunie didn't know where to begin. Of all the people she had ever known, Davina Clare was the last she could have imagined in Kintorran—or, indeed, anywhere out of London. She looked as if some freak wind had picked her up in Chelsea and dropped her without her noticing the change of scene. On this mild and sunny August day she had chosen to dress for walking in plastics: a large shiny white hat, black belted coat and long white boots. One of the Kintorran expressions with which Clunie was familiar was sardonic amusement at anything foreign or affected. She was very conscious of it now. "What have *you* got hold of?" it asked jocularly while Davina, still in King's Road, trailed along looking neither to left nor right.

The two girls had known each other for some time but only at party level, and the larger, less intimate parties at that. Clunie knew something about Davina. She was a singer. Davina, she was sure, knew nothing whatever about her. It was surprising that she remembered her at all.

"Whatever brings you here?" she asked. "Are you at the youth hostel?"

"Oh no," said Davina. "I'm staying with a relation. Some prehistoric aunt or something."

Clunie stopped again. "Not *Miss Bethune?*"

"That's her." Cool eyes flattened astonishment. "Lives up there—" she pointed, "—in a ruin. Why are you here?"

"Well, I've got a job in a hotel," said Clunie. "But we used to come every summer. We had a cottage." She added that she had known Miss Bethune—and Miss

54

Tullis—all her life.

"Lucky girl." Amusement showed briefly. "I never saw them before and I sometimes wonder if I'm seeing them now, quite frankly. They can't be real. And the ruin's pure nightmare."

Clunie laughed. 'They're probably more baffled than you are'"

"Oh they are," Davina agreed. "They don't understand a word I say. It's like being shut up in a nut-bin with a couple of crazy keepers. Aunt Charlotte bites. That's why I'm wearing these—" she stuck out a boot. "And the other one—Tay Mullis, Mully Tollis—keeps creeping up on me to see what I'm doing *now*. God!"

"'Give them time," said Clunie. "Molly's a kind old thing and a marvellous cook. And Miss Bethune just barks. She almost never bites."

Davina said, "They're a pair of old cats." Then she turned and for the first time looked at Clunie with friendly eyes. They were strange eyes, clear sea-green. "I'm being bitchy," she said and smiled.

In the whole human arsenal there is no more powerful weapon than a warm unguarded smile from someone who habitually scowls. Clunie had seen this smile before and knew that the warm front never lasted, but the bored remote face was transformed and in spite of herself she was disarmed. The hill grew steeper and Davina's steps lagged more and more. She had always been very slight but now it seemed that there was almost nothing in the black coat and she was so pale that Clunie wondered if she would get back to the castle.

"Would you like to rest for a bit?" she asked. "I heard you'd been ill. That's the doctor's house. I'm going to drop in for tea—Jean Graham's a friend of mine—and I'm sure they'd be delighted—"

"Jean Graham?" exclaimed Davina. "No, thanks very much. She came and drank coffee this morning and I don't want another dose. And I don't want any more doctors. Yes, I've been ill. Got a strep throat. Nearly killed me."

"Have a breather," Clunie suggested. Just short of the Grahams' house there was a gate leading to a small field and as Davina leaned thankfully against it she went on, "I'm terribly sorry about your throat. It's not going to affect your singing, is it?"

"It's not meant to," said Davina. "I can sing now—only not for long at a time. But of course it scuppered me. God knows when I'll ever get going again. It's too bloody easy to sink without trace—and quick."

"Oh *surely* that couldn't happen? You were doing so well. Didn't you land some marvellous contract? For an LP, was it?"

"TV actually. But it's dead now." A sour face came round. "That's the way it goes in showbiz. The ultimate rat race."

It was difficult to be cheering. Clunie spoke encouragingly of highland air and Miss Tullis's cooking. "You'll soon pick up and I'm sure you'll get going again."

"'I hate eating—good wholesome food anyway," was the gloomy reply. "And what am I supposed to do with the air? It's far too cold even to sit outside, let alone sunbathe.

The sun doesn't seem to operate in these parts—not noticeably."

Clunie said the weather had been exceptionally bad for the last week but she admitted that very little sunbathing took place on the shores of Loch Torran. Those who liked that sort of holiday went elsewhere. "Why did you come?" she asked curiously. "Didn't you know what it would be like?"

Davina shrugged. "I didn't, but I'd no option. No money, you see and I have to be somewhere."

"But—haven't you got any family? Parents . . ?"

"Oh, I've got the usual quota of parents—or had. In fact I'm well over the quota. I don't know about step-mothers —my papa may be dead for all I know—but I'm wearing my third step-father currently and he won't have me in the house. So my mum and I go our separate ways. The hospital contacted her and she fixed this up. Well . . . better get on."

She pushed herself upright. Clunie said, "I'll come with you. It isn't much farther," and they walked slowly on.

There wasn't much to say. Clunie remembered the first time she saw Davina. It was at a big party where she didn't know many people. A girl near her said, "Will you *look* at Davina Clare! Been to the rag and bone shop again. How the hell does she get away with it?" "She's a witch, didn't you know?" a man's voice replied and she looked round and there was Davina. After that she kept on seeing her—nobody could help it. Not that she was a delight to the eye. She wasn't. She wore a dingy black dress, which probably dated from the twenties, with a lot of fringe and a wilted pink rose: her blonde hair was lank and her expression off-hand in the extreme. But there was something final about her. Davina. Like it or not this is what I am. Later when she sang, standing with her guitar and the same take it or leave it air, she—and, indeed, the whole party—had listened spellbound. Witch, Clunie thought, was the word.

They reached the castle gates. "Here you are then," she said, turning her bike. "I'll leave you. Be seeing you."

Davina smiled again. "Well, I hope so. Do you realize you're the first human being I've spoken to since I got to this bloody place? Hey—what about your hotel? It's not that morgue down there is it?"

The Bethune Arms was a dignified hostelry, set in its ways, and Clunie gave a brief description of the Brig and admitted that there was more life about it. "The climbing brings young people, you see." She explained about the bothies, Harry's version of youth hostels, whose tenants swarmed into the bar in the evenings. "But there are no floor shows, if that's the way your mind's working."

The idea of people enjoying themselves without the aid of organized entertainment baffled Davina. "Don't they even have concerts or just informal sing-songs?"

"Not even TV," said Clunie. "They have a ceilidh sometimes."

"Cayley?"

"A sort of party where people sing or tell stories—any sort of turn—with some dancing as well. It isn't professional you know. Nobody gets paid."

"Oh, I wouldn't mind that," Davina said promptly. "It'd

be an audience—get me going again. Look, what's-your-name—Clunie?—put in a word, will you?"

Clunie said she would, if she got the chance, and Davina walked away up the castle drive with a more buoyant step while Clunie coasted back down the hill to the Grahams' house.

Tea was herself, Jean and Mrs Graham in the dining-room; a good solid meal in the Scottish tradition. Mrs Graham was an expert and indefatigable baker. Afterwards the two girls sat in the garden and in both dining-room and garden Davina was dominant. There was no sardonic amusement at the Anglified oddball here. Instead two different but equally familiar expressions. On meeting or even hearing of a stranger Mrs Graham's reaction was profound suspicion imperfectly concealed under a rather jolly social manner. Jean always feared the worst and in Davina she had found it.

"I haven't *seen* her," said Mrs Graham, "but I met Miss Tullis in White's yesterday and from what she said I'm afraid Davina is not an easy guest. It seems she makes no effort at all to adapt herself to the ways of the house. And Jean wasn't very favourably impressed, were you, dear?" She gave a little laugh. "I must say she doesn't sound a very *nice* girl."

"She's a horrible girl," Jean said bluntly.

"Well," said Clunie striving to combine civility with truth, "perhaps she isn't nice exactly, but she's really gifted and I don't think she's had much luck."

Two pairs of eyes bored into her. Mrs Graham said, "Of course you know her better than . . . Did you see much of her in London? How strange that you never heard of her connection with Miss Bethune. You must have been surprised to see her."

She had never been so surprised in her life, Clunie said. "I met her at parties and didn't really know her in a—a personal way. In London—or any city, I suppose—you can easily know people without knowing anything about their families." She looked at Jean. "You must have found that in Glasgow, haven't you?"

"No, I can't say I have," said Jean. "The circle I move in is probably narrower than your London one. All my friends are either university or people we know as a family. Anyway, Glasgow's not so big."

"Ah well," Mrs Graham came in tactfully, "when in Rome, I suppose . . . Now tell me about your mother, Clunie dear. And the Professor—we miss our summer neighbours. They will be very glad to have you at home again. And east, west, hame's best after all . . ."

Clunie rather feverishly agreed and reported the news of her family. Her parents were on holiday in Norway, which Mrs Graham couldn't quite like: what, after all, had Norway got that Scotland hadn't? And she shook her head over Alan's continued wandering in spite of its professional status.

"Still," she said indulgently, "he'll want to get married one of these days and then he'll settle down."

It was a relief when tea was over and she and Jean went out to the garden. Peace did not reign there either but she hadn't expected that it would and at least she didn't have to be polite.

Jean attacked at once. "You've changed, you know," she said.

"Think so?" said Clunie. "I feel much the same. What strikes you particularly?"

There was nothing exactly striking, Jean said, her clever bony face wrinkled in thought. It was generally agreed that fate had not been altogether kind to the Grahams. Jean had the brains and Malcolm the looks and if they could not have been more equally divided it was a pity they were that way round. The two concerned, however, felt no sense of ill-usage: Malcolm because he never thought about it, Jean because beauty is only skin deep. 'Nothing you can put a finger on,' she said. 'I just feel you're different. Of course you've been abroad a lot and then living in London . . . You're more sophisticated for one thing."

"Well, it would be rather a waste if four years of mind-broadening left me just where I was," Clunie pointed out reasonably. She added that she was gratified to be considered sophisticated. "Nobody in London was much impressed."

"I should hope not," Jean said darkly.

"But it was agreed that I have *style*," Clunie concluded with an air of ineffable smugness.

"H'mph!" said Jean. There was a short silence and then she asked, "Are you going back?"

"No," murmured Clunie who was beginning to feel sleepy. Jean wanted to know why and she went on reluctantly. There were several reasons, she said, none conclusive in itself: Tina's marriage, the breaking up of their gang. "And then somebody said if you stay away from Scotland too long you never get back."

"That's rather far-fetched, I'd have thought."

"Well, I don't know. People tend to stick wherever they are in the middle and late twenties. They form ties. I certainly didn't want to get stuck in the south of England, a day's journey from anything you could call a hill."

"Didn't you think of getting married? You must have met a lot of men."

Clunie shook her head, avoiding a pair of searching eyes. She knew what was behind that look. "Oh, I thought of it of course—who doesn't?—and I met a lot of nice guys but I didn't want to marry any of them."

"What are you going to do then? You don't mean to stay at the Brig being a receptionist forever, do you?"

"I can think of worse things to do, but I haven't been asked to stay forever. Morag will be back when she gets over her appendix." Clunie paused. "I don't know what I'll do. I'll have to decide on a new image."

"Image!" cried Jean. "Now there's an example of how you've changed. You would never have thought about images before."

"Maybe not, but they're worth thinking about."

"What? Building yourself up like some TV or pop personality?"

"Not necessarily. Deciding what sort of person you want to be—and what you can be. Everybody does it, more or less." As she spoke Clunie recalled with a prickle of irritation Malcolm's besotted face and the amusement on other faces in the bar at the Brig and amended her statement. "Well, not everybody. But you certainly do."

Jean began a lofty denial but it was cut short. "Oh yes, you do, Jean. You've been building up images for yourself since you were about twelve. You were the model school-girl, modestly scooping up prizes; then you were going to be a doctor like your father; and now you're going to be wise and compassionate, bossing people about in some social service."

It would be a good thing, said Jean, shifting her ground, if Clunie gave more thought to the under-privileged. "There's nothing more worthwhile or more truly satisfying than serving others. I didn't say anything at the time but when Tina came, that last summer you were here, the two of you didn't seem to think of anything but having a good time."

"We didn't—not so's you'd notice," said Clunie. She chuckled. "And what a good time we had!"

"And where has it landed you?" Jean demanded. "You're just where you were! Four years wasted."

"Oh I wouldn't say that. Not *wasted*"

"Why don't you go in for something really useful? Teaching . . . one of the social services as you call them . . ."

Clunie asked what she was doing now if it wasn't social service. "Helping Harry, serving the customers—with a smile. You should know by now, Jean, that it's casting pearls before swine trying to influence me. I have no— repeat *no*—missionary spirit. It wasn't issued to the Ritchie family. Think of Dad happily buried in the classics, and Alan: you don't imagine he goes hunting about for all those strange tribes to do them good, do you? All he wants is to know how they live . . . And I'm damn sure the underprivileged would be a hell of a lot worse off if I started butting in."

"It seems to me the best thing you can do is to get married," said Jean in a resigned tone.

Clunie laughed. "Meaning it's all I'm fit for? You may be right. I'd be a good wife and mother, I believe—given the right partner. But that's the rub, you see."

"It shouldn't be difficult. You're attractive."

"One has also to be attracted, however. To meet Mr Right, in short."

"Oh well, I dare say you will," said Jean and lost interest. She brooded for a little and then returned to Davina. *"That's* the real change in you. Clunie, how *can* you stand up for that girl?"

"What's wrong with her?"

It was as if a sluice gate had been opened. The permissive society, drugs, pornography, perversion, came pouring out. If you asked Jean, people who should know better and did nothing about it were greatly to blame. If you asked her, all this tolerance, making excuses, was simply shuffling off responsibility. "And if you ask me—"

"Oh do stop saying that!" cried Clunie. "I have asked you. What—is—wrong—with—Davina?"

"Well, if you want it straight, I think she's all wrong. She—"

"That's a damn silly thing to say. To save time I'll admit that her manners aren't what we've been brought up to. She's off-hand, she looks a bit of a mess—"

"She looks as if she needs a *good wash.*"

"She may need a good wash. I don't know where washing comes in her priorities. I might skimp it myself, knowing the amenities enjoyed by the castle. And at that they could be better than wherever she lives in London."

"Don't you know where she lives?"

"No idea. In a commune as like as not—or moving from squat to squat. I do know she's been ill—very ill, I'd say; she's got no home and the best her mother could do for her was to bung her up here to a great-aunt she'd never even heard of. No wonder she can't adapt herself. She doesn't believe Miss Bethune and Molly and the castle are real. They're survivals from a world Davina hasn't a clue about. Not," added Clunie honestly, "that she'd make much effort if she had." She grinned. "Never been taught to think of others. She just goes her own way."

After a pause Jean observed coldly that in her opinion Davina's own way would be highly immoral. "She's probably been on drugs. You've only her word for it that she had a strep throat."

Clunie retorted that Davina had certainly suffered from a strep throat because otherwise she would never have heard of it. "As for drugs, I wouldn't know. I'm not familiar with the symptoms."

"She's got very peculiar eyes."

"Would drugs make them that colour? Very likely she's had a go, but if she was really hooked she wouldn't sing as she does. As for her sexual morality I wouldn't bet on it. I wouldn't bet on my own if I had her background and temptation came my way. Would you guarantee yours?"

65

Imagination was not Jean's strong point. Yes, she said, she would. Everybody had the choice. "I'm not discounting background, but plenty of people with good backgrounds go wrong." She looked angrily at Clunie. "What about you? There's nothing wrong with your background but at least you seem to tolerate permissiveness quite easily."

Clunie returned look for look. "I'll tell you one thing, Jean. If I was on the receiving end of your brand of social work I'd go straight out and search for the nearest orgy."

There was a hard-breathing pause. As she simmered down Clunie realized that she might have been a trifle carried away by Jean's self-righteousness. Jean was rather shocked by the accusations—or near accusations—she had hurled at her life-long friend.

She cleared her throat. "I didn't mean to accuse *you* of —of permissiveness,' she began. 'Only—"

"Oh, shut up," said Clunie. "For all I know Davina may be everything you think she is. But I don't believe that anybody who's worked as hard as she must have worked at her singing is a complete mess. That's really all."

"Oh well," said Jean.

CHAPTER FOUR

THROUGHOUT THEIR LIVES Clunie and Jean had disagreed more often than not and since neither hesitated to say exactly what she thought of the other their quarrels were both frequent and abusive. The Davina quarrel ended as they normally did. Quite suddenly the storm was over, leaving no ill-feeling.

They had been talking amicably and enjoyably for an hour and Clunie was getting up to go when Malcolm came out of the house, his eyes glowing with pleasure. If he had known Clunie was here, he said, he could have been back sooner.

"I've just been nattering with Andy and Tosh." His face fell. "You're not going? Do you have to?"

"Well, I've got Minnie Stewart's bike," she said, "and I didn't have much sleep last night."

"Stay for supper," said Jean. "We'll put the bike in the van and run you home afterwards." As a further inducement she added that Dr and Mrs Graham were going out and grinned, the grin which made up for a lot of earnestness. "The annual dinner with Hake and his mum."

Clunie exclaimed. "Lord! Are they here?"

"Of course they are. Why not?"

"Why not indeed," Clunie echoed. "When we're all dead and gone, no doubt Hake will still be coming—and his mum too, very likely. She looks everlasting. Like those dried grasses. Well, I'll stay, thank you. I'm too old to bike

67

up hills and if Minnie wants a bike there are plenty about."

She sat down again with a pleasant sense of ease. It was nice to be here with Jean and Malcolm and without their parents. The generation gap always felt extra wide in the company of Dr and Mrs Graham. And how right Keith had been, she thought with amusement, when he said she would find everybody exactly the same only more so. Hake, for example. Eric Salmon had come and stayed in the Bethune Arms with his mother every summer as long as anybody could remember: man and boy, both rather stout. It was Alan who had dubbed him "the great muckle Hake", quoting a comic song. At the time it had struck them all as exquisitely funny and apt. As well as being called Salmon he looked like a fish. Fortunately he had been rather pleased at being distinguished by a nickname.

"He hasn't got a wife yet then," she said. "Poor Hake; I'm sure he'd love to be married but it can't be denied he has problems." She turned to Malcolm. "Tell me about this expedition. I heard a lot from Keith in London, but you know what he is. It all came out in such a spate I couldn't take it in. I just ate—he gave me a gorgeous dinner—and nodded now and again. The TV boys can't be sympathetic listeners."

"Too busy projecting their images," Jean said caustically and added, "Keith's hopeless. He's so scatty I don't know how he ever gets an expedition off the ground."

Malcolm protested. "Oh no! Keith's all right—first rate."

"He's efficient—nobody more so—when he thinks it

matters," said Clunie. "The expedition will get off on schedule, nothing vital will be forgotten and if he leaves a lot of exhausted wrecks behind it won't concern him a bit. What about your job, Malcolm? Are they quite happy to let you go?"

His school was very pleased about it, Malcolm said. "Mountaineering is such a good activity for boys—if it's done properly, that is—and I've got a lot of them very keen. The expedition's a great boost for them. And marvellous for me, of course."

"Marvellous," Clunie agreed, swallowing a giggle. He couldn't have the faintest idea what he was in for and she wondered again at Keith's taking anyone with such limited experience, but all she said was, "When do you go?"

December or January, he said. It wasn't finally decided, depending on who the other pair were and their commitments. "April's the time for serious climbing in Hindu Kush. So I'll teach this next term and be back to start again in September."

"If you ever go back to a humdrum job." She nodded at him. "There's money in the climbing business for hard men and tigers."

He laughed. "Don't look at me. I'm neither a hard man nor a tiger."

"Well, perhaps not a hard man," she conceded. "You couldn't be ruthless. But certainly a tiger."

Reminded, possibly, by the word ruthless, Jean suddenly reverted to gloom and Davina Clare. "Clunie *knows* her," she told Malcolm. "And Mother sticks to it that we must do something about her. We owe it to Miss Bethune."

Malcolm was unperturbed: it was the normal thing to do something about neighbours' visitors. "Well, that's all right," he said easily. "We'll have a loft party. Work off a few others at the same time. Hake for one."

"That girl won't think much of the loft," said Jean, sticking to martyrdom.

"Oh yes, she will," said Clunie. "She'll think it's a studio and instantly feel at home."

After supper when Clunie's yawns could no longer be stifled, Jean brought her tact into operation. Unlike her brother, she was observant. There was very little she hadn't known about what she thought of as the Keith-Clunie affair and she was fully aware of the state of Malcolm's heart. She was devoted to him with an almost fiercely protective devotion, and though she often disapproved of her she was very fond of Clunie. She wanted to get some reading done, she said. "Malcolm will run you back, Clunie."

Clunie had suffered much from Jean's tact in the past but this time it was unobjectionable. For one thing tact was one of the many things Malcolm didn't notice. All he said was that the front seat of his van was rather a squash for three anyway, and when they started the short journey to the Brig he began talking about climbing. Now the weather was better she would be able to get started again, he said. If she could arrange a time he would have a word with Andy. The instructors were pretty busy but Andy would certainly let him off.

There was little doubt, Clunie thought, that Andy would, but this was precisely the sort of thing she did not want: a special arrangement with Harry on her part, a special arrangement with Andy on Malcolm's. It was enough to get her firmly placed as Malcolm's girl and she had no wish to be Malcolm's girl. Though he had been a very sweet—and creditable—boyfriend that last summer in the glen when Keith's desertion had left her raw and smarting, they were now, both of them, past the boy/girl-friend stage.

"You know," she said, laughing a little, "I felt I could hardly wait to get my boots on, but now I've gone sort of —shy. Scared, really, I suppose."

"Well, that's natural enough," said Malcolm. "Four years is quite a long time. But you'll be surprised how quickly it comes back." He looked round, smiling. "As soon as you feel the rope round you and see the foot and hand holes on the rock you'll forget you've been away."

"Well, you may be right, but I've been wondering if I wouldn't be better advised to stick to hill walking. I have done that in Switzerland and Austria and after all you see more. When you pause on a climb you're just thinking about the next bit and if you're going to get cramp."

He was shocked. "Oh no. You can't give up. You were really good—well, promising. Walk if you like but climb too. Let's fix a time and I'll start you off gently."

"You'd be ashamed of me," she warned him. "Better wait till I've had a little private scrambling with Jean."

Jean had hardly done any climbing either, he said. "First it was her finals and now it's this postgraduate social sciences lark. I don't know what it's all about but she never seems to think of anything else. You'll be a lot safer with me. And I could never be ashamed of you. You know that."

"Well, that's handsome," said Clunie. "I'll take you up on it some time when Andy can spare you and Harry can spare me."

There was a short silence and then Malcolm slowed down. "Are you too tired to run a wee bit up Glen Trochy?" he asked. "You won't have been up there yet and it seems a pity to go in, it's such a lovely night."

Glen Trochy was a small glen, narrow and twisting, down which the Trochy Burn tumbled to join the river a little way below the bridge and from it rose the sheer rock face of Ben Trochy, one of the Torran giants. Clunie said cautiously that she *was* very tired. "It would be nice to go and look at it, but not far."

You couldn't go far, Malcolm reminded her. The road petered out. "I'm not going to make you walk or climb the Ben tonight." He turned on to the narrow road and drove on slowly. "Clunie, do you remember that last summer you were here?"

Clunie knew that she had made a mistake; she should have refused Glen Trochy. She did her best. "Yes, of course I remember it," she said very heartily. "It was a marvellous summer—one of the very best, I think. That day you and Alan and Jean and I did the Trochy gully and—"

"Yes, but . . . what I mean is . . . You know I was terribly in love with you and—well, I hoped you were a bit fond of me. I couldn't say anything of course. I hadn't even graduated. And then I thought you would be back next year. It was an awful shock when we heard your father had sold the cottage."

She said, "It was a shock to us too in a way. We just assumed it was there forever. But it would have been silly to keep it. Alan was hardly ever there—we were past the family holiday stage."

"I suppose so," Malcolm said doubtfully. There were passing places at regular intervals and he pulled in to one and stopped his engine. Through the open windows came the sound of the burn and the wonderful fresh scents of hill country, water and heather. He didn't speak for a moment and Clunie could think of nothing to say. There comes a time when you can't steer a conversation. After the pause he turned to her directly. "I'm still in love with you, Clunie. More than ever, I think. You've always been the only girl there could never be anyone else for me. Do you feel at all the same about me?"

She was a good deal moved by his seriousness and honest eyes. He was such a dear, Malcolm, and no girl could be unaffected by his looks, his glowing golden-brown colouring and splendid body. He was loving—and lovable. She would be safe with Malcolm and perhaps as happy as most people are, but . . .

"Did you never think of coming to see me if you felt like that?" she asked. "It's not as if I'd emigrated to Australia. Or you could have written."

"Well, I nearly did," he said. "I never knew where you were, though. I wasn't even sure of your Edinburgh address." This, Clunie knew, was quite possible. The Ritchies and Grahams did not correspond, even Christmas cards were not exchanged and Glasgow, not Edinburgh, was the Grahams' city. The friendship belonged to Kintorran and the holidays. "I could have looked you up in the phone book, of course," Malcolm was going on, "but we heard you'd got a job in London so it didn't seem much good."

"Didn't you go to Twickenham? I quite expected you to look me up. In fact I hoped you might take me to the match."

"Oh, did you? I'm sorry. I did go last year actually. I took some of the boys. But—" he paused and then said awkwardly, "—I feel such a fool in London. I suppose you got used to it, though I don't see how anybody can. It scares me to death."

"Why?" asked Clunie. "It's not all that different from Glasgow or any big city."

"Oh, it is. The sheer size of it."

"You don't see it all at once."

"No, but it gets you down all the same. Or it does me. It's—well, it's strange. And I didn't want to turn up looking like a—a great Heiland stot among your friends."

"Oh, Malcolm!" she cried helplessly. "You *are* a mug. The girls would all have been crazy about you. Tina was, that summer she came here."

Malcolm blushed vividly. "Oh shut up," he said and had to take time to recover. "Be serious, Clunie—*please*. I love you so much. I can't ask you to marry me yet. There's the expedition, and anyway I wouldn't want to get married before I've saved a bit—enough to start on. But—will you be engaged?"

He took her hand and Clunie left it in his warm clasp and sat looking at the hills. She was not thinking, or not consciously. She saw the familiar things, heard the gurgle of the burn and, superimposed, as it were, a lively dark-eyed face, charming and unreliable, and a voice that could beguile or repel her.

"Well?" said Malcolm and she turned to him.

"Oh Malcolm—no. I'm sorry. I like you so much—love you, I suppose, in a way . . . But it's not enough."

After a moment he asked diffidently, "Do you mind if I ask you—is there anyone else? I kept wondering if you'd meet some chap in London . . ."

"No," she said. "No, I didn't."

He looked at her with a small rueful smile. "You must think I'm daft, asking you straight off after four years. But you see I've always been thinking about you."

"You shouldn't, you know," said Clunie. "You should have looked round and thought about a lot of girls. You might easily have found one you liked better than me."

"That's not very likely," Malcolm replied. "And I'm not the kind that thinks about girls much." He brooded for a little and then cheered up and became resolute. "Well, I won't give up hope. You say there isn't anyone else, that's the great thing. And maybe it's just as well not to be engaged with the expedition to think about."

Solemnly Clunie agreed that the expedition gave him quite enough to think about.

"When I come back though, it'll be different," he said.

75

"And for now we can sort of go on from where we were that last summer, can't we?"

"Of course we can go on being good *friends*," she said. She gave his hand an affectionate squeeze and withdrew her own, adding a further warning in case, as was all too likely, he had missed the emphasis on "friends". "But don't go building false hopes. I'll wave a flag with enthusiasm when you come back from the Hindu Kush covered with glory, but it won't make any difference you know. Let's go back to the Brig now."

The very idea of flags and glory connected with himself dismayed Malcolm and his laugh was embarrassed, but he said, "All right," and put an arm round her shoulders. "What a tired wee girl . . . I'm a brute to have kept you out of your bed." He kissed her, patted her kindly and switched on his engine. Driving briskly along the narrow Glen Trochy road he went on to say that he had great hopes and he didn't think they were false. He was not such a fool as to think that it would make any difference if he did well in the Hindu Kush. "But you're not going to disappear to London again and you say you love me in a way and I love you so much I just feel we're meant for each other." He glanced round, smiling. "When I get back —well, we'll see."

As she went in to the Brig Clunie was intercepted by Alice Craig who observed that she looked worn out and ordered rather than invited her up to the private flat for a nightcap. "You'll sleep better with a milky drink inside you," she said.

It was less trouble to obey when Alice was bent on

doing you good and Clunie trailed after her, making no attempt to hide her yawns. She woke up, however, when Alice, placing a steaming mug beside her, asked, "Did you by any chance receive a proposal of marriage tonight? I saw that Jean helpfully left Malcolm to bring you home."

She protested. "Now, Alice, is it likely? All these years I've never seen nor heard from Malcolm. An old boyfriend doesn't turn into a suitor that fast."

"Not often," Alice admitted, "but if ever there was a faithful Honest John type, it's Malcolm. He's never even looked at another girl and it's not been for want of material—or encouragement. Comely climbers, winsome waitresses—"

"Bonny barmaids, charming chambermaids."

"They've cast themselves before him without raising more than a kindly smile."

"If he has any sense he'll have conducted his affairs in Glasgow, well clear of interested friends."

"He hasn't any sense—not that kind anyhow. He's just patiently waited for you to come back. It's sad in a way. So dull. But you might do worse, you know." There was a quick glance but Clunie was ready for it. "Of course you might do better, but you have to weigh the pros and cons. Nobody's perfect."

Clunie laughed. "You make it sound like making the best of a package deal."

"So it is, if you come down to it."

"Dear me! What's Harry been up to?"

"Nothing," said Alice. "He's far too busy." Her eyes, laughing now, met Clunie's. "Oh well, no girlish confidence, and no advice wanted from the Older Woman. Any news in the town?"

"Yes indeed," said Clunie. "Wait till I tell you. I met Miss Bethune's young relative—in fact I nearly knocked her down—and she's a girl I know. Davina Clare."

"No!" cried Alice. "How extraordinary! And you had no idea of the link? But how should you? 'Davina Clare' wouldn't bring Miss Bethune to mind. *Well!*"

She was a much more satisfactory listener to the Davina story than Mrs Graham and Jean. She laughed at the picture of Miss Bethune and Miss Tullis grappling with such a problem but though she sympathized with the hostesses she could feel for the guest. "After all they're two to one," she said.

Clunie doubted if numerical superiority would do them much good. "Davina's armour is pretty stout. The castle's a ruin inhabited by two old freaks and she's bored but she's not *affected* as they are. She couldn't care less."

"Still, the ladies can talk about her and support each other," said Alice. "Poor Miss Bethune though: rather a blow to the family pride. Well, we must rally round and do something about Davina. Will she create havoc in the bothy, do you think?"

"I really don't know," Clunie said, a little surprised to realize that she didn't know. Her own picture of Davina in mixed company was that of a successful singer with the nerve and ability to look a mess, eschew ordinary civility and get away with it. "I'd guess plenty of men would be interested in her but I don't recall any kind of havoc. Of course she wasn't such a novelty in London. She'd be a bit of an eye-opener to the bothy boys—or most of them."

Alice was philosophical. "Well, they all have to have their eyes opened some time. She must be quite an experience. I can hardly wait. Oh, by the way—Pat rang up."

"Don't say the new pump failed him?"

"No, he was safely back in Edinburgh. He's booked a room from Saturday."

"But we haven't got a room—not for the weekend."

"Oh, we always have room for Pat. He's part of the establishment. He says," said Alice looking bland, "that he's got business in the neighbourhood and some holiday due, so he's making this his base for a few weeks. We must hope he won't completely ruin life for Malcolm."

"Why should he do that?" asked Clunie.

"Think it out," said Alice.

On Saturday Clunie accepted an invitation to tea at the castle. She also, very thankfully, accepted the loan of Alice's little car.

Tea at the castle had been a regular feature of Kintorran summers. The treats were Miss Tullis's treacle scones and Harry Lauder on a very ancient gramophone which had a green horn embellished with roses. The habitable part of the castle consisted of a round tower and a straight bit, two storeys high. All the ground floors were of stone, as was the narrow spiral staircase, and as a small girl Clunie, fascinated by the round living-room and the castle's general air of belonging to the world of fairy tales, Pooh or Mrs Tiggywinkle, had wished ardently that she could live there herself. She still liked it but she could now see why the Bethunes of the 1860s had built and moved into Kintorran Lodge, and Davina, who had very likely never heard of Pooh or Mrs Tiggywinkle, could hardly be expected to appreciate its romantic quality. Miss Bethune, who was short, square and belligerent, with a marked resemblance to the elderly Scotch terrier which never left her side, gardened and wrote stirring historical romances, a feature of which were breathtaking chases over the heather. Miss Tullis kept house and knitted. She was the clinging type, slender and soft-eyed with a plaintive voice, and today she reminded Clunie of a trapped rabbit.

It was an uneasy tea party. Conversation was difficult. Davina took no part in it and Miss Tullis had been unsuccessful with the treacle scones and could talk of nothing else. She had added the baking soda twice over. She couldn't think, she said, how she had come to do such a thing. She had never done it before.

"Don't eat it, Clunie dear. Have a piece of the sponge— I know that's all right."

"It's very good," Clunie lied valiantly and persevered with her scone.

She and Miss Bethune worked hard. They agreed that it was a strange coincidence that she and Davina had known each other in London. Clunie was garrulous about the news of her parents and Alan's travels, but Miss Bethune was not so ready as she usually was to talk about her latest book and the work in progress. Altogether it was a relief to be able to plead receptionist duty and leave early.

"You will be going to the Grahams' party?" said Miss Bethune as they shook hands and Clunie thanked the ladies for having her. "It is very kind of them to invite Davina. It will be nice for her to meet young people and have some music. Won't it, Davina?"

"Yes," said Davina.

A thought struck Clunie. "There will be a car coming down from the Brig," she said. "We can pick Davina up."

Miss Bethune said there would be no need to trouble them. "I will drive Davina. But Jean did not say at what time she should be fetched. Do you know?"

"No," said Clunie, "and I don't suppose Jean does." Miss Bethune looked faintly surprised and she smiled. "The Grahams' parties just go on till they stop. But don't worry, Miss Bethune. It will be so easy for somebody to give Davina a lift."

There was a short bark of laughter from Miss Bethune. "We were told—politely—when to leave in our young day," she said. " 'Carriages at 11.30' " in the bottom left-hand corner of the invitation. Well, I shall be glad not to turn out."

"Thank God for small mercies," Davina remarked derisively as she went out with Clunie to the car. "I might be a prisoner under escort."

"Would you prefer to walk home by yourself?" asked Clunie. "Don't be so peevish." With a vision of the rusty black evening dress she added, "We don't dress up for these parties, by the way."

Davina looked amused. "Aunt Charlotte and Molly didn't *think* it would be formal dress. What's the form? Don't, for God's sake, say *games*."

"Of course," said Clunie. "Pencil and paper first—paper

provided, bring own pencil—followed by hunt the slipper." A horrified face came round and she laughed. "Idiot, Davina! You can bring own guitar."

The first sign of enthusiasm appeared. Nothing had been said about the guitar when Jean gave the invitation. She had never, Davina said, imagined that any party given by Jean Graham would be fun, but at least it would be a change. She gave a backward nod at the castle. "Death would be preferable to much more of that."

Clunie replied that Miss Bethune and Miss Tullis might prefer death to much more of Davina. "Can't you be a bit nicer? They're not too well off and they're doing their best to be kind. They *are* kind. They didn't have to have you."

"You're wrong," said Davina coolly. "It wasn't kindness that drove them. Think of the scandal if one of the Family died of starvation."

"Rubbish!" snapped Clunie. "You couldn't have died. And if you had who would have heard of it? You're not that famous."

One thing could be said for Davina; she did not readily take offence. She stuck her tongue out at Clunie and then the disarming grin appeared. "I might be nicer to the old cows if I knew how, but I don't. There's no line of communication."

Clunie thought that was probably true—or nearly. "Oh well," she said, "something may open up."

She was back in her office when Pat arrived and expressed surprise at seeing him back in the glen so soon. "Alice says you're going to combine business and holiday.

A sudden idea?"

"Well, recent rather than sudden," he said. "I wasn't sure till I got back to Edinburgh how things would fall out but it all fitted in. It's as good a time as any to get around this part of the parish and I'll work when it's wet and play when it's fine. I'll haul you up a mountain or two, I hope."

Clunie sighed and confessed that she wasn't sure if she had the nerve. "Looked at closely and surrounded by experts it's rather daunting. Malcolm offered to start me off, but the thought of Malcolm being kind and encouraging . . ."

"Quite so," said Pat. "Keith would be neither but he's not back yet, is he?"

"No, and if he were he'd very likely drop me through sheer exasperation."

"Well, I don't think his hillman's pride would let him go that far, but it's as well not to test it. No, I'm your answer. I'm out of form myself and of course we don't get any younger. We'll repair to some secluded rock and scrabble and pant in peace and privacy. If we can find a secluded rock. What with the Finlay Expedition and Andy's school and training courses the glen's fairly humming."

"Oh, you're out of date," said Clunie. "Finlay's been relegated. There's a new bigger headline. Miss Bethune's got a young relative staying at the castle."

He was as interested as any newscaster could wish. "Has she though? I didn't know she had any young relatives."

"Nobody knew till the girl was here. But the strangest thing is that I know her. We coincided at parties in

London."

"Well well! What's her name? Is she a young Miss Bethune?"

Clunie gave an involuntary laugh. "No, not at all. She couldn't be less like Miss Bethune and her name's Davina Clare."

"H'mph!" said Pat. "A bit fancy but I don't suppose she chose it. Davina . . ." he tried it out. "I've never met a Davina."

"I don't expect you have," she said with some relish. "They're quite rare. Of course when Alice told me about a young female relative at the castle and—practically in the same breath—that you were coming back I saw the hand of Fate." She shook her head. "But it would be wrong to raise false hopes."

Pat's face was as solemn as her own. "Is she booked?"

"Not booked. At least I don't think so. She's a singer."

"A singer! Well, what a joy in the long winter evenings. Not that I'm very musical but I like a good tune."

"You might learn some duets," said Clunie, unable to resist it. She reverted to solemnity. "No, I don't think you've much chance, Pat. Davina's dedicated. What's more, I doubt if she has any idea of a Woman's Place. However, you'll see for yourself. The Grahams are doing something about her. They're having a party on Tuesday and you're invited."

Pat sighed with pleasure. 'I *am* glad I came . . . What about a climb tomorrow?"

Normally there was little to do in the hotel during climbing hours on Sunday but tomorrow, Clunie said regretfully, Harry and Alice were going to be away. "I'll be kicking my heels, I expect, but I have to be here."

"Oh well," said Pat, "plenty of time."

"Provided you're not fully engaged in pursuit of Davina."

"There's that of course," he said. "You'll just have to take your chance."

CHAPTER FIVE

NEXT DAY as Clunie was not available Pat accepted a friendly invitation and attached himself to the "school" which Andy McKillop ran with Tosh as a permanent assistant and a migratory corps of instructors. Of these Malcolm Graham was the most regular and Pat spent a pleasant morning in his company helping a group of boys and girls on graded climbs. He was a good deal impressed. On this, his own ground, Malcolm was not only an accomplished performer, he was authoritative and he was a first-class instructor.

After the lunch break Andy handed his own group over to Malcolm and bore Pat off to climb the Torran Mhor face. He knew fine, he said, as they walked away together, that when Keith came back he would get no more good of Malcolm so he might as well let him do the work now.

Pat had never had a better climb. For him climbing had never been the one absorbing passion but once back on the rock the fascination gripped him. The elation of returning skill, the "feel" of his body responding to the challenge . . . there was nothing like it. Though he had known and admired McKillop for many years it happened that he had never before climbed with him and he wondered how Keith compared with him. In their young days he had occasionally tied on with Keith, but at that time Keith was no more experienced than himself and was given to rash and ill-considered moves in which only his remarkable aptitude averted disaster. Andy was different. His moves were precise, a treat to watch, and though Pat didn't mind admitting that he was fully stretched he never felt anything but secure.

When they were down Andy told him he was no bad, no bad at all, which was fulsome for Andy. "I wonder you haven't given more time to it."

"I doubt if I would have been much better if I had," said Pat. "I'm a plodder with good balance and a big reach, but whatever it is that puts you and Keith where you are I haven't got. Inspiration?"

"Madness maybe," Andy said dryly. "Plenty call it that and I wouldn't say they're wrong. I wonder myself whiles what it is that drives men to go and kill themselves on something like the Eiger Direct. How daft can you be? But if the thing's in you, away goes everything else. Mind, a chap can combine top class climbing with useful employment; a lot do: teaching, plumbing, medicine . . . it doesn't matter what. But climbing comes first. He'd go hungry or in rags for it."

They were walking back to the road and Pat, glancing at the disreputable figure striding along beside him, smiled. The famous McKillop would never have been a dressy man or even ordinarily tidy but the ragged state of his garments was not due to poverty and not altogether to indifference. There are many kinds of image. He remarked innocently that probably the happiest men in the world were those like Andy himself, Tosh, and to some extent Malcolm Graham, who managed to make a livelihood round a ruling passion whether it was climbing, stamp collecting or poetry. "Not that many fortunes are made that way but we don't all want a fortune. I dare say you don't do too badly either, one way and another."

Andy's head came round sharply and then he grinned. "Aweel," he said in his broadest Scots, "a man can aye dae wi' a wee bit mair." But he admitted that there was more money in the climbing business than would have seemed possible even ten years ago. "What you have to do," he said, reverting to his normal speech, "is make up your mind how professional you're going to be. Malcolm now, he isn't professional at all—not in the sense you mean."

"And you wouldn't call Tosh a real pro, would you?"

"No I wouldn't. He's a damn good engineer is Tosh. He picks up a good bit on his climbing—instructing and so forth—but the workshop is what he depends on. It's nothing great but it suits him. But Keith and me—we're pros all right."

"Hard men?"

"Och, that's dressing it up. Showmen."

Something in his tone made Pat look round. "Well, that doesn't worry you surely? Why should it? You've got a special ability and you're doing a good job with it."

Andy said it didn't worry him all that much. "I get sickened whiles at the way every damn thing's getting commercialised and wonder what the hell I'm doing adding to it, but then the TV or some paper comes along with a good offer and I jump at it."

Pat laughed. 'I don't blame you. There's nothing wrong with professionals, as professionals, and even commercialism has its uses. Think of all the chaps who never heard

88

of climbing till TV showed it to them. I agree we don't want queues at the foot of every climb in the country and fixed ropes and beer cans all the way up but we're a long way from that yet."

"Well, we are," said Andy. "That's the way we're going though, and it's the kind of thing that moves fast. Still," he added cynically, "you can count on the mountains themselves to thin the ranks." They had reached the road and as he walked round to the driver's door of his vehicle nostalgia seemed to overtake him. He was not a man, he said, who spent his time regretting the past, "but man, we had great times in the old days. These kids with all the organizing and the gadgets and know how get a lot of fun out of their climbing and they're good—some of them— but I doubt if they get the kick out of it that we got, setting out on push-bikes or our feet with a hank of clothes-line and a couple of bob in our pockets." He glanced at Pat. 'That's a long way back from your time. And it's a different world from Keith Finlay's."

"But even in those prehistoric days there were tigers hitting the headlines," Pat argued. "Irving, Mallory— Hillary, dammit. You weren't all that old, Andy, when he and Tensing got to the top of Everest. I can barely remember it in fact I probably don't."

"That's true enough," said Andy. "But it wasn't like now. They hadn't the mod cons. Some folk even grumbled about them using oxygen." He sat still, filling his pipe and gazing into the past. "But by gosh, they were heroes. In some ways it's far harder to be a hero now. Expeditions are common. Anybody can go and a hell of a lot do."

Pat said he had even been to the Hindu Kush himself. "Jo and I went in a university party but we don't boast about it. It was a mistake. God, it was hell! Fortunately nobody actually died but it was a near thing for some. Dysentery." He lit his own pipe. "You know, Andy, I'm wondering what Malcolm's going to make of it. Has he any notion at all of what it's like?"

"No, and you needn't waste your breath telling him. He hasn't the imagination. But he won't get any of the local plagues. They'll be better prepared than you were."

"That won't be difficult. I'm surprised, though, that Keith's picked him. There are plenty of good climbers with far wider experience."

Andy, his pipe well alight, reached for the starter. "Well, it's like this," he said, "there's quite a few wouldn't go. Competition's keen and Keith has a reputation. Mind, I don't say he means it: I don't think he does—not exactly—but it's his own reputation he's thinking about."

"He was always a competitive sort of chap."

"Aye. What they call a great competitor. So he picks a good reliable second—and Malcolm's damn good, mind you—who won't push to the front of the picture. And Malcolm will be all right. He'll take what comes in the Hindu Kush like he does on Ben Nevis in a blizzard." The car moved forward and as it picked up speed Andy gave a laugh. "I reckon the threat to this expedition is Clunie. It's to be hoped they don't fall out over her."

There was a short pause before Pat asked, "Is it likely?"

"Well," said Andy, "Keith had a notion of her at one time. He lost interest and Malcolm filled the gap but there's no saying Keith might not be interested again. From something Malcolm said he has hopes of announcing an engagement when he comes back from the Hindu Kush and as we've said, Keith's competitive."

Only the insistence of her mother that courtesy to Miss Bethune demanded it had persuaded Jean Graham to arrange the party for Davina. There was nothing she wanted less, she told Clunie who was called in to advise, than to do anything about the girl or even see her again. She didn't know how she was going to have the face to introduce her to their friends. At least it would be a very small party: only those who could be trusted to understand the predicament.

Clunie argued that the mixture should be diluted. Integration, she agreed, would be difficult, though she refrained from pointing out that the determination of the hostess not to blend with the principal guest didn't help, and she suggested some additions to the trusties, including a couple of pleasant young marrieds who were English and would prevent Davina from feeling alone among the natives. But Jean, though she asked for advice, rarely took it. She conceded the English couple since they were on the list of people who must be done something about and seven guests were finally invited to meet Miss Bethune's young relative. Clunie and Pat and a local brother and sister, Ross and Elspeth McAdam were the trusties: Hake joined the English couple to be worked off.

The young Grahams did their entertaining in the loft above what used to be the stables. Furnished with throw-outs and white elephants they had added to its amenities over the years and thrown nothing away so that it combined a rare variety of styles. "A Little Child Shall Lead Them" kept company with abstracts and climbing photographs on the walls: there was a rocking-chair, wicker-chairs, a veteran piano and a splendid Victorian sofa. Christian Bonnington and James Bond rubbed shoulders with *Little Women* on the bookshelves and a brass standard lamp provided a mellow light and a strong smell of paraffin. To old friends the loft was a place where they had played Happy Families, danced, sung songs and, at a pinch, slept. Davina, as Clunie had foretold, thought it was a studio.

"What a fabulous place!" she exclaimed. "Aren't you clever! Where did you get all this marvellous tatt?"

"Oh—here and there," Clunie would have replied lightly, but not Jean. Jean conscientiously explained how the collection had come about and drew Davina's attention to the dolls' house and train set. Davina lost interest. She sat down on the sofa to take stock of the company and didn't think much of it either.

The company, for its part, was struck dumb. Her appearance threw them out. In spite of herself, the highland air and Miss Tullis's wholesome food had done her good so that she was looking better, and she had washed her hair which shone pale gold in the lamplight, but her idea of informal dress was not that of Kintorran. She wore black; immensely wide trousers and a top lavishly decorated with spangles. In the context of jeans and cotton frocks it looked bizarre in the extreme and the other girls would have felt sorry for her if pity had not been so obviously unnecessary.

As Jean mumbled introductions the girls were dismissed with scarcely a glance. Ross McAdam, Eric Salmon and the married Englishman got little more and a head to foot stare at Pat met such bland amiability that it was quickly withdrawn. Malcolm was different.

It was some time before Clunie saw what was going on. She was busy since Jean, in her resentment, was missing on half her cylinders. Malcolm, with Pat and other old loft hands, was moving about with drinks and food; she herself was supporting the English pair in their efforts to converse with Davina but they were getting nowhere. Davina was fully engaged in looking at Malcolm.

He was worth looking at. His hair shone, his skin glowed with a golden tan and his athletic body moved beautifully. Clunie's father described him as a magnificent young animal and had once remarked with a shocking lack of delicacy that if They ever got to the point of imposing selective breeding—which, if the present lunatic trend continued, was not impossible—Malcolm's services would be greatly in demand. But he was pleasant as well as handsome and he was a good host. He had always been better than Jean in this respect, and being quite uncritical and not observant he had not been alarmed either by reports on Davina or Davina in person. She was just another girl and this was just another party which he expected to enjoy in the usual way.

It was during a discouraged lull after the English pair and Clunie had admitted defeat that Malcolm's world turned upside down. Davina was staring at him and as if he felt it he turned and looked at her across the room. Meeting his look the strange blue-green eyes widened and the bewitching smile began and grew, parting her lips. Malcolm, with an air of not knowing what had hit him, went straight to her. She moved a little, making room for him beside her on the sofa.

"That," murmured Pat in Clunie's ear, "is what was known in the Naughty Nineties as the Glad Eye. A masterly performance. I'd better go and talk to Jean before she bursts her boiler."

He went over to the flushed and outraged Jean, commanding her attention, and Clunie only had time to see Elspeth McAdam's stricken face before being pinned by Eric Salmon.

From their earliest youth Hake had been rather a bad joke. Though he was a good deal older than the Ritchie-Graham gang he had attached himself to it, oblivious to insult, and in later years Clunie had caught his blameless fancy. Even with Keith and then Malcolm in possession as recognized boyfriends she had spent a lot of ingenuity in dodging Hake and now she was horrified to see that, the way being clear, he proposed to move in. The eyes of a fish cannot glow but the ardour was unmistakable.

"It's grand to see you again, Clunie," he murmured confidentially. "Kintorran hasn't been itself at all these last years."

"Well, that's nice of you, Hake," she replied. "Oh—I shouldn't call you that now. Eric."

He laughed. "No, no. I like Hake. And anyway I

wouldn't mind what you called me. I'm afraid I'm a bit old-fashioned—a square." He glanced at Davina and then back to Clunie with a whimsical smile. "I don't admire modern girls. You haven't changed at all. Just the same simple Scots lassie . . ."

"Oh, I hope not," said Clunie with a cool sophisticated smile. "I'd hate to think I'm as simple as I was four years ago."

"Well, you're older, of course," he allowed, "but you're very different from . . ." Another meaning glance.

"Davina? She's a friend of mine, you know. We saw quite a lot of each other in London." This slight exaggeration served its purpose. In the momentary bafflement which followed she excused herself. "I must speak to Jean."

Ross McAdam, who had taken charge of the gramophone, was about to put on another record and she said, "Hold it, Ross," and went over to Jean. "What about asking Davina to sing? She's brought her guitar."

"I *will not*," Jean hissed between clenched teeth.

Pat spoke soothingly. "You might as well. Break things up a bit."

"I won't speak to her."

"Then I'll do it," said Clunie. She raised her voice. "Hey, Davina! What about a song?"

Davina was more than ready. Abandoning Malcolm she got up, took her guitar from its case, and stationed herself unerringly beside the standard lamp. "I only know one Scotch song," she said, "so I'll begin with that as a compliment." She smiled at Malcolm, played a few chords

95

and sang *The Four Marys*.

There had been a lot of singing at other parties in the loft. The McAdams were both good natural singers, Clunie could play the piano if the accompaniments were familiar or not too difficult and all of them could raise their voices tunefully enough to join in, but the first song from Davina told them that tonight they would do better to keep their mouths shut. Davina was a professional and not one to suffer amateurs gladly.

Her talent, in fact, was limited and most obviously so in her choice of songs, for though her repertoire held old folksongs, ballads and—unexpectedly—some very charming little French songs, the bulk of it was of the modern variety of "folk" and there was no evidence that she knew the good from the bad, the true from the false. But within her limits she was very good indeed. Her voice was charming and highly individual, she sang with feeling and musicianship which made the most inane numbers almost convincing and above all she was a spellbinder. 'There was Mary Seaton and Mary Beaton and Mary Carmichael and me," she sang and brought all the pathos of the tragic Queen of Scots into the loft.

Listening, Clunie felt that she could forgive her almost anything. It was such bad luck that the throat infection had stopped her when she had so nearly arrived . . . How could she be expected to adapt herself to the castle and Kintorran? . . Miss Bethune and Molly—Jean—even the McAdams . . . Artists have to go their own way, be themselves.

One song followed another till Davina was tired and

most of the listeners were well content. When she stopped it was growing late and nobody wanted to start anything else. For a little while talk was easier since Davina's knowledge of show business and its personalities provided material, then she turned back to Malcolm and the party soon broke up. The lousiest party she had ever attended, thought Clunie as she saw Hake approaching again.

Hake wanted to drive her home: his car was at the Bethune Arms but it wouldn't take five minutes . . . Well then, what about fixing something up? Golf? A walk? Dinner—"Mummy would love to see you . . ."

It was the final straw. "Sorry, Hake," she said coldly. "I'm afraid I can't fix anything. We're very busy at the Brig. Goodnight." She turned to Pat. "We can take Davina home, can't we?"

"If she hasn't made other arrangements," said Pat and she turned her back on him.

Davina said that Malcolm was taking her home and the hand which was not carrying the guitar grasped Clunie lovingly by the elbow. "What a fun party! Who'd have believed it? I'm really grateful, you know."

"Well, thank your hostess, not me," said Clunie.

"Oh I will." Davina giggled. "I'll gush all over her. She hated every moment and don't tell me *she'd* have asked me to sing. How was I? It felt all right."

It sounded more than all right, Clunie assured her and left her waiting complacently for Malcolm to fetch her.

"What about the clearing up?" she asked Jean. "Want a hand?"

Jean said shortly that she was going to put out the lamp, shut the door and go to bed. "Thanks all the same," she added grudgingly. "And if you thank me for this party I'll hit you."

"An empty threat," said Clunie. "G'night. Sleep well." She turned to Malcolm. "Night, Malcolm."

"Oh—goodnight," he mumbled without looking at her.

The drive back to the Brig began silently.

"Interesting evening," Pat remarked at last. "Rum creature, Davina." He glanced round briefly. "Not a home-maker, as you so kindly warned me. Not my type at all, in fact, which is just as well, considering everything."

Clunie said nastily that Hake didn't like modern girls either and he retaliated with a sympathetic, "Bad luck" before reverting to Davina. "Surprising sort of relative for Miss Bethune to spring on the community. How do they get on?"

"They don't. Miss Bethune hasn't a clue about Davina and Davina hasn't much about her."

"A good deal less, I should imagine. Miss B. is quite a shrewd old party."

"Are you implying that Davina's dense?"

"Oh, she's clever enough in her own line—not that I know much about it. But in all other departments I'd rate her as pure bone."

"Let's take it you don't know *anything* about Davina," said Clunie. At this moment she didn't know what she thought of Davina, but she wasn't going to be told what to think by Pat. Not only was she ruffled by the party, she was annoyed with Pat himself. They had hardly exchanged a word since the cheerful talk when he arrived. She knew he had climbed with Andy on Sunday but instead of telling her all about it in the bar afterwards he had left her to be embarrassingly and boringly monopolized by Malcolm. On Monday he had simply vanished. She could only suppose that he again regarded her as a nuisance, or a potential nuisance, though they had got on so well during the long hours of the mug-hunt. Probably, like other men, he was chary about getting involved and she wished she hadn't talked so much. Clearly the hatchet had been buried in a very shallow grave.

Now she said coldly that she wouldn't call Davina shrewd. "Artists very seldom are and you won't deny she's an artist."

"That's a big word," said Pat.

"I'm not saying hers is the biggest kind of art. All I'm saying is that it's one kind and she's good. She must have worked really hard and she's absolutely serious about it. It's the only thing she cares about."

Pat was silent. If there was any expression on his face she couldn't see it.

"Can't you grant her that?" she demanded. "Or are you too prejudiced? I suppose Harry Lauder is your ideal."

There was an aggravating twitch at the corner of his mouth but he said gravely that Sir Harry was before his time. "M'father heard him once and was quite impressed."

"You must have heard him on the castle gramophone."

"No," he said, "I never had the privilege of hearing the castle gramophone." He paused. "I don't think I'm prejudiced. Not particularly. Davina's good at what she does and she sang a few good songs, but most of what she sang was tripe. Pretty tedious unless you happen to be the sort of adolescent moron it's aimed at."

"Obviously I am," snapped Clunie, forgetting that she too had thought it a pity about the tripe. "And I *have* heard Harry Lauder at the castle—they've got dozens of his records—and *he* got away with a lot of damned phoney Scots songs. The trouble is—"

"I know," said Pat. "We're all so parochial. Like Hake." He drew into the car park and walked round to open her door.

"Thank you," she said and added stiffly. "Sorry if I was rude."

"What?" The grin appeared in his eyes. "You're never apologizing? That's something new. Where's your spirit?"

She gave an involuntary laugh. "Oh, I've still got it but it's rather reduced at the moment. Of all the ghastly parties! I could have stuck a hatpin into Jean."

"Well, she had a lot to bear when you think of her principles," said Pat. Clunie started wearily towards the house and he picked her up as if she were a small child.

"Hey!" she protested. "What do you think you're doing?"

"Don't panic. I'm just giving you a carry because you're worn out."

"I hope all the people looking out of their windows understand that."

Pat said soothingly that they would probably think she was a bit tight. "Nothing to worry about. Might happen to anybody." He set her on her feet and opened the door. Only the dim all-night lights were burning and he locked up according to instructions and turned round to face her. "You're not heartbroken," he said.

She looked at him, frowning. "What do you—do you mean Malcolm? Well, hell! Of course I'm not heartbroken. It's pathetic. I wouldn't have believed even Malcolm could be such a—such a *dope*. But why should you think my heart comes into it?"

"I didn't think so—not really," said Pat. He took her hand. "The thing is there's a rumour going round that your engagement will be announced when he gets back from the Hindu Kush. Perhaps I shouldn't have told you, but I think it's better that you should know."

"Yes," said Clunie. "Much better. Thank you." She thought about it for a moment, wondering who had told him. On the whole she would rather not know. The source of the rumour was only too easy to identify. "I was a fool," she said abruptly. "He said he would ask me again after the Hindu Kush and I sort of let it pass. I thought he might forget about it."

"*Forget* about it?"

"Well, it can't have gone all that deep, can it—judging from the evidence? But you'd think he'd have had the sense to keep his mouth shut."

"Ah," said Pat, "that's one of the things that separates the men from the boys. The men don't talk. Malcolm's a nice guy and a damn good climber but his best friend couldn't call him mature."

"Poor Malcolm," Clunie said sadly.

Pat's grasp of her hand tightened. His other hand lifted her chin and he kissed her. It was a good hard kiss but not lingering. Before she got over the surprise he let her go. "There now! See what you've made me do," he said. He turned her round and pushed her towards the stairs. "Away to your bed before passion bursts its banks . . ."

Clunie went upstairs with a warm bubble of laughter inside her. The whole episode was so characteristic. Nobody but Pat would have kissed her like that, without making a thing of it. Only Pat would have told her of the rumour about Malcolm and herself—warned her. That, however, was something that could be left till tomorrow. Meanwhile the unpleasant taste of the party had gone and her last thought before she fell asleep was that Pat's withdrawal of the last few days was not caused by unfriendliness. The hatchet was still buried.

In the morning, when she thought about it, she realized just how annoying the rumour was and she was more than ever grateful for Pat's warning. There was nothing the glen relished more than the news that a girl had lost her man—been jilted, they would believe if Malcolm had been confiding his ill-founded hopes to all corners. For some reason a man in the same plight was not nearly so rich a haul, probably because of an underlying feeling that he was to be congratulated on getting off the hook. Well, she would just have to take it. Pat would help.

"How was the party?" asked Alice, dropping in to the office on her morning round.

"Hell," said Clunie. Though Alice liked gossip as much as anyone hers was rarely malicious and she could be relied on for a fair degree of discretion. It was better that she should get the facts undistorted and Clunie decided to come clean—or at least reasonably clean. She gave her a graphic description of the party, the capture of Malcolm, and Jean's consequent paralysis. "The rest of us worked like slaves well, apart from Hake and he may have done his best—but the tension! . . Honestly, Alice, you never saw a faster bit of work. One look . . ."

Alice was fascinated. *"Well!"* she exclaimed, wide-eyed and sat down to digest it. "Of course Malcolm's a sitting duck," she said. "He's never been exposed to anything really high powered. I'm not underestimating your appeal, dear," she added kindly, "but you're not in Davina's class evidently."

"Nowhere near," Clunie agreed. "Mine's just natural wholesome appeal, guaranteed harmless."

"Well, I dare say you could do quite a lot of damage if you wanted to," said Alice. "The difference is you don't want to. Poor Malcolm though. Years of being faithfully in love with you and bowled out by a bitch. On heat."

"Now, Alice! No need to be coarse. A *witch* is what Davina is. Later on she sang and had everyone spellbound. Except Jean."

"Well, no doubt it eased the tension. But doesn't it just show you? It's no good bringing a boy up in blinkers. He's got no resistance. You can't see Alan or Pat—or Harry when he was that age—going down like that."

Clunie pointed out that none of them had been exposed to direct attack by Davina, but Alice retorted that the *femme fatale*—sufficiently *fatale* for innocents like

Malcolm—wasn't all that rare.

She got slowly to her feet and paused for a moment, deep in thought. "I must do *something* about her," she said at last. "It would be rude not to. And," she added more briskly, "silly. After all young men take tosses every day though most of them get it over earlier in life. Besides, I want to see this witch."

"Well don't," Clunie implored her, "lay on another jolly party."

"I won't," said Alice. "For one thing Harry and I are too old. Nobody over forty should attempt it. I'll think about it."

Pat was the next caller. "Are you looking for a fight?" he asked, eyeing her warily.

Clunie raised her eyebrows. "You mean because you kissed me? No, not at all. It was kindly meant, I'm sure."

"I live for others," said Pat. "It's not a bad day, what about that climb? You haven't been out yet, have you?"

"I haven't, but you have and covered yourself with glory, according to the bar. Hardly a fair start. But I couldn't go today even if you hadn't sneaked ahead. Harry and Alice are taking the day off."

"Well, when can you? Tomorrow? I swear I won't undermine you with my superior prowess."

"Tomorrow should be okay," she said. 'I'll just have to ask Harry.'

"We'll fix it tonight then," said Pat. "God willing and weather permitting of course." He reached through the hatch and gave her hair a tweak. "Be seeing you, Sunshine."

As he disappeared along the passage the phone rang. "Brighouse," said Clunie.

"Is that you, Clunie?" said Jean's voice. "Look—I must talk to you. Can you come to tea? Mother's going out."

Clunie said it was impossible. "I'm on duty all day."

"You must have *some* time off. What about lunch? No—Mother won't have gone. Well then, just say when you can come. Any time."

"Jean," said Clunie, "if you think I'm going to bike down *and* up just to hold a post-mortem on your horrible party think again. There's nothing to talk about."

"You're wrong," said the telephone angrily. "I'll come to you . . ."

Jean arrived, rather flushed and out of breath, early in the afternoon and Clunie, having arranged for a stand-in, heartlessly insisted on going for a walk. She said she wanted air. "Tied as I am to my office I must get out when I can."

"You seem to be in one of your facetious moods," Jean said resentfully.

"Well, it's better than making mountains out of molehills."

"Molehills!"

"Come on," said Clunie and set a brisk pace along a winding old road which led eventually to another glen. It was a cloudy uncertain sort of day which muted all the colours and the hills had a look of brooding. "Now," she said, "you can get it off your chest—or unburden your soul, if that's what you prefer."

Jean took a deep breath. "I simply don't understand

105

you, Clunie. You seem to think—what happened last night is funny."

"I don't—at least not very funny. I think it's a pity."

"A pity? Well, that's putting it mildly." Jean paused. It was very difficult to say what she wanted to say while they were belting along at five miles an hour. "Do go a bit slower," she said.

Clunie slowed down slightly; not much because round the next bend was a hump-backed bridge and if they had to have a heart-to-heart session that would be the place. It was out of sight of the hotel and they could stare at the burn and chuck a few stones in to relieve the tension. They climbed down to the bank where there was a comfortable cushion of heather and plenty of stones. The burn gurgled cheerfully past on its way to join the river.

Jean assembled her thoughts which had been somewhat disrupted. She had a prepared speech and she was determined to use it, though it would need a little adapting in view of the listener's attitude. Clunie selected a flat stone and bending sideways flicked it across the pool in three hops. "Cock, hen, birdie," she said. "I'm listening."

"Well," Jean began, "first I want to tell you I know Malcolm's let you down and I'm—I can't tell you what I feel about it. Malcolm's miserable about you himself. He feels terrible. And of course it's been an awful shock to Mother and Father "

"Jean!" Clunie cried sharply. "What's this? Do you mean to tell me you've told your parents—held a family conclave because Malcolm fell for Davina?"

"Well, of course we had to—"

106

"For heaven's sake *why?* Malcolm hasn't let me down. We weren't engaged—you know that."

"I don't know why you weren't," burst from Jean, the prepared speech gone forever. "You said not till after the expedition, but you *were* a pair and you know he never looked at anybody else. If you'd just agreed to the engagement or—or an understanding, *this would never have happened.*"

Clunie was dumb. She had never been so angry in her life, not even with Jean, but a shouting match would do no good. Jean, repenting her outburst, began to apologize but she stopped her.

"You've got it wrong," she said curtly. "It seems Malcolm did too. I did *not* say I'd be engaged to him after the expedition but he's been going round telling everybody—"

"Telling everybody?"

"Well, somebody told Pat as if it was all settled."

"Who told Pat?"

"I've no idea. Andy or Tosh probably. I refused to be engaged and he said he'd ask me again, that's all." Clunie bent to pick up another stone. "He probably wouldn't have taken a final 'no' even if I'd said it—as I should have done." She flung the stone into the water with one great splash. "And I don't believe," she added, "it would have made any difference if we had been engaged. Or even married."

"That's nonsense," said Jean.

Clunie eyed her sourly. "I suppose you think being engaged to me would have protected him. Malcolm's—

what? Twenty-four? Twenty-five? If he can't look after himself by now it's time he learnt. Let's hope Davina will be a lesson to him."

"She'll *ruin* him," cried Jean. "You don't understand. It's *serious*. She's as madly in love as he is and he's talking about getting married before his term begins. In London," she added as a last straw.

The idea of Davina married to a schoolmaster domiciled in Glasgow was ludicrous. She could easily be, as she would say, crazy about Malcolm and a love affair would greatly enliven her stay at the castle, but to her, Clunie suspected, love affairs were no more than agreeable diversions. Indeed Malcolm's deadly earnestness might be as much of a shock to her as her lack of it would be to him. It would be useless, however, to say any of this to Jean.

"I'll have to get back now," she said and got up. "Don't worry too much. It'll work itself out."

Jean sighed. "I wish I could think so. If only you'd—but I won't say any more about that."

"Don't even think it," said Clunie. "And kindly make it clear to your parents—and Malcolm—that he was perfectly free to fall in love with any girl he fancied. What he was *not* free to do was to babble about me as if I was half-engaged to him. That I do resent."

This seemed to be a new idea to Jean. Having thought about it she admitted that Clunie had cause for resentment but it was second nature to defend her brother. Malcolm, she said, probably hadn't been so definite as gossip made it sound. "If they were chipping him about you he may have said something like—oh, waiting till he's back from the Hindu Kush. He wouldn't think there was any harm in that."

"H'mph!" said Clunie.

They walked back to the Brig and parted friends, though sombrely.

CHAPTER SIX

WHEN CLUNIE returned to her post after seeing Jean mount her bicycle she was informed by an ill-used stand-in that the phone had never stopped ringing and Morag never went out when the boss was away. The phone kept on ringing. Half the tourist population of Scotland seemed to have set its sights on the Brighouse Hotel. Harry and of course Morag, she thought rather crossly, carried in their minds a complete, or virtually complete, list of rooms available on given dates but she had some way to go before she reached that standard of expertise and the fact that those who telephoned usually wanted accommodation for one night or at most two added to the difficulty. Later in the afternoon new arrivals began to check in and a further complication arose when strangers asked her to recommend a hotel for their next stage. It was then her duty not only to recommend hotels but to offer to ring round till she found one which had vacancies, a service which was rarely refused.

She was engaged in one of these negotiations when, to her astonishment, Pat came in escorting Davina. Pat, taking in the situation, gave her a speaking look over the shoulders of the waiting clients, indicated Davina and with a word to her disappeared. Davina, looking slightly amused, turned away and studied the display of postcards.

The postcards and the board showing notices about places to visit, Highland Games and times of meals were both exhausted before Clunie was free to attend to her visitor.

"What a busy little bee," said Davina, perching herself on the high stool provided for the use of clients without encouraging them to linger.

Clunie pressed a hand to her forehead. "If you hear a zizzing noise it's my brain," she said. She looked in the mirror and gave her face and hair a little rapid attention. "Hallo. How did you get here?"

"Pat McThing brought me," Davina replied carelessly. "I was looking for a hitch and he happened along. He says he'll take me back if Malcolm doesn't show up." Malcolm, she explained, didn't know she was here and might or might not drop in on his way home from whatever he was doing. "Something about rescue techniques. Greek to me but don't try to explain. I wanted to see you because I'd like to know if it's true I seduced your steady. Your intended."

"Who on earth suggested that?" Clunie demanded. "Malcolm? Surely not! Even Malcolm—" She stopped.

"Couldn't be that simple," Davina finished for her. "No. He's troubled in his mind, but I put that down to inexperience and being Scotch."

Miss Bethune and Miss Tullis rushed into Clunie's mind and out again. Pat? Certainly not. "Jean!" she exclaimed.

Davina nodded. "She came to see me this morning."

Clunie groaned, wondering if she was glad or sorry she hadn't known this when she saw Jean and Davina's smile lit her eyes. "Yes, do murder her," she said. "I'll help. You may not believe it, but I don't lure men from other girls.

111

At least not unless I hate the girl. So if I've done the dirty on you I'm sorry. Not that it's very helpful to say that now. Jean said you were practically engaged but I didn't believe her. You weren't, were you?"

"No," said Clunie, "but a lot of people think we were. You won't know but in a place like this everybody knows *everything*—and more than there is to know. Just a minute . . ." She turned to attend to a couple who wanted to order packed lunches for tomorrow. Davina, though she didn't move, effaced herself, becoming part of the background.

As soon as Clunie was free she went straight on from where they had left off. She said she knew nothing whatever about places like Kintorran but she was learning. "Aunt Charlotte and Molly come back from the shops bringing the news with the fish and discuss it for hours. Well, what else have they to talk about? They've never mentioned you and Malcolm though." She looked directly at Clunie. "You know it simply didn't occur to me last night that you might be interested in him. If asked I'd have said Pat Thing was more your type."

Clunie laughed. "If asked I'd have said you never gave it a thought."

"Well, maybe I didn't exactly think," Davina admitted, "but I'm quite observant."

"You don't give that impression."

"It pays off better not to, but you'd be surprised. As of now. I'm glad to see you're not mourning—or even very angry with me."

"I'm not angry with you at all," said Clunie. "But what

112

are you going to do with Malcolm now you've got him? Are you in love with him?"

"Oh yes," Davina said earnestly. "Well, look at him. Maybe you're used to it but I'm still reeling from the impact. Achilles—no, he was the one with the heel. Male gorgeousness personified, whoever he was."

"But with a Scotch Presbyterian background, don't forget. It's different from Ancient Greece in many ways. Are you going to marry him?"

"*Marry* him? Of course I'm not going to marry him. Can you see me living in Glasgow married to a teacher?"

"Frankly, no," said Clunie. "But it's what's expected of you."

Davina stared at her, not without suspicion. "You're not telling me you can't have a nice passing affair in Scotland? I don't believe you."

"Not with Malcolm you can't. He's already told the family that he hopes you'll be married—in London, to add insult to injury—before his term starts next month. I expect he's planning to leave you with his parents when he goes to the Hindu Kush."

"It's not true!"

"Yes it is. Jean cannot tell a lie."

"Hell!" said Davina. There was a short silence and then she asked petulantly, "What *is* this Hindu Kush?"

"The Hindu Kush," said Clunie instructively, "is a mountainous area in Afghanistan. Malcolm is going on a mountaineering expedition led by Keith Finlay. They'll go in December or January to get themselves acclimatized and organized for the real climbs—the assaults—in April.

113

Have you heard of Keith Finlay?"

"No. At least I believe Malcolm mentioned him but I wasn't listening. Who's he?"

Clunie explained Keith Finlay and threw in a little about expeditions in general and the Finlay expedition in particular. "You must have heard about Everest expeditions. This is the same sort of thing on a small scale."

"They must be mad," said Davina. "I can't see the point of it. And it'll be hideously uncomfortable."

"Oh, it'll be that." Clunie smiled. "All climbers are more or less mad, I suppose. I'm not much of a climber. I'm scared to death half the time or else plain miserable but it gets you. It's so glorious . . ."

"Well, if you say so," Davina said in a tone of extreme scepticism. She brooded for a moment, frowning. "Malcolm—what a nit,' she said bitterly. 'I'll have to—"

The sentence was never finished. Hurried steps sounded on the stone floor of the porch, the door was pushed open and a bloodstained figure in climbing gear stumbled in. He was a very young man, near to collapse and Clunie darted out and was beside him before he was properly in. Afterwards she was surprised that Davina was almost as quick as she was, but there was no time to think about it then.

"In here," she said and between them they supported him into Harry's office and got him seated. He held his hands stiffly in front of him and the palms were raw and bleeding.

"Mike," he gasped. "The belay gave—I couldn't hold

114

him—"

"All right, Willie," said Clunie. "We'll take care of it." He was one of the regular bothy boys and she knew him quite well. She looked at Davina. "Go through to the bar, will you? That way—" she pointed. "Tell the barman—and Pat if he's there." Davina vanished and turning back to the boy who was very near to fainting, Clunie put her arm round him. "It's all right," she said again. "Just try to tell me . . . is he badly hurt? Were you able to get to him?"

He nodded. "Aye, I got down. He was knocked out but he—he came round a wee bit."

Pat came in as he was speaking. He had been enjoying a quiet beer in the newly open and almost empty bar, wondering what Davina was saying to Clunie and when the castle had supper. It was doubtful if Davina either knew or cared. He would give her another twenty minutes and then if Malcolm didn't turn up he would rescue Clunie, buy Davina a drink and take her home.

It was at this point that Davina suddenly appeared in the doorway leading to Harry's office. She looked round and beckoned to him.

"Clunie wants you," she said. "Somebody's fallen off a mountain and a boy called Willie has come for help. He's just about all in."

"Brandy, Tom," said Pat, on his way. "Bring it, Davina."

"He kind of came and went," Willie was saying jerkily. "I think it's—it's his legs mostly but I—I couldn't—I was frightened to touch him . . ."

Clunie looked up, her arm still round him. "It's Mike," she said, "but Willie knows where he is."

"That's the main thing," said Pat. Davina came in and he took the glass she handed him.

"Brandy?" Clunie said doubtfully. "Is that all right?"

Pat nodded. "We've got to keep him going. Come on, Willie. Take a swig."

Willie obediently drank, gasped and coughed and presently announced that he was better. "But no more climbing for me, by God."

"Well, there you're wrong," Pat told him. "You're going to help us get Mike down. Is that a First Aid box you've got there, Tom? Give it to Clunie and she'll see to these hands. No sign of Andy yet?"

"Not yet," said Tom. "They shouldn't be long, but we'd better not wait."

Pat agreed and Tom, who was standing in the doorway where he could keep an eye on the bar, said, "Bessie's not on yet. I'll send for her and Benny or one of them can go in there till she comes."

"Tom," said Clunie, "could you wait a little before sending for Bessie? Just till we know a bit more." Tom nodded and she told Pat that Bessie was Mike's girl.

"I see," said Pat. "Now, Willie, tell us as exactly as you can where Mike is."

"Well, we were on Trochy," Willie began more composedly, "—and we thought we'd have a go at the Steeple . . ." Pat's eyebrows rose a little and Clunie glanced up sharply. The Steeple was recognized as Very Severe, dangerously exposed in places. "We were going fine," the boy went on with a note of defiance, "and then . . ."

The story was soon told and Mike's position described.

116

Clunie listened as she dressed the sore hands and when Pat asked, "Got all that, Clunie?" she nodded.

"Could Willie have some coffee before you start?" she asked.

Tom, who had come back, said he had laid it on along with a flask for Mike. "I'll go and collect the gear now. If Clunie could raise Andy on the R/T before his party leaves it would be a good thing," he said to Pat. "He and Malcolm have been doing rescue training with some Army lads and they might as well use it if we can catch them. Come straight along with all their equipment."

"And if the Army's left they can damn well turn round and come back," said Pat.

No more than half an hour after Willie had stumbled in the three men drove off in the hotel Land Rover which would take them as near to the casualty as a vehicle could go. There would be a long haul and a difficult one for the stretcher party, as Clunie knew. She could see in her mind almost exactly where Mike lay, for though she had never climbed the Steeple she knew the look of it well and had, indeed, watched ascents through binoculars. She gave one anxious look at the weather, praying that it would stay clear and not too cold, and then concentrated all her wits on what she had to do.

After some delay she got Andy on the radio. He was on his way back with Malcolm and his trainee soldiers had already left, but he undertook to contact them and ask for assistance.

"Have they a doctor with them?" asked Clunie and he replied that they had and he could climb.

"We'll look in and collect more muscle men," he said. "And, Clunie—food and hot drinks. None of us have had much since our breakfasts. Say twenty minutes."

"Okay," said Clunie. She rang the police and ambulance service and then went through to the kitchen, which knew exactly what was required of it, and to the bar where Bessie, who seconded Tom, was in charge.

"Who's here?" she asked her. "Andy says they're going to need muscle men."

The two girls looked round. It was still too early for the regulars and there were no obvious muscle men. "I'll get Sandy to take word to the bothy and stick up a notice for Tosh," said Bessie. "Is—is he bad? Where did he come off?" Her normally rosy face was pale but she was composed, well in control, and Clunie smiled at her. "It doesn't sound too bad, love," she said. "They were on the Steeple."

Bessie exclaimed. "The *Steeple?* Just him and Willie? How daft can you be? Oh well, we're all more or less daft I suppose. I'll whistle up Sandy . . ."

In the office the sight of Davina studying the hotel tariff brought Clunie up short. "Good lord!" she said. "I'd forgotten about you. Sorry."

"Don't mention it," said Davina. "It's been highly educational. This pub isn't cheap, is it?"

"Not cheap, but it gives good value," said Clunie and looked rather helplessly at the added complication. "What on earth are we going to do about you?"

"What would you do about me?"

"Well—get you home. I don't suppose you fancy

walking."

Davina was explicit. She did not fancy walking. "I'll just hang around till Malcolm comes."

"Malcolm will be helping to get poor Mike off the Steeple. It'll take hours."

"Hours?"

"Could be all night. Have you any idea what's involved?"

"No. How could I?"

"You *have* noticed the mountains?"

"Not to say noticed," was Davina's reply. "I'm not interested in scenery and I'd rather not think about swarming up one of them. It makes me feel quite ill. As for falling off . . . How did that boy—Willie—get his hands in such a mess? They looked as if they'd been burned—or flayed."

"So they had," said Clunie and explained what happens when one man is trying desperately to hold another and the falling man's weight drags the rope through his hands. "Look, Davina—" she said, "—the Steeple is about two thousand feet of sheer rock. Mike's lying on a ledge nearly halfway up. They've got to get the stretcher to him, lift him on to it without damaging him any more—and they'll have practically no room to work—and then they have to strap him on so that he can't possibly slip or even move, and bring him down."

Davina was staring, her eyes horrified. "It's not possible! Down sheer rock? How can they?"

"I can't tell you how they'll do it," Clunie said. "It'll take a lot of strength and a lot of know-how and a hell of

119

a lot of courage. But they'll do it. I can tell you that." Since she seemed to be holding her audience she went on to describe as much as she could of the techniques of lowering a stretcher on ropes, stage by stage, with men waiting wherever there was a foothold to guide it. "And when they've got it down," she concluded, "there's two miles or so of carrying over rough ground to the road. That's where the muscle men come in. The more the better."

There was silence. Clunie looked at her watch, thinking it was time Andy and Malcolm came and wishing Harry was back. And Tosh—where *was* Tosh? And was the kitchen getting on with the provisions? How would they know how much would be wanted? Were there going to be enough men? Her job was to stay by the radio and telephone, but she *must* see—

"Well," said Davina out of the silence, "everybody young goes for kicks more or less. They're a bit soft if they don't. Getting killed or smashed up falling off mountains is no crazier than drugs or mucky sex and pop festivals. It's better, if anything. Positive."

Clunie was slightly startled, having again forgotten Davina, but she looked round on her way to the door and laughed. "Well said, Davina. And don't forget the muggers and the football hooligans."

The kitchen had done what was expected of it. Sliced in loaves sufficient quantity had been found, a tactful blend of butter and margarine with slabs of corned beef or cheese slapped between slices, and boiling water poured on to powders and sugar. Boxes of sandwiches and

120

Thermos flasks of good strong soup and coffee were ready for loading when Clunie went out and a group of muscular young men were also ready for loading. The dining-room staff meanwhile was sailing into action, serving the punctual seven o'clock diners who were not climbers and unconscious of crisis.

As so often after what seems an endless period of waiting, everything happened at once. Andy and Malcolm drove in, two Army vehicles containing officers and young soldiers rolled up from the opposite direction and Tosh strode over from his workshop.

Andy, coming into the office for Clunie's report, was followed by Malcolm who gave an audible gasp. "Davina!" he exclaimed. "What—"

"Hallo, darling," said Davina, raising a hand in greeting.

Andy gave one surprised, irritable glance from one to the other and turned his back. "Now, Clunie, where have we got to?" he said and as they talked Clunie heard Malcolm's agitated mutter and Davina's voice clear and unperturbed in the background.

"I just came to see Clunie," she said airily.

"Mumble mumble?"

"Oh, Pat Thing gave me a lift. He was going to take me back if you didn't come, but then this schemozzle blew up and he's somewhere on that ghastly mountain. But I'm in no hurry. In fact I'm—"

"Okay, then," Andy concluded. "We'll signal them when we get there and they'll send up a rocket to let us see exactly where they are. You'll get this lot on the blower: you know what to tell them. Come on, Malcolm."

121

"You could take Davina home in my van, couldn't you?" Malcolm said to Clunie, looking over her head.

Andy disposed of that idea. "We'll need your van and Clunie can't leave here," he said curtly.

"You needn't worry about Davina, Malcolm," said Clunie, hoping he might get the message, though it was unlikely. "Oh . . . Andy, this is Davina Clare who's staying at the castle. Andy McKillop, Davina."

"Hallo," said Davina.

"How do," said Andy. "Come on, Malcolm . . ."

Malcolm looked despairingly at Davina and followed him. Ignoring a heartless giggle behind her Clunie said, "I must nip out and see them start."

"Me too," said Davina.

They ran out and joined Bessie who had also deserted her post for a moment. The convoy started with Andy leading and the licentious soldiery in the five-tonners blowing kisses to the girls. Clunie, blowing kisses back, heard a faint sniff beside her and turned quickly.

"Cheer up, Bess," she said. "Look at these toughs." She waved a hand at the fast-disappearing convoy. "And Mike's as tough as any of them."

"Oh, he's tough all right," Bessie agreed. "If toughness'll do . . . Here—I must get back to the bar. Will you—?"

"I'll keep you posted," said Clunie and hurried back to her own job, Davina still at her heels.

When she had got through what was left of the callout drill she turned back to her uninvited guest. "Now what's to be done about you?" she said to her. "Miss Bethune would come for you, wouldn't she?"

Davina said that Miss Bethune no doubt would but she would rather stay where she was. "It's more interesting than the castle."

"But won't they be worrying? Do they know where you are?"

"Oh yes. At least I said something about wanting to see you. They'll just think I've stayed to dinner." She looked hopefully at Clunie. Appetizing smells were seeping delicately through from the kitchen.

A menu lay on Harry's desk and Clunie passed it over, pointing out the prices. "Not on, dear," she said firmly.

Davina sighed. "I've read it from cover to cover. It sounds lovely. Couldn't you sort of smuggle me in with you? After all you must eat. And, think what a help— what a *support*—I've been in your hour of need."

It was more than likely that if Harry and Alice were at home Davina would get her free dinner, but it was not for the receptionist to order it and in any case Clunie had no idea when she herself was going to eat. "You must be a lot better," she remarked. "Last time we talked about food you said you hated it."

"That was *wholesome* food," said Davina. She looked faintly surprised. "I hate to admit it but I *am* better. I'll have to start watching my weight."

"Well, missing your dinner will be a start," Clunie pointed out. The R/T came to life and Pat's voice spoke.

"We've been talking to Andy," it said, "and everything seems to be in hand. We're with Mike—more or less. There's not a lot we can do for him but we've given him some dope and got him warmed up a bit. Did you alert

Doc Graham? Over."

"No," said Clunie. "Should I? There's an Army doctor with the party and he can climb. Over—oh, Pat—damn!"

Pat was already talking again. He thought she should call Dr Graham because of Willie. "Tom's going to take him down now and we'll get somebody to run him to the Brig. He should go into hospital for tonight. He says he's damned if he will but he needs looking after."

Clunie said she would see to it. "Pat—is there anything I can tell Bessie?"

"Oh yes," said Pat. "Mike says tell her he's thinking about Christmas and she'll be climbing with him before then. Mind you, I doubt the last bit, but you needn't stress it. You okay? Harry back yet?"

"I'm okay. No, they're out to dinner."

"Wish I was. I'll take you out to dinner one of these days."

"Thanks. I'll remind you," said Clunie. "There's food on the way but an awful hungry lot of troops with it. Don't let them eat it all."

The first thing was to deliver the message to Bessie. Clunie went to the door of the bar and beckoned and as she returned, Bessie eagerly following, the telephone rang. It stopped.

"Brighouse Hotel," said Davina in dulcet tones and grinned at her over the receiver. "Oh hallo, Aunt Charlotte. Yes, I'm helping Clunie. Somebody's fallen off a mountain. No, don't bother. I'll get home somehow but I don't think I should leave while I can be of use . . . I knew you'd think so . . ."

Clunie gave her a speaking look but Bessie was waiting. She delivered the message. Bessie listened, gulped and finally burst into tears.

"Oh dear!" she sobbed. "I'm sorry. If I can just have a minute—"

"Of course you can," said Clunie. "Sit down."

Davina went to the door. "What we all need is a stiff drink," she said. "I was a barmaid for a time. Leave it to me." She vanished and in a moment reappeared with three glasses. "Brandy," she announced complacently and put one of the glasses into Bessie's hand. "Drink up, mate. It'll do you good."

Bessie, her tears dried by astonishment, was grateful but didn't know what Harry would say.

"Well, we'll have had it before he misses it," Davina pointed out. "There's hardly anybody in there so take your time."

"Who in the world is *she?*" asked Bessie.

"Davina Clare, Miss Bethune's young relative," said Clunie with some relish.

"Miss Bethune's—" Bessie stared. She was a local girl. "Is *that* . . ? My God!" She paused and then, looking rather puzzled asked, "What's she doing here then?"

Clunie explained. "Oddly enough I knew her in London—though I'd no idea she was related to Miss Bethune. But she really came to look for Malcolm," she added lightly. "The Grahams had a party last night and they fell for each other at sight."

"Oh," said Bessie. From under her eyelashes she stole a look at Clunie but saw only amusement. "Well," she said,

"I'd rate her as sudden death, that one."

"You wouldn't be far wrong," Clunie said laughing. "She's not a bad sort though."

Bessie, with some reserve, remarked that it takes all sorts and rising from Harry's chair went back to the bar.

As the door closed behind her, quick light footsteps sounded in the porch, the inner door was thrust open and Keith Finlay came in. He looked towards the office with a smile which changed abruptly when he saw the occupant.

"Good God!" he exclaimed. "Clunie!"

"Hallo, Keith," said Clunie.

CHAPTER SEVEN

"WHAT ARE YOU—where's Morag?" Keith demanded with every sign of annoyance.

Not being one to wear her heart on her sleeve Clunie replied with unruffled calm. "I'm a temp recep," she said amiably. "Morag is in hospital. Appendix."

"Oh. What made Harry think of you? Did he advertise, or what?"

"No, I wrote asking if he had a job for me."

Keith had had time to get over his surprise and her off-hand tone had its effect. "I see," he said and gave her a moderately friendly grin. "I remember you had a sudden attack of nostalgia during that dinner in London but it seemed to pass." He perched on the high stool. "Where's everybody? The place is uncommonly quiet."

"They're bringing Mike Shaw down off the Steeple. All the regulars, about half the British Army, and Pat McKechnie."

He had looked up sharply. "He hasn't killed himself? He should never have been on the Steeple."

"You must tell him. I'm sure he'll be grateful," said Clunie. "It sounds as if he's pretty badly hurt but he was able to send a message to his girl. Bessie."

Ignoring the impertinence Keith said he'd better go along and help. Then he paused, looking doubtful. "Trouble is I haven't had anything to eat."

"Haven't you been to the Lodge?"

"Yes, but there's nobody there except the Wilsons." He seldom gave notice of his arrival and the servants, a married couple who, in Kintorran's opinion, had an easier job than was good for them, never hesitated to send him to the Brig for his dinner, protesting that there wasn't a morsel of food in the house.

"Well, you may as well eat," Clunie said. "From the reports everything's under control at the Steeple."

As she spoke Davina came through from the bar. "Clunie, they're going to bring your dinner on a tray," she said, "but they don't know what to do about me. *Do* tell them how invaluable—"

Seeing Keith she stopped. He rose to his feet and Clunie introduced them. While the two pairs of expert eyes appraised and appreciated, the familiar young relative—we knew each other in London ran its course, this time with unusual enthusiasm from Davina.

"We nearly died of shock—" she said, "—but was I glad to see a fellow human. I couldn't have *survived* without her. And now, though I've been working like a slave in this crisis she's so mean she won't stand me dinner."

"No!" exclaimed Keith, suitably shocked. "Clunie, I'm surprised at you. But never mind—Davina?—Davina. I haven't had dinner either. We'll have it together. First, though, a drink."

"Lovely," said Davina with her smile.

And what could be smoother? thought Clunie as they walked away. Two birds with a perfect left and right: Davina getting her dinner and an agreeable acquaintance;

Keith making it plain that he was in no way involved with her, Clunie. The complacent backs disappeared into the passage and with a sigh she went back to Harry's office. Keith had employed this gambit before: she had so often watched him walk away with other girls, without, she was glad to think, showing what she felt. Now she was used to it and no longer suffered the searing agony of earlier days. The ache she did feel was almost more for him than for herself. It was not her Keith walking away with Davina. It was the fan club idol.

Somebody kicked the back door of Harry's office and she opened it to find the headwaiter with a loaded tray.

"Soup, veal and a hunk of *gâteau*," he said. "Okay?"

"Perfect," said Clunie. "Gosh, how hungry I am! Thanks a lot, Bennie. Oh—how come the booze?"

The schooner of sherry, Bennie said, was from Keith. "Is it right that the girl he's got with him is the one staying at the castle?" Clunie confirmed the rumour and he gave a whistle. "I'll say they're fast workers. Well, Keith always was but the girl's having no trouble keeping up. Quite a dish, but not my type. I like them cuddly." He nodded at the R/T. "How're they doing? Are you receiving them?"

"Some—and learning a lot of new words," Clunie said. "I thought I knew them all but I was wrong. Andy and Malcolm are up on the ledge now. They've got Mike in the casualty bag but it's going to take ages to bring the stretcher down. He's complaining of pain in his back."

"That'll mean a cable—if they can rig it," said Bennie knowledgeably. "Do they know Keith's here?"

129

"No. Should I tell them?"

Bennie thought they might be glad of him. "If he's no in too much of a dwam. Though his dwams never seem to hinder him on the hills," he added fairly. He gave the tray a professional glance. "Anything more, Mahdam? We'll send coffee." He went away but immediately reappeared. "Better no say anything about the back," he said with a jerk of his head towards the bar. "No sense bothering her. She's doing fine."

Clunie left the covers on the hot dishes while she called Pat on the radio.

"Understood," said Pat. "Will consult and inform you. Is Keith there?"

"At the moment he's dining with a lady. Guess who."

"Oh? Well, he can finish his dinner but don't let him go."

"Roger," said Clunie and sent a message to Keith to stand by.

She had reached the coffee stage when Miss Bethune came in accompanied by Hamish the Scottie. "Thought it would save trouble if I fetched Davina," she said.

Clunie, who had leapt to her feet, invited her to sit down. "Keith's taken Davina to have dinner, but they must have finished—or nearly. Will you have some coffee, Miss Bethune?"

"No thanks, never touch it at night," said Miss Bethune, seating herself in Harry's chair. Hamish sat down by her feet and stared inimically at Clunie. "I'll wait. You'll all have enough on your hands getting that poor laddie off the Steeple without thinking about Davina. Is that the wireless thing?" Her stare at the wireless thing was as inimical as Hamish's. "Don't understand wireless. Too old. You've probably never thought about it but it's an interesting thing how people seem to be born with the ability to cope with the inventions of their time. It was cars in my day. My father always bought bad ones and he was a hopeless driver. Used to shout 'Whoa!' in a crisis."

Clunie laughed. "It sounds terrifying."

"It would have been if he'd ever got above twenty miles an hour," was the reply. "We suffered most from mortification. Has Davina really been of some use?"

Davina certainly had been of use, Clunie said. "The boy who brought the news of the accident had terrible rope burns and she helped me with the dressing." She suspected that Miss Bethune was less shockable than the young generation imagined—much less than Molly—and though she did not mention Davina's professional experience as a barmaid she said she had been of great use in the bar. "They're very short-handed, because the Craigs are away for the day and the barman is out on the rescue."

"Dear me!" said Miss Bethune. "Well, I'm glad to hear it. I should have thought her far too vague and scatter-brained to be even moderately safe behind a bar. It's always seemed to me to be very exacting work. However, I admit I'm far from understanding Davina. Do you?"

The question was accompanied by a piercing stare and Clunie hesitated. "I don't really know her well," she said. "We used to meet at parties sometimes but that was all. I think there's more to Davina than she . . . well, than she lets on."

Miss Bethune, in a very dry voice, said that from what Davina chose to "let on" nobody would suspect hidden depths.

"Oh well, that's just her line," said Clunie. "She's serious enough about her singing and she must have worked very hard at it. Of course I'm no expert, but I think she's really good. She's—unusual. Did she tell you about the television contract she lost through being ill?"

"No, she hasn't told me anything," replied Miss Bethune. She thought for a moment. "H'm. Interesting," she said. "Her upbringing was deplorable—you may say she hasn't any—but she has good Bethune blood in her. I must confess I wish—"

She broke off with a start as the R/T came to life. It had been silent for some time as Andy was communicating with the Army on a different frequency. Now Pat's voice came through.

"Clunie? Can you hear me? Come in please."

"Yes, Pat. I hear you loud and clear."

"Andy wants Keith here. There's some fear that Mike has back injury and it's going to be very difficult to get him down with the stretcher horizontal. Will you tell Keith to proceed to the base and await instructions? Got that? Repeat please."

Clunie repeated it.

"Good," said Pat. "Did you get Dr Graham? Willie's in pretty poor shape."

"Dr Graham should be at the base by now."

"Is Harry back yet? No—well you'll stand by till he can relieve you."

"Wilco," said Clunie professionally and heard him give a laugh.

"Roger, Sunshine," he said. "Out."

Clunie got the kitchen on the intercom and told them to ask Keith to come to the office and then met a pair of eyes which, though still piercing, were amused.

"The marvels of science," Miss Bethune remarked. "I'm glad they're no concern of mine. The Rescue Service seems to keep its spirits up pretty well. As in war, no doubt. There were a lot of jokes in the blitz: good, bad and merely coarse, but they all helped."

The door opened and Keith came in with Davina who started at the sight of her great-aunt. She began to speak but Miss Bethune held up a compelling hand and said, "Wait."

Clunie, controlling a slight quiver in her voice, gave Keith the message. He received it without comment and said his gear was in his car and he would get off at once. Then he turned to the castle ladies with his charmingly frank smile.

"How do you do and goodnight, Miss Bethune," he said. "I'll drop in, if I may, to see you and Miss Tullis." He thanked Davina for giving him her company at dinner, said goodnight and was gone. Miss Bethune followed, sweeping the reluctant Davina with her, and Clunie was left to her solitary vigil, enlivened only by Bessie and Bennie and other interested persons coming in to hear the latest news.

She was able to hear almost all the exchanges on the Glen Torran frequency and with the knowledge she had it was easy to imagine the scene: the brilliance of searchlights coming on as daylight faded; the lesser beams of torches and headlamps illuminating the slow meticulous rigging of ropes and the progress of men climbing up or down to positions from which they would guide the stretcher past a danger point or accompany it over a difficult pitch. She saw it too vividly for her own comfort. Against the black bulk of the mountain background the Steeple was mercilessly exposed. It was a hazardous business bringing Mike down and so many men she valued were up there on the rock: Keith, Malcolm, Pat and Tom; Andy and Tosh and the bothy boys; farmers, shepherds and game-keepers she had known all her life. But personal danger never stopped the Mountain Rescue Service.

The news that the stretcher was safely down came through just before eleven o'clock. Mike, said the report, was bearing up well and had taken a keen interest in the proceedings which suggested that there was no cause for grave anxiety though the extent of his injuries would not be known till after X-ray. Now the long carry to the ambulance had begun. It would be a good deed, the message concluded, to telephone the news to the Kintorran cottage hospital and give Willie a better night.

Soon after this call had been made the Craigs arrived and Harry, when he was in the picture, peremptorily ordered Clunie and Bessie, who was with her, to bed. "I don't want any argument," he said. "There'll be no more news tonight and you need your sleep."

"Come with me," said Alice. "Ovaltine all round and a

sleeping pill for you, Bessie."

It was easy to see, thought Clunie, why the permanent staff stayed at the Brig and the temps came back year after year.

Next morning Davina rang up. "Did they all get down?" she asked.

Everybody got down safely, Clunie told her, and Mike's injuries were not so serious as had been feared. "He has a lot of broken bones and it'll mean plaster for quite a long time but then he'll be as good as new. They really mend wonderfully—they're so healthy—but Mike's been lucky. It was silly to try the Steeple on their own like that."

"Was it?" said Davina. "I wouldn't know. It all sounds pretty silly to me. I mean you can have fun without the jaws-of-death stuff. Still, as both my new boyfriends are dedicated I'll keep my mouth shut. By the way, I haven't stolen your man *this* time, I hope? I couldn't see you taking Malcolm seriously but Keith—"

"Oh no, you're welcome," Clunie said. "Keith's an expert at the agreeable passing affair." A little giggle came over the line and she added a warning. "But don't count on it. He's as career orientated as you are and pretty busy at the moment."

Davina swore. "Damn this Kush thing. What a bore it is. Oh well, there are the two of them. They can't both be busy all the time. Do you think one or both will call this morning? If not I might thumb a lift and call on you."

"I'm not at home," said Clunie. "I'm going climbing."

"Are you really?" said the phone. "Well, hold on."

135

Clunie put down the receiver with a slam. There was no telling what Davina was. She changed with every mood as a chameleon changes colour. All the same, though she might not be a very admirable character she had entertainment value of a kind.

"What's funny?" asked Pat arriving at the desk.

Having somebody to share it turned Clunie's rather sour amusement into a genuine laugh. "Davina," she said. "She's expecting both Keith and Malcolm to call and hopes for a bit of drama if they coincide."

"Oh? When did Keith enter her life?"

"Last night. He gave her dinner. She won't get her drama, though. Keith's much too fly. He'll chat up the old ladies and bide his time."

Pat agreed. "They might be a tricky pair to drive—" he observed, "—but she's obviously an expert."

"Who next, one asks oneself?" said Clunie. "You, very likely."

"Well, I haven't felt any symptoms *so far*. Not that I've had much chance with Malcolm blocking the line."

"Oh, you won't feel any symptoms. Davina just strikes. Bessie says sudden death. It's rather hard on me," added Clunie in a tone of strong complaint. "Two good boyfriends falling to a left and right. But I think I can depend on Hake."

"That must be a great comfort to you," said Pat. "Meanwhile, if you can turn your mind from romance, what about this climb?"

Though she had told Davina she was going climbing Clunie was not so sure about it. Pat was saying that he had

136

had a word with Harry and they could get off more or less at once.

"I've ordered lunch." He looked at her doubtful face. "You're not turning chicken?"

"Oh, no. No, certainly not," she said. "I just thought you won't want to haul me up a mountain after last night."

"I've no intention of hauling you up," said Pat. "You're going to haul me. Get moving now. It's a grand day, don't waste it."

It was a grand day, with bright sunshine and a brisk wind sending cloud shadows racing across the hills. Clunie thought of poor Mike, encased in plaster and tied to a hospital bed, but as they drove her spirits soared. The picture of the nightmare glare and black background of the rescue scene dissolved in the smiling daylight and in her climbing boots her toes wiggled with joyful anticipation. She felt she could tackle the Steeple though she wasn't going to—not yet—and she was given no option. Pat had the whole thing planned.

"You don't want to overdo it your first day," he announced.

"No," said Clunie, but she added pointedly that he would no doubt be glad of an easy day himself after the rigours of the night.

"Me? Not at all," was the reply. "I played a subordinate and comparatively static part. Anyway I'm a strong man, not a poor weak woman who hasn't been on a hill for years." He paused but Clunie refused to rise and he smiled slightly and went on, "What we're going to do is go down Glen Trochy, ascend the Lum and walk off."

The Lum was a moderately difficult climb on Ben Trochy, culminating in the pleasantly challenging chimney which gave it its name, and Clunie said scornfully that she had climbed it when she was about fourteen and many times since. "I could do it in the dark."

"Maybe you could at one time," said Pat, unimpressed. "But you've got to remember you're older now and you know what pride goes before." He turned into the narrow Glen Trochy road and glanced round. "Is this where Malcolm proposed to you the other night?"

Clunie was, in fact, recalling her last visit to Glen Trochy and felt rather startled. "That's a most improper question," she retorted. "I'm surprised at your lack of taste. What made you think of it?"

"Well, it's a good place to propose. Undisturbed, romantic scenery. I wouldn't mind using it myself. And it was in your mind."

"You've no idea what was in my mind," snapped Clunie. "My face is inscrutable—famous for it."

"Not to me it isn't," said Pat. "I will say you don't give much away but my penetration is exceptional. We'll stop here. Just enough of a walk to limber up and not too far when we come down." He drew the car into a gateway and looked round at her. "Cheer up, Sunshine. I won't ask any more embarrassing questions—not this trip anyway."

Clunie still felt jolted. She wasn't sure why. Anybody might guess that Malcolm would choose the Glen Trochy road for his proposal—it was a most obvious place—but she wondered if she only imagined that Pat was more interested than his words and tone suggested. She was not

138

inexperienced and Tina and she had agreed that a girl has to be very thick if she doesn't know when a man is in love or at least attracted to her. But—Pat of all men!

He had opened the back door of the car and was sitting on the floor putting on his boots. He looked unusually serious and for some reason the jolted feeling had given way to one of constraint which she knew she must get rid of.

"No wonder you have to sit down," she said. "Your feet are an awful long way off. How do they let you know if they're cold?"

"Oh, the word gets round." He threw his shoes into the car and stood up to his full height. "And they're not out of reach, you know. Watch . . ." Stretching his arms above his head he began to bend down and then straightened again. "No, on second thoughts we'll keep that for another day. You're having enough treats for—"

"Pat," she said sharply, "did you hurt your back last night?"

"No, no, just a touch of lumbago. As I've said before we don't get any younger." He put a hand to his back and hobbled round to open the boot.

Clunie ignored the act. "Did you strain it or give it a jerk or what? I'm sure you shouldn't climb till it clears up."

He looked at her over the car. "I'm quite safe. I promise I won't peel."

"Don't be stupid," she snapped. "I'm not thinking about that. I don't want you to risk making it worse because you think I have—or might develop—a trauma after last

139

night. *I* promise *you* I haven't and won't."

Pat went on looking at her and to her annoyance she felt her colour rise. She turned away but he came round and put his hands on her shoulders. "Look at me," he said. Reluctantly she raised her eyes and now there was no mistaking what was in his.

For a moment they looked at each other very seriously and then taking her hands he said, "Clunie, I never intended this. It's far too soon to say anything and you don't want to hear it, but it would be worse to say nothing—at least I think so. We wouldn't know where to look. Some time, before very long I hope, I'm going to ask you to marry me."

"Oh, Pat," she said, distressed. "I've never even thought . . . I don't know—"

"You don't have to know. I haven't asked you yet."

"No, but . . ." She stopped and there was a little silence.

After waiting for her to go on Pat broke it. "I would like you to tell me one thing, but you needn't if you don't want to. I know you aren't in love with me. Are you with anybody else? I couldn't see you marrying Malcolm, but Keith . . ? He may give Davina a spin, but he won't really fall for her. And there's Hake, of course."

"Oh, poor Hake," Clunie said remorsefully. "It's a shame to laugh at him—though we always have." She hesitated, but Pat's straightforwardness had moved her. And, oddly enough, the constraint had passed. She looked at him easily, feeling comfortable. She could say anything to Pat.

"You know," she said, "I really did think I might marry Malcolm—some day. There he was: nice, faithful, as I

140

thought, and I would like to be married." She gave a small laugh. "Jean thinks it's the only thing I'm fit for and she's probably right."

"I'd put it differently," said Pat. "I've never known a girl better fitted for it."

"Well, that's handsomely said. Thank you. But—Keith . . ." Clunie's eyebrows drew together in a frown. "He's such a *nuisance*." There was a smothered laugh from Pat and she said, "Well, it's true. I don't even like him very much; at least I like him sometimes and at others—more often—I really dislike him. And *yet* I fell in love with him, quite desperately. He was in love with me too for a bit and he still is, in a way, but marriage doesn't fit in with his plans. Not marriage with me, anyhow."

"Has he told you so?"

She shook her head. "Oh no. We've never talked about it. We've never talked about anything personal, as a matter of fact. We're not on sufficiently intimate terms." She looked up with a gleam of laughter and then, serious again, went on, "Don't imagine that I've been languishing all these years. I haven't: I don't think I'm in love with him now, but I can't be sure he's out of my system. The reason I'm telling you all this," she concluded apologetically, "is that I'm afraid I'll never fall in love again. I never have."

"So you thought perhaps Malcolm might *do*," said Pat. What he thought of Keith Finlay was unprintable and he had a profound desire to tear him limb from limb but neither his face nor voice gave any hint of such extravagant emotion. Instead he said in matter-of-fact tones that in his view she never would fall in love again *like that*. "The first time it hits you with such a wallop. It takes you by surprise. If you're lucky you may have a few moments of heaven, but it's ninety-five per cent hell. Agony."

Clunie looked sceptical. "Do you speak from experience? I wouldn't have believed it. Who was she?"

"Never mind who she was. Do you think me incapable of passion?" Pat demanded. "I'll show you if you like. It's not what we came out for but I'll willingly change my plans."

"No, no," she said hastily. "*Of course* I believe you if you say so. It's a little unexpected, that's all. So I suppose," she added, "you think I might *do*, both of us having passed the age of romance."

Dropping her hands Pat took her by the shoulders and gave her a brisk shake. "Clunie," he said, "I've a good mind to—No. We'll go and climb the Lum. Come on and behave yourself."

CHAPTER EIGHT

"What about your back?" asked Clunie.

"Och, forget it," said Pat, shrugging on a knapsack. "It's a wee bit stiff, that's all. We'll eat on the top," he added, explaining the knapsack, and reached into the car for a coil of rope. "I don't think we need any further aids, do you?" Clunie didn't and he shut the car and took her hand. "Forward then."

"Hey!" she protested. "We're not on these terms."

Unrepentant he held on to her hand and told her not to fuss. "It's nice—friendly—and it doesn't commit you to anything. I'll drop it if we see anybody coming as you're so sensitive."

They saw no one and the half-mile walk to the foot of the climb was very pleasant. They didn't talk much. Clunie's delight in being back where she belonged, among her own mountains, was intense, and it was undoubtedly heightened by the warm comradely clasp of Pat's hand. Neither was given to rhapsodizing but the hand told her that he shared her feeling.

She had never been an ambitious climber though she had natural aptitude and a considerable degree of skill. For her, collecting ascents of Very Severes held no appeal and even while looking with a climber's interest at the Jungfrau or the Eiger she had felt no great urge to climb them. She admired the Alps and the Dolomites. The hills of Scotland she loved and the joy of climbing lay in the contact: the feeling it gave her, as nothing else could, of being part of the mountain.

"You were rated as one of the coming tigers, weren't you?" she said, breaking a comfortable silence. "Lined up with Keith and people. Did you never feel tempted to go on with it?"

"Well," said Pat, "I wouldn't say never, but it didn't last long. For one thing I wasn't anything like as good as Keith."

"Couldn't you have been as good though?"

"Not a chance. Keith's an ace. And then I lack ambition—I can't be bothered to compete. Andy says I haven't the essential madness."

"I dare say that's true—I mean that you haven't got it. It's certainly a part of it." She laughed. "Big of Andy to admit it. Keith doesn't. He says Alan's a maniac, which he is, but when I pointed out that he's one too he wouldn't have it."

"I wouldn't say Alan's a maniac," Pat said judicially. "A maverick, rather."

"Oh he's a maniac," said Alan's fond sister. "If I've got it right a maverick's just an incalculable, rather aimless wanderer from the beaten track. Alan's as mad and as purposeful about his ethnology as Keith is about his climbing. Davina's another," she added. "She doesn't mind living in squalor or being cast off by her friends and relations so longs she's let alone to get on with her singing. It's an enviable state really. I wouldn't mind being a maniac."

Pat smiled. "Well, it leaves no room for doubt. But leaving aside discomfort and unpopularity—which doesn't bother them—their range is so limited."

"You can't say Alan's range is limited, Pat."

"Not his geographical range. And his mania is wider than Keith's or Davina's, it's in a different class; but he hasn't much time for anything else. Keith doesn't see a mountain, just a climb, and I wouldn't think Davina ever listens to music, apart from assessing the performance of her rivals. I'd rather be what I am: an ordinary bloke doing an ordinary job. Of course I'm lucky. It isn't a routine job and I have a lot of freedom."

Clunie was interested. She had no clear idea of the function of an agent, or factor. "You obviously move about," she said, "but where do you operate from? Where do you live?"

"Now that—" Pat said cordially,"—is the kind of question I like to be asked."

"Don't make too much of it."

"No, but it shows a friendly interest. Well, I operate from Edinburgh and I have a flat there. When I'm on what you might call field work I stay in one of the Finlay hotels. It suits all right, but when—and if, of course—I marry, I'll have to change my way of life."

"I'll bet," said Clunie.

He gave her a dignified glance. "That was rude. Unlady-like."

"So it was," she agreed. "Accept my apologies. It slipped out. You were saying?"

"I was saying that in the event of my marriage I would make other arrangements." Though Edinburgh was the headquarters of the Scottish part of the Finlay empire, he

145

went on, it was not essential for him, Pat, to live there. His centre could be anywhere within limits: Inverness, Perth—even Kintorran. "It would depend on what the missus felt about it, but I fancy the kind of girl I have in mind wouldn't care to live in Kintorran all the year round. What do you think?"

Clunie couldn't undertake to give an opinion. "Some like country life, some don't."

"True," said Pat, "though not particularly helpful. Well, there's another alternative: two homes: one town, one country among the hills. What do you think about that?"

"You must be very well off."

"I am quite well off, in a modest way. But your father and mine contrived to keep two houses and academic incomes aren't exactly lavish. I must admit, though, that Glenvarroch nearly did for us."

"But it's practically a mansion. An ancestral home. Ours was just a holiday cottage."

"Glenvarroch's a damned rickety old barrack," said Pat. "Lord! When I remember the crises . . . the overdraft . . . We tried paying guests once but if it wasn't actually counterproductive there was no visible profit. M'mother fed them too well and thought it only civil to lay on sherry before dinner. That's how Jo came into our lives."

Clunie was laughing. She remembered Mrs McKechnie and could not see her as a successful businesswoman. "Jo was a paying guest, was he?" she said. "I thought you were at school together."

"So we were, but we didn't know each other. Different Houses and Jo has brains. He just answered the ad and he's

146

been one of the family ever since, involved equally in its ups and its downs. He little knew what he was letting himself in for. Well—here we are." They had arrived at the start of the climb and he made one of his expansive gestures. The Lum. How does it look?"

"Beautiful and friendly," said Clunie. She went and put her hands on the rock which was warm from the sun and turned to smile at Pat. "I was scared at the thought of starting and no doubt I'll be scared again, but at the moment I'm full of confidence."

Pat, uncoiling the rope, warned her against overdoing it. "No recklessness if *you* please. Just remember you hold my life in your hands, not to mention your own. Are you going to lead through?"

"No, we'll take turns," she said, and when he asked casually if he should lead the first pitch to let her get the feel of it she agreed readily. Only when they reached it did she realize that this meant that he led the last and most exposed. She had been managed, but by then she was glad of it. The Lum was friendly and the conditions perfect but she was rusty. In the lead she was slow, hesitant sometimes about the next move, and she grew tired. It was a relief to stay on the comfortable ledge which the Lum characteristically provided at this stage knowing that Pat would pull her up all right if she got into difficulties.

Watching him she thought what a good climber he was. It was true he was not in Keith's class: Keith on a mountain seemed to float up and there was grace in every movement. Pat was not graceful, but for so big a man he

147

moved lightly and in one respect at least he was superior; he considered his second. Clunie had tied on behind Keith and been hard put to it sometimes to follow his lead, an experience which she did not enjoy and which was liable to result in one of their periods of estrangement.

Pat disappeared from view and presently she heard him shout "Come on," and felt a slight reassuring tug on the rope. She took a deep breath, blew it out again and reached for the first handhold. At the top he was waiting to give her a hand and she grinned at him and flopped thankfully on to the ground.

"You were quite right," she said when she had got her breath back. "The Lum was plenty. I underestimated that last pitch."

"You did it in good time," said Pat. "You're quite a climber, aren't you?"

"For a poor weak woman," Clunie added for him.

They ate their lunch, lounging in the sun on the top of Ben Trochy with their eyes on the incredible view of mountains, lochs and glens. There was no need to talk. Occasionally they pointed things out to each other. Clunie drew Pat's attention to a hovering kestrel, he spotted a group of deer about a mile away—in that clear air it was possible to see detail at great distance—and they both sat up to watch the progress of two climbers on the face of Torran Mhor.

They got back to the Brig soon after four o'clock and went in by the side door which was normally used by regulars. It was a quiet time, too early for newcomers to arrive and before those out for the day returned, and they stopped in the empty vestibule while Clunie thanked Pat for the climb.

"It was perfect. I couldn't have had a nicer start. How glad I am that you bullied me into it."

"My pleasure," said Pat. "Nothing I enjoy more than bullying the weaker sex. We'll go out again soon and tackle something a bit stiffer."

"Oh, your back! I forgot about it," she exclaimed, reaching round to give it a friendly rub. "Is it all right?"

He said he had forgotten about it himself and bending his head kissed her smiling, up-turned face. "Don't look at me like that if you don't want to be kissed," he said. "I'm only human."

It seemed at the time to be the natural, indeed inevitable, finish to a lovely time and Clunie was laughing when Keith pushed the door open and came in. For a fraction of a second he hesitated—it was too brief to bring him to a halt—and then walked swiftly past without a word.

Pat glanced at the flushed face beside him. "Pay no regard," he said, but Clunie went upstairs feeling jangled. She had heard one of the girls say that necking with guests was among the few sins Harry really went to town about and she felt as if she had been caught doing just that and was both guilty and besmeared. This immediate reaction, however, was exaggerated and by the time she had bathed and changed she was ready to take Pat's advice and pay no regard.

Snatching a cup of tea from the kitchen she went back to her office where she found Alice with Harry. They had already heard from Pat that she had acquitted herself creditably. Harry was a climber himself, though he rarely found time for it, and he was always pleased to encourage his young staff.

"You should get in as much as you can," he said, "especially while Pat's here. He's as good a man as any to bring you back into form—not so daft on it that he'll try to force the pace."

"Don't forget I'm one of your paid employees," said Clunie.

"Oh, it's only a matter of arranging things," was the easy reply.

"Flexibility is our watchword," added Alice. "I must say it's done you a power of good. You were a bit pasty when you came—that's London of course—but you look fine now." Her observant eyes moved calmly from hair to face and on to a dark blue dress piped with white. "You look a treat in fact, doesn't she, Harry? You're one of the lucky ones: you tan, I peel. And you do know how to dress. That's London too, I suppose, to give credit where credit's due."

Clunie was catching up with her work, checking bookings made during the day, guests due to arrive that evening and calculating an approximate number of diners for the kitchen staff, when Keith emerged from the passage.

He was in a temper, she observed, noting the well-known signs; his normally lively face set and rather pale, his dark eyes expressionless. Pay no regard, she reminded herself, and greeted him cheerfully.

150

Keith with an unconvincing air of nonchalance perched himself on the high stool and said he had come in early because Page and Carter, the second pair in his Hindu Kush team, were due to arrive. "Complete with wives, poor devils."

"Alas!" said Clunie shaking her head. "How ill-judged. But they don't imagine they're booked in here, do they?"

"Oh no, they've got Dormobiles. They're just reporting here. And I'll give them dinner. That'll be six if I can get hold of Malcolm. You might see I'm told when they turn up, will you?"

"Will do." She made a note of his party for the kitchen. "Where will you be?"

"The lounge, I suppose, till the bar opens. Somewhere around anyway." Very nonchalantly indeed he lit a cigarette and looked at her with narrowed eyes. "So it's McKechnie now, is it? How long has he been a special friend of yours? I thought you couldn't stand him."

"How right you were," Clunie remarked affably, "when you told me I'd find everybody in the glen exactly the same only more so. *Everybody* remembers that when I was a kid I fought with Pat McKechnie. Even you with all your experience and renown." A tinge of colour in Keith's face gave her some unworthy satisfaction and she went straight on. "We seem to get along quite amicably now— *so far*—but there's hardly been time for civility to wear off. I hadn't seen him since I was about fourteen till he turned up the other day."

"Fast work then." Keith blew out a thin stream of smoke. "Unless you include embraces under the head of

151

civility. The influence of the permissive society, perhaps, and a presbyterian conscience only intermittently active."

The best line to take with Keith in a temper was refusal to rise. Though he could be exceedingly nasty it didn't usually last long. But Clunie had a temper too. She was not going to refer to the scene outside her flat and the suggestion then made but she wanted to hit back.

"You must have had an overdose of Grandpa Walter," she said. "I don't believe even he, knowing Pat and me as well as you do, would have been all that shocked because I gave Pat's stiff back a rub and he gave me a kiss after a good climb. But then he was far from dense, wasn't he? He founded the Finlay empire after all. I dare say he could tell a hawk from a handsaw."

Keith was now pale again and the dark eyes were hard but there was no comeback. Clunie was not surprised. In this sort of battle he was not very quick on the draw and with his strong instinct for self-preservation he was astute enough to know it was safer to keep his mouth shut.

He got off the stool and after a moment's hesitation said in a milder tone, "Actually I was going to suggest a climb, but if you've got it all laid on with McKechnie I don't suppose there's much point."

"None at all." She laughed. "I haven't got it laid on with anybody but I told you in London I haven't the nerve to tie on with you."

"What? Do you think I'd drop you?"

"Oh no, I'm sure you wouldn't—though I might find myself wishing you would. The strain would be too great. I'd crumble."

"Tchah!" He gave a short bark of laughter. "You're a little devil, Clunie. You always were. Well . . . it's no business of mine if you want to kiss McKechnie."

"Just what I was thinking," she said. "I'll see you get the message."

With a brief nod he walked rapidly away and Clunie, hearing sounds of arrival in the porch, retreated to Harry's office to cool off. Quarrels with Keith were nothing new and more often than not she won easily on points, but they left her feeling battered and humiliated; humiliated because, though she had no illusions about him, he still had the power to attract and hurt her. His climber's conscience would never allow him to drop her—or anyone—on a mountain, she reflected wryly, but he had dropped her often enough on the flat without hesitation. This comparison she suddenly found funny and, much cheered, she returned to her duty.

Clunie was not yet a hardened receptionist. She took a liking to some guests and a dislike to others and, as Alice told her with amusement, let herself in for a good deal of time-consuming and frequently boring chat. Mr and Mrs Nesbit, who were waiting at the desk, needed, she felt, encouragement. He was a twinkling little man and his wife was what Pat would call a home-maker and probably a great knitter, but in bad hotels—even in good ones when pressed—they would be served last and they wouldn't complain. Well, they would be properly treated at the Brig. She beamed at Mr Nesbit as she gave him the register and then pressed the bell and took the key from its hook.

"You'd like to go straight up, I expect," she said. "Would you care for tea presently? We serve it in the lounge—just along the passage."

They looked at each other. "Well . . . if we're not too late," said Mr Nesbit doubtfully.

"I'd *love* a cup of tea," said his wife in a burst of confidence. "Not if it's a trouble though."

"No trouble at all," she assured them. A boy in a white coat appeared and she gave him the key. "Take Mr and Mrs Nesbit up, Roddy, and they'd like tea. They'll ring when they're ready."

"Righty-ho," said Roddy picking up the suitcases and added more formally, "This way, Mahdam."

Mr Nesbit twinkled at Clunie. She smiled back and forgot about him. Keith. Why was she sorry for him? Nobody could be more unreasonable. Suspecting her of pursuing him and furious because Pat kissed her . . . She felt a pang of remorse for having slanged him so ruthlessly, but it was not a severe pang. There was no placating Keith in a temper and why should she try? Keith had everything: success, charm, plenty of cash in the background. But it had been too easy. Though he was less simple than Malcolm he was very little, if any, more mature.

A little later the Hindu Kush pair and their wives burst in led by an exuberant man who hastened to introduce everybody. He was Bill Carter, this was his wife Wendy, these were Alf and Maureen Page. The girls said, "Hallo," Wendy with a friendly grin, Maureen with a weak smile. Alf Page, hatchet-faced and glum said, "Ump," which was

154

the only sound he ever addressed to Clunie.

"And who—or whom—have I the honour of addressing?" asked Bill. She told him and he said, "Glad to know you, Ginnie. Keith around?"

Keith would be in the bar by now, she said. "I'll get someone to let him know—"

"No need, no need," cried Bill. "Just point us in the right direction."

They surged off, leaving her wondering whether the moroseness of Alf or the jocularity of Bill would impose the greater strain on the expedition.

Her next caller was Davina who emerged unexpectedly from the passage. She looked discontented.

"You again!" Clunie exclaimed. "Who brought you this time?"

"Malcolm," said Davina. "He invited me to dinner."

"What a whirl of engagements."

Davina sighed. "Yes, but poor darling Malcolm's been foiled. He's caught up in this ghastly party of Keith's and we've got to dine with them. Malcolm didn't want to, naturally, but he's feeble. Can't say no. It's going to be pure hell."

"Well, you'll get two dinners," Clunie said consolingly. "Malcolm will be able to afford to take you out again."

"If I survive this," said Davina. "Honestly, Clunie, have you seen these people? The end. And Keith's actually *asked* them to go crawling up these Hindu things with him. They'll drive him mad."

Clunie confessed that she was inclined to agree, though she had no doubt that Bill and Alf were very good

155

climbers, and Davina, who was not interested in their climbing ability, added that Keith was looking like a thunder cloud already. "But that's probably me—because of being with Malcolm I mean."

"Very likely," said Clunie. She saw Mr and Mrs Nesbit meekly hovering and advised Davina to go back to the bar before Keith and Malcolm came to blows.

Davina thought they would hardly do that—yet, but she could do with a lot more to drink if she was to get through this party. "Oh—one thing," she said. "Why I really came. I wish you'd introduce me to the Craigs and sort of put in a word about my singing."

"Well, I told you we don't have floor shows," Clunie reminded her. "But you'll meet Alice. She means to do something about you—because of Miss Bethune."

"Oh . . ." Davina made a face. "Like Jean . . ." She turned to go and then remembered something. "By the way, I'm glad to see you're in one piece."

"One piece?" said Clunie and then laughed. "Oh yes. I held on as you advised."

She was still smiling as she noted the Nesbits" request for morning tea and a packed lunch, but her mind was not with them. She thought that Jean, however unwittingly, had done a good deal for Davina. Certainly she had started something and she, Clunie, hoped a little uneasily that it would end without real trouble. Malcolm madly in love for the first time in his life, Keith in his present mood and Davina without scruples . . . At least potentially an explosive mixture.

"I wonder," said Mr Nesbit, "if I might ask . . . was that

Miss Clare talking to you just now? Miss Davina Clare?"

Clunie looked at him, greatly surprised. "Yes," she said. "Do you know Miss Clare?"

"Oh no, I can't say I know the young lady," was the reply. "I have seen her but she was quite a child at the time. She wouldn't remember me." He gave a little laugh. "Even as a child her appearance was striking and it has changed very little. She resembles her father more than—" He broke off as if he had caught himself on the verge of an indiscretion. "Is she staying in the hotel?"

"No, she is staying with her great aunt, Miss Charlotte Bethune, in Castle Tornay."

It was Mr Nesbit's turn to look surprised. "Indeed? Is that so? I fancied that all the family left the district when Sir James Finlay bought the estate."

Clunie believed they did. "Miss Bethune has been here as long as I can remember, but she is the only one I know anything about. Did you know the family, Mr Nesbit?"

"Not personally, no," said Mr Nesbit. "I acted for Mrs Clare at the time of Sir Alistair Bethune's demise. That was when I saw Miss Davina."

"Mr Nesbit is a solicitor," Mrs Nesbit put in helpfully. "A Writer to the Signet."

"Oh, I see," said Clunie. "Would you like to talk to Davina? She's dining here with friends. I know her quite well and—"

He laughed. "Thank you, I won't trouble you. It would bore her very much, I'm sure. Does Miss Bethune live in solitary splendour in Castle Tornay?"

"Not splendour," Clunie said. "There isn't very much of

the castle left. Miss Bethune lives in what there is with a friend. Miss Tullis."

"Indeed?" Mr Nesbit repeated with the same note of surprise. "Well, I am glad to hear that Miss Davina is staying with her great aunt. Thank you, Miss Ritchie. Are you, by any chance, the daughter of Professor Ritchie?" Clunie said she was and he smiled. "Now I *do* know Professor Ritchie. We meet quite frequently. And I know your brother by reputation. A brilliant young man in my opinion . . . Shall we go in to dinner, dear?"

Mrs Nesbit nodded and smiled at Clunie. "I'm really quite hungry. This air and such a lovely smell of good cooking . . ."

The staff had meals in an extension near the kitchen which was used for guests when the dining-room was full, and they ate before or after the main dinner was served. By the time Clunie went in most of the guests, including Keith's party, had left the room but Pat, who was guest or staff as he felt inclined, was drinking coffee with Alice at the manager's table.

Alice waved urgently to Clunie to join them. Her eyes were bright and interested and she began at once. "Well! I have *seen Davina*."

"Oh?" said Clunie. She sat down rather stiffly. "Gosh, I'm so empty! I'll be more responsive, Alice, when I can forget the pangs."

"This pub's nothing more nor less than a sweatshop," said Pat. "Wait and I'll get you a drink. What's your Union?"

"Amalgamated Engineering. Thank you. Sherry would

be welcome but what I crave for is soup. Thick soup."

"Coming up," said Bennie appearing at her elbow. "Stay where you are, Pat. Ye'll jist obstruct the traffic." He could be heard relaying the order. "Sherry for Clunie, Tom. A schooner. On Pat."

"Sweatshop!" said Alice bitterly.

"He didn't really mean it," Clunie assured her kindly.

"It's not that bad. Did you talk to Davina? She's more than eager to talk to you."

There had been no opportunity, Alice said. Pat pointed her out. Not that there was any need with Malcolm's glazed eyes never off her. He's *besotted*, silly boy." She paused reflectively while sherry and soup were placed before Clunie and as Bennie left added, "I really feel quite sorry for the Grahams, and you know as well as I do that it's not very easy to feel sorry for the Grahams, good kind people though they are."

Clunie and Pat did know. Good kind people though they were there was an armour, or lagging, of self-satisfaction about the Grahams, except for Malcolm who had hitherto been protected by an unquestioning faith in human nature and a benevolent deity somewhere above.

It was Pat's opinion that Malcolm's passion would die a natural death, particularly if people didn't keep on at him. Davina would go away and the expedition would take his mind off it. "After all, most of us go through it and come out unscathed."

Alice hoped, rather doubtfully, that he was right and that her own boys, now aged sixteen and thirteen, would get it over early. "It's like mumps: nothing to worry about in children as a rule but quite serious for grown-ups. What does Davina want to talk to me about? Singing? Oh. Well, I must do *something* about her but the singing will be for Harry to decide. If you ask me he won't be too keen."

"He may not be too keen," Clunie said to Pat when Alice had left them, "but I'll bet he gives in."

CHAPTER NINE

HARRY CRAIG was not eager to have his hotel used for the promotion of Davina Clare's career and he was no fonder than most men of being pressurized, but Davina, displaying unexpected tact, handled the matter lightly and with charm, leaving the pressure to be applied modestly by Malcolm and noisily by Keith with a chorus of his young followers. Clunie prudently kept out of it.

There was nothing very unusual about music in the bar at the Brig and no sufficiently definite reason why Davina should be refused the opportunity. Harry agreed with Alice that something must be done about Miss Bethune's young relative and this would be as easy a way as any of showing proper attention. He gave in. Alice was not surprised: the beguiling smile that began in the limpid sea-green eyes was a powerful weapon. She was not proof against it herself, the smile and the look of fragility, though that was probably due to lack of fresh air and the wrong food.

"And she's the most persistent little madam *I've* ever come across," she confided to Clunie later. "You'd give anything to say no, but what's the use? She'd just keep on till you collapsed from sheer exhaustion—not arguing, just looking."

Clunie laughed and agreed. "But she's worth backing. She's really good."

"Well, if you say so," sighed Alice. "Anyway, Harry will cope."

Being an experienced manager Harry did cope. Davina would not have the stage to herself, silencing everybody else as she had done at the Grahams' party. It was quite a long time, he said, since they had had a ceilidh at the Brig. They would have one on Saturday. This being Thursday it didn't leave much time, but they didn't need much time: word—quite enough—would get around, and he went on to outline a draft programme.

Pat, watching appreciatively in the background, saw Davina's eyes widen when she heard that Tosh would give them a tune on the pipes and Andy one of his recitations. A squeezebox would come over from the bothy and Alice was always available to play the piano. Elspeth and Ross McAdam were added to the list and Clunie said, "This will interest you, Davina. You'll never hear Scots songs better sung."

"Oh?" Davina turned to Malcolm. "Weren't they at your party? They didn't sing then."

Malcolm with some embarrassment said nobody seemed to think of it. "I mean they're . . . well, they're not professionals like you."

"And you sang first," added Clunie. "You'll have to place her, Harry."

"I'll place her," said Harry.

Davina's smiling charm had passed through incredulity to resentment. "I don't quite see how," she said coldly. "Am I expected to sing Scotch songs?"

"Lord, no," said Keith. "We're not that parochial. Sing whatever you like."

"Well—" said Andy in a doubtful tone which made

several people look at him sharply, "—of course there's nothing like the auld Scots sangs. Mind you I'm not saying there aren't plenty of other good songs but they don't go down so well."

As Davina snapped that she hadn't *got* any Scotch songs Clunie shot a dagger glance at Andy which made him grin, and gave her a warning prod. "Sing *The Four Marys* again, Davina," she said, "and you've got some lovely old folk songs—Welsh, Irish *and* English. All the same you should think about the Scots ones. They're not all dialect."

"Well, she hasn't far to look," Harry said unexpectedly. "Miss Bethune was a great singer in her day, so I'm told."

Davina's jaw dropped. *"Aunt Charlotte?"*

From a corner an old gamekeeper spoke up. "The Bethunes were all singers," he said. "Great ones for a ceilidh they were. But Miss Charlotte's brother—no the laird, the other one, Mr Hugh—he was the best. They used to say he could charm the deer down off the hills." He paused, his faded blue eyes on Davina. "He would be your grandpa. You've a look of him."

"Oh?" said Davina. "I'm afraid I don't know anything about him."

Clunie felt sorry for the old man who had clearly hoped to go on with reminiscences of the Bethunes for some time, but Davina's tone was final and Harry moved on.

Next, he said, he wanted dancers. "You lot—" he nodded at the boys and girls, "—can romp through a few reels and *Strip The Willow*, but I've got some foreigners and English booked in and I want them to see something better than that. A good foursome at least. You, Clunie, Pat—"

163

"I haven't got my kilt here."

"Get it."

"Sir!"

"Malcolm—"

"Oh, leave me out, Harry. I'd really rather—"

"I'm very good in a foursome and my kilt's at the Lodge," Keith offered.

Andy looked meaningly from his five foot eight to Pat's towering height. "Is it a comic turn we're wanting?" he asked mildly.

"No," said Harry. "You'll do as you're told, Malcolm. Now the other girl." He looked a little doubtful. "Would Jean—"

"Elspeth," Alice said hastily.

"And I," said Keith, "will sit beside you, Davina, and explain what's going on. What's more I'll push you through a romping reel if you're game."

Davina made no response to this offer but drew Clunie aside. She was very angry and making no attempt to conceal it. "Look," she said, "this isn't what I expected. I'm not sure about going on with it."

"What *did* you expect?" Clunie demanded. "A song recital by Davina Clare?"

"No—well, not that exactly. But I didn't see myself in a muddle of pipers and comics and local amateurs."

"Well, that's what you'll get," was Clunie's reply. "You needn't think you'll budge Harry. You can pull out if you like. He won't mind, I can tell you that. There have been plenty of good ceilidhs at the Brig without you and will be plenty more. You wouldn't have got this if you hadn't

164

been related to Miss Bethune."

"What's that got to do with it?"

"Everything. Same as the Grahams. Did you think they wanted to ask you to a party? They didn't. They wanted to show civility to Miss Bethune, a highly respected neighbour."

"How bloody stupid!"

"Think so?" said Clunie. "I wouldn't be surprised if a good many people are thinking the same, but they won't be thinking about the Craigs or the Grahams."

There was a short pause and then Davina said, "I've got to think of my reputation, you know."

"I didn't know you'd got one."

"Well, that's the point. You can do what you like when you've arrived but at my stage you can't afford to appear in the wrong sort of company and what's-his-name— Harry —said there'd be a lot of visitors."

Clunie had had enough. She was going to bed. "You can make up your mind if you're going to honour us, but let me tell you the McAdams could make you look nohow even though they're not professional singers."

"They couldn't!" exclaimed Davina angrily and then asked, "How?"

"They're well known and popular and what Andy said was quite true. With this audience—the majority—they'll go down better." Davina's face was still sullen but it was also doubtful and Clunie relented. "Cheer up," she said. "Ross and Elspeth are much too nice to upstage you. If you come along and join in the party you'll do your reputation nothing but good—however many snooty English visitors are here to listen." She turned away and then looked back. "Oh, one other thing. Harry and Alice are Mr and Mrs Craig. They're quite keen on civility."

Davina scowled.

Next morning Pat announced that he had business in Fort William which might as well be done today so that he could go on to the rickety ancestral home and pick up his kilt. "What about coming too? Nice drive. You might see the Monster."

Clunie shook her head and said that not even the possibility—in any case remote—of seeing the Loch Ness Monster could lure her from her duty.

"Pity," said Pat. "Another thing though. I hope it's clearly understood that you're my partner in this foursome of Harry's."

"That'll be a relief to Malcolm," said Clunie. "By the way, who won last night?"

Pat said he didn't know who drove Davina home, but he would put his money on Keith. "As soon as he'd shaken off the other Hindu Kush chaps old Malcolm was finished. Never got a word in, poor sap."

"Keith can be a swine sometimes," Clunie remarked dispassionately. "It's not even as if he wanted her—at least not much."

"Hardly at all," Pat agreed. "I doubt if Keith knows what he wants." He changed the subject. How were her legs? he asked. Had they recovered sufficiently from the climb yesterday to dance reels tomorrow? She enquired about his back and they danced a few experimental steps, setting to partners across the reception desk.

"We'll do," said Pat.

As he went out Mr Nesbit came to the desk to pay his bill. Mrs Nesbit and he had enjoyed their stay at the Brighouse, he said, and were glad they had included Glen Torran in their tour. "It's a wee bit out of the way, not like Glencoe, let alone the Great Glen which you can hardly miss, but it's none the worse for that."

In response to a polite enquiry he told her where they were going next and then said, "By the by, I'd quite like to get a glimpse of Castle Tornay. Is it easy to find?"

"Oh yes. Like the Great Glen you can hardly miss it," said Clunie. "It's on a kind of hump on the left as you go down into Kintorran. But it's not a show place, you know. You can't go over it, or even up to it."

"I wouldn't want to," he said. "It's just curiosity. Seeing Miss Davina brought things back. I'll say goodbye then, Miss Ritchie. My kind regards to your father . . ."

They shook hands cordially and Clunie was left feeling some curiosity herself. Though she was not given to scenting mystery where no mystery existed, she didn't think she was imagining something a little mysterious about Davina. It was strange that until she arrived at the castle nobody knew that Miss Bethune had a young relative: in Kintorran people did know about relatives, especially in such families as the Bethunes. And though the relationship was acknowledged, Miss Bethune had made only one brief reference to Davina's "blood". Now there was Mr Nesbit. Were busy solicitors usually so interested in clients for whom they had acted on one occasion many years ago? However, thought Clunie, it was no business of hers: probably the leftover of one of those family estrangements which go on and on after everybody has forgotten why they started.

Speculation was a popular local sport to which Alice was much addicted but when presently she came into the office her mind was occupied not by Davina's origins but Davina now. "You know," she said seriously, "I dread to *think* what's going to be the end of this Davina—Malcolm —Keith triangle."

"Well, if I were you I wouldn't waste any worry on Keith or Davina," was Clunie's advice. "Malcolm will suffer but you must just have faith. Think of his upbringing."

"Ye-es," said Alice looking doubtful. "Of course Keith's as hard as nails and he hasn't a scruple in him. We all know that. Davina . . ." She mused for a moment. "I haven't seen a sign of scruples in her either. I think she's as ruthless as Keith and even more selfish. And yet I can't help liking her. It's charm, I suppose."

Clunie laughed. "Isn't it difficult? How often would I gladly slap Davina and then she says—or does, or just looks—something and I see things from her angle and feel quite fond of her."

Alice said that having lived in London and being of the same generation Clunie was in a better position to see things from Davina's angle than herself. "But I've been about enough to know you've got to take people as they are. Now this ceilidh. Harry thinks we should invite Miss Bethune—and Molly of course. He's got this thing about Miss B. being a great singer in her day. What do you think? I don't know, frankly."

"Lumme!" said Clunie and thought about it. "What a surprise for everybody if they came! But do you think they would? It's a bit late for them, isn't it? When are you blasting off?"

About nine, Alice thought. After dinner was cleared up. "It is rather late for them but they needn't stay long. In fact it's to be hoped they wouldn't, but it would be civil to ask them and I can't see that it would do any harm. There wouldn't be climbers at the ceilidhs Miss B. went to in her youth, but she must have seen plenty of tight or tightish gamekeepers and shepherds."

"Oh yes," Clunie agreed. "Queen Victoria herself attended the ghillies' balls at Balmoral and our company won't be any coarser than they were."

"Well, we'll ask them," said Alice. "I'll write a note." She went on to say that she was driving Bessie to visit Mike in the afternoon. "So will you take the little car and organize Kintorran?"

There was quite a lot to be organized in Kintorran. Not only was Clunie to deliver the note at the castle, and if possible bring back a reply, she must cheer up Elspeth McAdam who was showing a marked lack of enthusiasm at the prospect of singing in front of Davina Clare. She must also arrange with Elspeth what they would wear in the foursome reel so that they neither clashed with the men's kilts nor with each other. Finally, Alice thought she should drop in at the Grahams' and sound Jean. It was to be hoped that Jean had enough sense to appear at the ceilidh and be reasonably civil to Davina but there was no telling.

Clunie was glad to have a reason for calling on Jean. Though it was only two days since their scene beside the burn, life had been so full and so eventful that she felt they were out of touch in a way that had never happened before and it must not be allowed to go on.

She went to the castle on her way down to Kintorran and rather to her surprise Davina answered her ring. "It's an invitation to the ceilidh," she said handing over the note. "I'll come back if it isn't convenient for them to give me the answer now."

"Great God Almighty!" Davina exclaimed. "Have the Craigs had a brain storm or what?" She looked at the envelope with dismay and then her face cleared. "But they won't come—can't in fact. Molly's ill."

Clunie said she was sorry. "What's the matter with her?"

"Me," said Davina. "It's one of her turns—she's famous for them—but I brought it on. She bursts into tears whenever she catches sight of me. And it's not as if I was being provocative," she added resentfully. "I've been quite *conciliatory*. She's taken to her bed now."

"I suppose the strain's been too much for her," said Clunie. "What about Miss Bethune? I thought when she came to fetch you the other night that she might be beginning to get on your wavelength."

Davina said she was—just. "We've talked, believe it or not. I told her what Harry said about her singing and that old man saying how good her brother—my grandpapa— was and she was quite pleased. She said she'd hunt out her songs for me. At which point Molly gave a loud howl and rushed from the room. Oh well . . ." She shrugged and then held up the note. "What about this? Want to wait?"

"I'll come back," said Clunie.

In the main street where she had shopping to do she met Hake and found that the snub administered at the Grahams' party had been ineffective. She was not surprised. Hake had always been difficult to shake off.

"Well met!" he cried merrily, coming towards her with manful stride. He was just off for a round of golf. "What about coming with me? Have you had a game yet?"

She shook her head. "No time, no clubs, no inclination."

Clubs could easily be borrowed, he assured her. "And you must have *some* time off."

"Of course I have, but it's rather irregular and I'm concentrating on climbing." This was safe ground. Hake played golf, fished and went for strapping walks but he did not climb. It deflated him momentarily but as she walked on he went with her, making a most unexpected remark.

"You had old Sandy Nesbit at the Brig last night I hear."

"We did have Mr and Mrs Nesbit," she said. "You know them, do you?"

"Lord yes. Known Sandy Nesbit for years." Hake smiled, swelling a little. "Matter of fact, I worked in his office for a while."

"I thought yours was a Glasgow firm."

Hake, now fully reflated, told her condescendingly that his family firm had been established in Glasgow for generations. He had merely spent a couple of years in Edinburgh to widen his experience. "Quite a good firm,

Nesbits. It was a coincidence meeting him here because I felt I should know something about Davina Clare but I couldn't place her. One sees so many people," said Hake, world weary. "But seeing old Nesbit brought the whole thing back. He acted for her—Davina Clare's mother—when Sir Alistair Bethune died. There was a bit of a wrangle over the Will."

"Oh yes?" said Clunie. They had reached Alice's little car and she stopped. "Well, I must get on. Good—"

"Interesting case," Hake went on, his stout form planted between her and the car. "I wasn't concerned in it myself before my time—but I read it up. She—Mrs Clare—was a by-blow of Hugh Bethune's you know. Quite a lad *he* was evidently. And—"

"I have always understood," Clunie broke in, "that no lawyer *ever* spoke of his clients' affairs."

Hake was taken aback. "Oh well—" he said, "naturally one has to be discreet. But—"

"One of my uncles is a solicitor and he doesn't even talk to his wife about clients. Will you move, please? I want to get into this car."

"Oh look, Clunie—" Hake protested, moving reluctantly, "—there's no need to make such a . . . I mean, I just thought you'd be interested, knowing Davina and Miss Tullis and—"

Miss—! Clunie swung round so fiercely that he took an involuntary step back. "Hake," she said, "if I hear even a whisper of this I'll write to Mr Nesbit and I hope you'll be struck off the rolls—or whatever they do."

"You don't suppose I'm the only person in the glen who

knows about it do you?" said Hake defensively. "Everybody knows."

"So far as I'm concerned there's nothing to know," snapped Clunie, slamming the door of the car.

She drove off smartly in the wrong direction which, however, was quite a good thing. By the time she turned round her wrath had cooled and she felt she had been overdramatic. Though Hake was a fool and fond of scandal there was no real malice in him—at least not much—and he had only been trying to impress her. Quite probably he wouldn't think of mentioning it to anyone else even if he was not frightened by her threat. For her part she was going to put it out of her mind . . . She wondered if Pat knew.

The McAdams were refreshingly normal. Though Elspeth still dreaded the thought of singing before Davina, a real pro and a terrifying girl anyway, she had already resigned herself and her mother, a plump, comfortable woman, combined with Clunie to laugh her out of her remaining doubts. The two girls arranged what they would wear and a few minutes later Clunie rang the Grahams' bell.

Mrs Graham opened the door and it was immediately obvious that here things were not normal. "Oh—Clunie!" she exclaimed, sounding a little dismayed. "Eh—come in, dear. Did you want Jean? She's in the loft." She forced her irritating titter as she added that Jean's nose was never out of her books these days. "I tell her she would do better to take a holiday but no, she won't hear of it."

"I'll see if I can prise her loose," said Clunie. "No, don't call her, Mrs Graham. I'll go up."

All the signs of deep study were present in the loft except one. The kitchen table with the crack along the middle was stacked with books and papers but the face Jean raised, far from being that of an absorbed student, was distracted. It was also very unhappy.

"Oh hallo," she said without enthusiasm.

"Hallo," said Clunie and shut the door. "Deep in your books?"

"Well . . ."

The books, several of them open, were formidable and Jean had a pen in her hand but nothing had been written on the page in front of her. Clunie glanced at it.

"Heavy going?"

"Well . . ." Jean threw down the pen and sat back in her very uncomfortable wooden chair. "It's this thesis," she said irritably, "and I simply can't concentrate."

Clunie sat down on the sofa. "Have you been sticking at it too much?"

"You know perfectly well it isn't that, Clunie. I'm worried sick. Things go from bad to worse. I suppose you've heard about the latest development?"

"If you mean that Keith's back and indulging in light dalliance with Davina—yes. Only to be expected, don't you think? I'd have thought you'd welcome it?"

A scowling face came round. "How could I *welcome* it?"

Her old friend, thought Clunie, was woefully lacking in what Pat called nous. Painstakingly she pointed out that Malcolm's family had been appalled at the prospect of his

174

marrying Davina. Was it not, therefore, desirable that his eyes should be opened? "Keith's not in love with her nor she with him but he's very good at dalliance and if she plays along Malcolm will surely see that she's not serious about either of them. He won't like it naturally, but he'll get over it. Isn't it the best thing that could happen?"

"It would be if Malcolm was like that," Jean allowed, "but he's not."

"He got over me fast enough."

"Oh, Clunie!"

"I'm not complaining. What you want now is a sultry brunette or a ravishing redhead. However, you have got the Hindu Kush."

"Oh, you just don't—or won't—understand," cried Jean. She rose abruptly and paced about the loft while Clunie sat still and listened—off and on. She felt as if she were attending a lecture, something she never did if she could help it. Malcolm, Jean explained, was the victim of a cataclysm—

"Just a minute. That"s not the same as a catalyst, is it?"

"Of course it isn't. A catalyst—"

"All right, all right. Don't bother. A cataclysm's something like an earthquake. Go on."

With an effort Jean went on. Malcolm's whole personality—or almost the whole—had been changed by his passion for Davina. Though far from indifferent to the sufferings of his family and Clunie—

"You can leave me out."

—nothing was *real* to him except Davina. "Not even the expedition," Jean concluded despairingly.

"He's not giving *that* up?"

"No! He doesn't think there's any need. *That's* where you're so wrong. Of course he doesn't like Keith making a—sort of making a set at Davina, but he just thinks every man must be attracted to her and she's so sweet and—and simple—"

"Simple! Davina!"

"—there's no harm in her . . . well, responding." Jean halted her pacing to glare. "You may laugh, Clunie, but that's what he thinks."

Clunie rose to her feet. Further discussion of the Malcolm-Davina problem would be a waste of breath and she was tired of them. "What I came for," she said, "was to make sure you'd show up at the ceilidh tomorrow."

As she expected there was an outcry. Jean couldn't do it. To have to listen to that girl, applaud her singing . . . It would be the height of insincerity. *Dishonest.*

"Rubbish! " said Clunie dampingly. "You needn't clap hard. Do you *want* to set all the tongues in the glen wagging more than they are already?" Jean's scowl became doubtful and she pressed home her advantage. "The best thing you can do for Malcolm is to come and look as if you liked it."

When she returned to the castle Miss Bethune herself opened the door. "Come in, Clunie," she said. "I have a note to Alice Craig half-written but I want a word with you before I finish it. Davina told you that Miss Tullis is far from well?"

"Yes," said Clunie, following her along the stone-flagged passage. "I'm so sorry. Is there anything we can

176

do? I'm sure Alice—" She stopped, partly because she couldn't commit Alice, partly because the round living-room startled her. In all the years she had known it, it had never changed: chairs stood in their places, Molly's knitting was rolled up neatly on her work table, Miss Bethune's papers in orderly array on her desk and the round table in the middle was either laid for tea or empty except for a bowl of flowers. Today it was not merely untidy, its whole character seemed different. Molly's knitting lay on the floor, the ball of wool some distance away from it, and on the round table was Davina's guitar and a litter of songs. The Scottie, sitting with his back to a dying fire, wore an expression of most profound dudgeon.

"Out of the way, Hamish," said Miss Bethune giving him a nudge with her foot. "Drat this fire. It's nearly out." She threw on a log. "Sit down, child. Is the hotel up there full?"

Clunie collected her wits. What was today? Friday of course. Yes, they were full for the weekend, she said. She thought there might be a vacancy or two at the beginning of the week. "Why, Miss Bethune?"

The reply came briskly. "I'm thinking about Davina. You can see for yourself I'm no housekeeper—never was." An impatient hand indicated the surrounding muddle. "So I thought if the Brighouse could take Davina for a few days . . . No use sending her to the Bethune Arms. She'd turn the place upside down. However, if you're full up, that's that. She must stay here till we can arrange for her to go back to London."

Like Miss Bethune, Clunie could see no further

alternative. It was usual in such cases for a neighbour to come to the rescue, but who would take on Davina? Not the McAdams. Certainly not the Grahams. Kintorran Lodge came to mind—Keith would be delighted—but only as a joke. She said hesitantly that there might perhaps be a room in the private flat. "I don't really know. Would you like me to ask—"

"No, no," Miss Bethune broke in. "Say nothing about it. If there should be a cancellation perhaps you will let me know." Clunie said she would and Miss Bethune sighed and stared worriedly at the fire, now finally killed by the log.

"It may be just as well to have a day or two to think things over," she said with most uncharacteristic doubt. "Davina doesn't want to go." She glanced at Clunie with a bleak gleam of amusement. "I dare say that surprises you. It did me. Apparently she resents being what she calls thrown out on her ear. I assured her it's no such thing: she is not to blame for Miss Dulles's illness though she is the immediate cause of it. I can't make her comfortable or even *feed* her properly, but she says she knows more than I do about convenience foods, whatever they are."

Clunie laughed. "I'm sure she does," she said. "They're really very nice, Miss Bethune—some of them. And it will be a help, won't it, if she does meals?"

"Well," said Miss Bethune with more of her normal decision, "it is not, after all, urgent, so long as Miss Tullis is confined to her bed. I'll just finish the note to Alice. I would have liked to go to the ceilidh. It is a long time since I went to one. But it can't be helped."

CHAPTER TEN

WHEN SHE RETURNED to the Brig, Clunie had a surprise which temporarily banished everything else from her mind. In response to a call from Harry she went through to his office and in the doorway stopped dead and shrieked *"Alan!"*

"The bad penny in person," said Harry and a young man rose to his feet, patted Clunie kindly on the head and said, "Hallo, sister."

He was an exceedingly thin young man a few inches taller than she was, who would have resembled her more closely if his skin had not been darkened and his hair bleached by tropical sunshine. Just now he was almost emaciated and an unhealthy tinge showed through the sunburn.

"I thought you were in Ecuador," said Clunie with a slight air of resentment. The family was used to Alan's unheralded arrivals but as a rule it was possible to calculate roughly when he might be due. This time he had, by his standards, only just gone.

"Quite right," he said. "I was in Ecuador but I picked up a bug."

She looked at him anxiously. "What kind of bug?"

"Don't ask me. I don't know one bug from another. Somebody flew me to a doctor and he sent me home."

It was always hard work quarrying information out of Alan but Harry had already made some progress, and between them they gave Clunie the facts. On his arrival in

Edinburgh, knowing that his parents were in Norway, he had gone to the family doctor who sent him straight into hospital where everybody, he said, had a happy time identifying the bug. Not a lethal bug, he added.

"Why wasn't I let know?" Clunie demanded crossly. "Dr Shields knew I was here."

"He told me. But what would have been the use? I wasn't ill—not *ill*. They threw me out as soon as they'd finished their damned tests and decided I wasn't a danger to the community. I just have to report to old Graham, hand him a sealed letter and swallow pills."

"You're going to stay here, are you?" Clunie asked and looked a little doubtfully at Harry.

Alan said his intention was to bag a bunk in the bothy and Harry laughed.

"Try that on Alice," he said. "You'll find yourself in the flat where she can count the pills to make sure you're taking them."

"Ministering angels," said Alan gloomily and added that the bothy would be luxury compared to what he was used to.

"Very likely," said Harry, "but you can save your breath."

He went away and Clunie, left alone with her brother, put her arms round him and kissed his lean cheek, a demonstration to which he could only be said to submit. "Poor old thing," she said. "Have you had a horrible time?"

Not too bad. The worst bit was in hospital. All these humiliating tests . . . Why can't they let you be ill in

180

peace?"

"You might die."

"So what? We've all got to die some time. Still," he admitted with a faint grin, "there's some work in South America I'd hate to leave unfinished."

It was not until some time later that Clunie was able to give Alice her Kintorran report. On her return Alice, as Harry foretold, immediately took charge of Alan, installing him in the private flat and ordering him to attend Dr Graham's evening surgery and remember to take the sealed letter. Alan, aware that it was no use arguing with a ministering angel, shrugged his shoulders and obeyed. Alice next described Mike's condition: he was extensively plastered and pretty dopey but quite all right. She then turned to Clunie and the ceilidh.

"Are Miss Bethune and Molly coming?"

"No," said Clunie. "Here's a note. Molly's having one of her turns."

Davina had been right in saying that Molly's turns were famous. As she took the note Alice remarked that it was only surprising that she hadn't had one sooner; Davina was bound to bring one on. "She must be quite a strain for them both but Miss Bethune's made of sterner stuff. How she's put up with Molly all these years, I'll never know." She read the note, frowning slightly. "She wants to send Davina here as soon as there's a room. Well, that's not on."

"Why not?" Clunie asked curiously.

"Because she can't afford it," said Alice and added that the Brig didn't take neighbours in trouble as customers.

"We could have had Davina in the flat if Alan hadn't got the room, but I'm not going to turn him out and I'm not sure it would be a good idea anyway."

"There's a further point," said Clunie. "Davina doesn't want to come. She resents being bundled out of the way as if she were to blame for Molly's turn—which Miss B. admits she isn't—and she says that at least she knows more about convenience foods than Miss B."

Alice expressed surprise.

"She's full of surprises, Davina."

"But even if she does know about convenience foods I can't think she'll be any *use*."

"Alice," said Clunie, "have you ever seen the castle as run by Miss B.? You wouldn't know the place. I don't suppose Davina will be reliable—she'll abandon the fish fingers without a backward glance if Malcolm or Keith asks her out—but she can't be worse than Miss B."

"Well, well." Alice looked amused. "I've called, of course, when Molly's had a turn but, now I think of it, never in the holiday season." In reply to a raised eyebrow she explained briskly that Mrs Kidd usually gave the castle extra time when Molly had a turn but in the season she helped at the Bethune Arms. After reflection she added that the problem of Davina had better be left for the present. "Now, did you fix things with Elspeth? And what about Jean?"

Elspeth and she had agreed to wear tartan skirts and white blouses, Clunie said. She would have to buy or borrow a blouse. She thought Jean would come but she was still very sticky. "She said she'd think about it."

182

Alice approved of the tartan skirts and hoped Jean would think straight. "The trouble with high principles is that people's thoughts get so complicated." She went away, leaving Clunie in a state of giggles, but came back immediately to say there was no need to buy a blouse. "You can have one of the boys' white shirts."

The hotel was full and as Harry was helping his hard-pressed dining-room staff, it was late when Clunie went for dinner. She found Bessie eating a hurried meal and sat down beside her, saying how glad she was to hear of Mike's progress. "I told you he's tough and how right I was."

Bessie nodded. "They'll let him home as soon as he's able to get around a bit. You know, the loo and that. It'll mean a lot of work for his mum—not that she minds that but I wish we weren't so pressed here. The bar's full tonight and it'll be like this every weekend till the weather gets really bad. They *couldn't* let me go."

Knowing Harry and Alice, Clunie thought they would contrive it somehow.

"That's just it," Bessie said dolefully. "They're so kind I'd feel terrible if I let them down. So would Mike."

"Everybody would pitch in."

"Nobody can be in two places at once though." Bessie finished her pudding and began to drink the coffee that was already before her. "You know that girl Davina? She's in the bar again tonight. Remember she took over for a bit the night of the accident and she seemed to know her way about. I just wondered . . ."

"Well," said Clunie, "it's a thought. I'll throw out a

feeler if you like, but I don't think she'll be here long enough to be any good."

A few minutes after Bessie left the room Davina came in. "Mind if I watch you eat?" she asked and sat down. She looked depressed. "Who's the yellow man in the bar?"

"That's my brother, Alan."

"Oh. Sorry. Why's he that colour?"

"Sunburn—tropical and he's rather ill. Just out of hospital, in fact."

In that case, Davina said, she didn't blame him for his colour. "I was a dirty grey when they let me out. Is he a climber?"

"No, but he's just as mad," said Clunie. "You might call him an explorer. Where's your go or stay argument got to? Is it settled?"

"Yes, it's settled." Davina picked up a fork and drew patterns on the tablecloth. "I lost. Molly had a fit of hysterics after you'd been and Dr Graham came down on the go side."

"After I'd been? How could I make her hysterical?"

"Oh, it wasn't you. It was the idea of me coming here. So I have to leave the country."

"Oh surely—" Clunie began and stopped. "It sounds a bit excessive," she went on, "but you wouldn't have stayed much longer anyway, would you?" She remembered Davina saying the day they met that she had to come to her great aunt because there was nowhere else she could go, but then she was an invalid. She must have what Pat called howfs in London, haunts where she would find friends who would take her in and let her sleep on the

184

floor. "After all, you're well now."

The fork was still busy and Davina did not look up. "Oh . . . yes. I'd be all right, but Aunt Charlotte says I must go to my mother. She's going to ring her up." She threw down the fork. "Well, I *can't*. My mother doesn't want to know about me. I can't make Aunt Charlotte see that. She says, even if we don't get on, Mum's responsible for me and she must at least know I'm going back."

"But," said Clunie, "you're of age. Your mother isn't responsible for you."

Davina gave her a cynical glance. "She'd be the first to agree with you. But I can't budge Aunt Charlotte. I can't have the money for the fare till she's contacted Mum and that's final. It's not even her money," added Davina bitterly. "Mum sent it to her."

There was really nothing to say. Clunie went on eating automatically, hardly aware of what she ate. It was so surprising that Miss Bethune should act in this way. Though her eye was bleak and her manner abrupt she was kind-hearted and about the last woman she, Clunie, could have imagined losing her head. Molly would, of course, panic on the slightest provocation and if there was any truth in the hints dropped by Hake it explained the trapped rabbit look and the failure of the treacle scones. But Miss Bethune had received Davina: she if not Molly should know that the surest way to set tongues wagging was to send her away suddenly. And not only was it hard on Davina, who felt herself unjustly blamed for Molly's turn, the atmosphere of crisis, with Davina's mother added, would seem the worst possible thing for Miss

185

Tullis.

"Malcolm's the last straw apparently," Davina was saying. "I could murder him. There's Keith too, of course. Nobody seems to bother about him but Aunt Charlotte brought them both in. I asked what kind of carry-ons she visualized. Well, I mean where could you carry on—apart from petting in cars? But it wasn't very tactful, I suppose. She got really angry. The Grahams are so up-tight even the doctor isn't his usual self and she *can't* have neighbours upset and Molly made ill." She got up abruptly. "Oh hell! I'll go back to the bar and get tight."

"Half a tick and I'll come with you," said Clunie. "Who brought you tonight?"

"Keith. But Malcolm's here too. They're in a Hindu huddle at the moment. I can't think of anything more boring. Keith'll have to come out of it long enough to buy me another drink."

Clunie finished her meal and as they made their way through the dining-room said, "What puzzles me is why your mother throws you into such a tizz. Nobody can force you to go to her."

"No?" Davina looked round. "You don't know much, do you? You can be forced to do almost anything if you've got no money at all. What do you think made me come here? And don't talk to me about social security. They don't just hand it across the counter, and you have to eat while they're making up their minds if you're—what's the word?—eligible."

The more Clunie heard the more confused Davina's plight appeared. It was unthinkable that her mother, however badly they got on, would refuse to help her while she found her feet again: even more unthinkable that Miss Bethune would send her great-niece away without money enough for emergencies. She said so but Davina shook her head.

"She thinks I lead such a shocking life in London that she won't take the responsibility of letting me go back without being sure Mum's alerted to keep tabs on me."

"What kind of shocking?"

Davina shrugged. "Every kind. You name it. Well, a lot of the time it's fairly squalid; Molly'd have a hell of a turn if she saw some of the holes I've lived in. But it suits me. And I'm not *depraved*. At least I don't think I am."

"I'm sure you're not," said Clunie. In her experience the consciences of maniacs were individual, to put it mildly, but they had them, and there was a world of difference between a maniac, working for some object or ambition regardless of comfort and appearances, and a dropout who merely talked about his creative urges. She thought of the scene last night about the ceilidh, but she didn't mention it. Obviously Davina was still in.

At the bar, Alan was talking to Pat and she steered Davina over and introduced him to her. "Davina wants to know why you're such a peculiar colour," she said. Alan replied that he would be happy to explain his complexion and she turned away to intercept Malcolm who was hurrying to Davina's side.

Malcolm shied like a nervous horse and Clunie, though she was not going to let him escape, began mildly. She had seen Elspeth, she told him, and they were going to wear their tartan skirts and white blouses for the exhibition foursome. "I haven't actually got a white blouse but Alice is lending me one of the boys' shirts."

"Oh," said Malcolm. "Oh yes. That—that should look very nice."

"We're giving them the whole works complete with the Reel of Turlock, did you know? I hope I don't lose my way—or have a heart attack. There's nothing more strenuous. It goes at such a lick. Do *you* remember it?"

"Oh yes, I—I think so. Yes, it is—er—strenuous. I'm sure it'll come back to you all right. I mean you—well, you've done it so often."

"But not for a long time," she said and took him through a verbal rehearsal with gestures. Pat drifted over to join in and Malcolm gradually relaxed and even laughed with something like his normal good humour. But his eyes kept returning to Davina who, with a glass in her hand, was exchanging slanderous hospital stories with Alan and he could not be held for long.

"What can I get you?" Pat said to Clunie. "It's a good twenty minutes since you came in and you haven't had a drink yet."

She said she wasn't a heavy drinker. "Tomato juice— shandy—I really don't mind."

"Oh we can do better than that without exceeding," said Pat and led her to the bar. "Clunie's tired," he said to Tom. "What do you recommend?"

Tom smiled benevolently at Clunie. "Well, what about a wee whisky and tonic? You like that, don't you?"

Yes, she said, it was effective and agreeable, and a

moment later she found herself seated in a corner with the drink before her.

"Now then," said Pat, "what's on your mind?"

"What makes you think—"

A negative side-to-side gesture stopped her. "I've told you before I can read you like a book. Come on, open up. You didn't get far with Malcolm, did you?"

"No," she said, "but at least we're on speaking terms—I hope. I got really tired of being avoided and looked squinny at. I couldn't have believed even Malcolm could be so dumb."

"He isn't—when he's in his right mind," said Pat. "What were you trying to do?"

"Oh . . . to get some degree of thaw. But . . ." She hesitated and glanced up at him. He was filling his pipe and looked utterly dependable. Even more so than usual, she thought, because of the pipe. Pat, glancing down, caught the gleam of laughter. He cocked an enquiring eyebrow and she explained.

"Yes," he said. "You'd think by this time a pipe would be discredited as a sign of reliability and integrity and sagacity—a real sound chap, but no. Every conman should smoke a pipe. It's infallible. Proceed."

She did so reluctantly. "Well, we used to be good friends and I had an idea that if he thawed enough I might tip him off to be a bit more discreet about Davina. He isn't doing her any good. But there wasn't a hope, and it's probably too late anyhow."

"Is he doing her any harm?" asked Pat.

"Yes, he is. So is Keith, but not so much." She told him

189

about Molly's turn and Miss Bethune's decision that Davina must go. "She says she can't have Molly made ill and neighbours upset—meaning the Grahams. Davina's to go as soon as Miss B. can fix it with her mother. It really isn't fair that she should have all the blame shoved on her."

There was a pause while Pat lit his pipe and then he said, "I hate to be ungallant but don't you think Davina's asked for it? Very likely Malcolm would never have noticed her if she hadn't deliberately bowled him out. Keith would, but as you say he's not so damaging—or so vulnerable."

Clunie agreed. "The fact is, Davina's as simple in her way as Malcolm is in his. All he knows is Glen Torran and a narrow little circle in Glasgow. She only knows King's Road, Chelsea."

"Which is just as narrow though it would be astonished to hear you say so. You have a point. Poor Davina. No doubt she didn't mean to bring on Molly's turn either."

"No, of course she didn't. And the sad thing is that she and Miss B. were just beginning to get on. She told them what she'd heard about the Bethunes being singers and Miss B. was quite pleased and talked about Scots songs. She dug a whole lot out for Davina to see."

"How much do you know about her background? The Bethune connection?" Pat asked.

"All she's told me about the Bethune connection," said Clunie truthfully, "is that Miss B. is her great aunt. I'm not sure if she even knew Hugh was her grandfather till old Jimsie mentioned him. As for background, she hasn't any.

She doesn't know if her father is alive or dead and her stepfather won't have her in the house. So, when she came out of hospital, her mother pushed her off here."

Her tone was indignant and Pat smiled. "No marks for Mum then," he said. "And quite a lot for Davina."

"What do you—what marks?"

"Well, she could easily have been funny about poor old Molly," said Pat. Clunie was silent and he looked round at her. "Don't you know about that?"

She shook her head. "I don't think I want to."

"Oh? Why?"

It was not easy to be precise. "It seems so mean . . . Hake . . " She hesitated and then told him about Mr Nesbit's interest and Hake's indiscretion. "I threatened to get him struck off the rolls."

"You did? I'll bet that frightened Hake. What an interesting mixture you are."

"What of?"

"Soft-hearted to a fault and, when roused, ferocity personified."

"Dah!" said Clunie.

"And with too lively an imagination," he added and stood up. "You'd better have the facts before it runs away with you but first I'll fill up the glasses."

"I don't want to be tiddly," she said crossly.

"You won't be if you don't mix your drinks," was the calm reply.

He walked away to the bar and Clunie's brother strolled over and sat down beside her, remarking that the only drawback to an evening spent in the bar of the Brig was the standing about.

"You look a bit drawn," Clunie observed. "You'd better go to bed soon." She looked at the glass in his hand. "Is whisky good for this bug of yours?"

"I don't know," said Alan. "It's good for me, I know that. The bug can take its chance. Your friend Davina's quite an experience, isn't she?"

Clunie looked round at him. "Are you aflame?"

"Well, no," he said with some regret. "She's seductive but boring. One of those tedious fanatical types."

Pat, arriving with two large whiskies and a small one drowned in tonic found Clunie, her head on her hand, helpless with laughter. Alan said he couldn't think what was the matter with her and asked severely how much she had had to drink.

"One small whisky and tonic," said Pat. "It can't be that."

Clunie sat up and pointed at Alan. "He—he thinks Davina's one of those—tedious f-fanatical types."

" 'Wad some power the giftie gie us, to see oorsels as ithers see us,' " Pat quoted in a detached tone which set Clunie off again. "Never heed her, Alan. You're a sensible man in your own way and not nearly as tedious as you might be. Clunie's fighting spirit's up. She thinks Davina's being made a scapegoat because of the great Bethune scandal."

Alan stared at him. "What Bethune scandal? Oh—d'you mean the divorce? Dammit that was about fifty years ago. What's it got to do with this creature—Davina?"

"Well, nothing, you might say." Having distributed the

drinks, Pat sat down. "Except, of course, that she's descended from it."

"Divorce?" Clunie looked from one to the other. "What—I mean who divorced who?"

"Do you mean to say you never heard about it?" Alan demanded. "You must have."

"Well, I didn't. How did *you* hear?"

He said he couldn't remember. "Probably from one of Pat's informative little talks."

"More than likely," said Clunie tartly.

Pat denied it. The first he had heard of it was from Sir James Finlay when he was appointed to his job. Old Finlay, he said, held the view that the best way to deal with a secret was to make sure everybody knew it, thereby removing the spice and leaving very little to say. Sir James suspected that the only person in Glen Torran who was unaware that her story was common knowledge was the heroine—or victim. The plain truth was that Miss Tullis had been married to Hugh Bethune who had quite soon left her for another woman. She divorced him and instead of going back to her own maiden name, took her mother's.

"Is *that* all?" said Clunie, confirming Sir James's view.

"I suppose you thought 'e'd done 'er wrong," said Alan.

"Well, he certainly done 'er wrong," she retorted, "but I admit I thought it was a different wrong." She sipped her drink, looking over at Davina who was sitting at the bar flanked by her admirers. No wonder the sight of her upset poor Molly, reminding her of pain and humiliation. But impatience came in. Though divorce caused more stir fifty years ago than it does now, why should the innocent party still be in such a state? It wasn't sense—but then Molly was not sensible. "I suppose she's been round Miss Bethune's neck ever since," she said. "Isn't it surprising that she came back here?"

"They didn't come till after the war," said Pat. "Molly hadn't been here much anyway—if at all: the whole affair, engagement and marriage, was over within a year, I believe. So she could kid herself that nobody recognized her and Miss Bethune's shrewd enough to share old Finlay's view. Besides there's very little money and they have the castle for free."

Alan got up announcing that he was going to bed. "You know," he said, "I can't help sympathizing with Hugh Bethune, sinner though he was. Treacle scones are not enough."

Alice Craig was quite as indignant as Clunie when she heard that Davina was to be banished and immediately began racking her brains as to how she could be squeezed into the Brig without expense to Miss Bethune. But Clunie didn't think Miss Bethune would budge from her decision and Harry when consulted was quite definite. They could do nothing about Davina.

"It would be rank interference," he said. "The girl didn't want to come to the castle in the first place. If Miss Bethune thinks it's time she went back where she belongs, what's she got to grumble about?"

"Nothing, I suppose," Alice admitted. "Only she doesn't seem to belong anywhere, poor girl, and she's still far from strong. And what sticks in my throat, Harry, is that she's a stranger in the glen and she's being thrown out for no fault of her own."

Now she was just being sentimental, said Harry callously. The glen meant nothing to Davina. "She'll forget about it—*and* Malcolm *and* Keith, not to mention Miss Bethune and Molly—as soon as she's in the train. I wouldn't say she's blameless either," he added. "She's making a proper fool of poor old Malcolm."

"Well, he *is* soft, Harry."

"Maybe he is but I don't like to see him played up the way she's doing. I hope to God there isn't real trouble between him and Keith."

Alice was sobered. Harry didn't often speak so forcibly and there was much in what he said. But she was not entirely convinced. Though Davina might not be over scrupulous she could hardly be blamed for misjudging her effect on Malcolm: the Grahams, in her opinion, were making an absurd fuss about nothing, and finally she had no patience with Molly's delicate sensibilities.

Harry laughed. "Well, do as you think best," he said. "But young Davina's been a hell of a nuisance to a hell of a lot of people. I'll be glad to see the last of her myself."

"Oh, do you find her disturbing too?" asked his wife innocently.

Later in the day she called at the castle and was received by Miss Bethune who looked worn, and Hamish who was even more morose than usual. Miss Tullis, she was told, was no better.

"Oh dear, I am sorry," she said. "Is she eating anything?

195

I brought a chicken—cooked."

Miss Bethune gave a short bark of laughter as she thanked her. "Very thoughtful as well as kind. I'm no cook. Nor is Davina, thought I must say she's quite ingenious in finding things that don't need much cooking. She has gone to buy some now. Some kind of fish you boil in its bag. Come in, Alice, though we are somewhat disordered as you will see."

The round living-room was as Clunie had described it, except that the ashes of the dead fire had been sketchily swept back into the grate and an electric heater placed in front of it. Possibly another example of Davina's ingenuity.

Alice murmured that disorder is inevitable when there is illness in the house and asked more minutely about Miss Dulles's condition. "Is it her heart?"

"Nerves," said Miss Bethune. "Having Davina here has been altogether too much for her. It was a risk, of course, but what could I do? The child had just come out of hospital after a serious illness and somebody had to look after her."

"It must have been a strain for you both," said Alice. She smiled. "Davina's a modern of moderns, isn't she? I was going to suggest that she should come to us, Miss Bethune, but—"

"You have no vacancy, have you?"

"No proper vacancy but we could squeeze her in some-where. Clunie says, though, that you feel she should go to her mother."

Miss Bethune sighed. "So she should if we could find

196

her mother. She is the most irresponsible . . . Nobody answers the telephone and we have no forwarding address. She may be anywhere."

"Well then . . ."

There was a long pause. It was difficult to know what to do for the best, Miss Bethune said at last. "Though Miss Tullis finds it a great strain having the child here, I am afraid she would be even more upset to think of her at the Brighouse."

"But why?" said Alice. "I don't follow—"

"My dear Alice, *think*," Miss Bethune commanded her testily. "Everybody in the glen knows that Miss Tullis was married to my brother Hugh who bolted with another woman—Davina's grandmother. You knew it, didn't you?"

Alice swallowed. "Well, yes, Miss Bethune. But surely—it's such an old story it must be forgotten now."

Miss Bethune's head was vigorously shaken. "No. Anything that concerned the Family was naturally of the deepest interest. And my concern now is for Miss Tullis. She has never got over it and seeing this girl brought it all back. Davina has a considerable resemblance to my brother. It was a shock too to find that she had heard the story from her mother—as something of a joke, we gather. Miss Tullis may be oversensitive, but to some extent I share her dread that Davina may repeat it and laugh—"

"Miss Bethune," said Alice, "I don't know if you can convey it to Miss Tullis without causing her further distress, but I am absolutely certain that Davina has not talked of it.

"She promised me she wouldn't," Miss Bethune admitted, but I was not sure if she could be trusted. She obviously thought it a great fuss over nothing. Which in a way—" she added realistically, "—I suppose it is. But it was a tragedy for us." She paused for a moment. "My brother was not a bad fellow, you know. He was in the Navy and died very gallantly early in the war." He was, she concluded, a good deal spoilt, being the youngest of the family.

"And I have heard that he had great charm," Alice said smiling. "Old Jimsie the keeper says he could charm the deer off the hills with his singing. I haven't heard Davina sing, but I think she has inherited the charm."

Along with Miss Bethune's realism ran a strong vein of romance. She straightened her shoulders and lifted her chin a little. "She may," she said. "We have Stuart blood. My grandmother was a Stuart."

Murmuring respectfully, Alice got up to take her leave and hurried home to tell Harry.

"What?" he cried. "Mary Queen of Scots and Bonny Prince Charlie and all? Well, poor Molly! She hadn't a chance."

"No," said Alice. "And how typically Stuart to die gallantly leaving others to pick up the pieces. But, Harry—the waste! Those two women spending their *whole lives* brooding over their shame."

Harry pointed out that they needn't have wasted their lives—if they had wasted them. "They've probably quite enjoyed their tragedy. Stuart blood or no Stuart blood the Bethunes were a pretty dull lot so far as I can make out.

What about Davina? Is she coming here?"

No, Alice said, Miss Bethune had decided that until Davina went back to London—which it was hoped would be within a few days—it was better that she should stay at the castle.

"Much better," said Harry.

CHAPTER ELEVEN

THE CEILIDH that night was much like other ceilidhs at the Brig. For many of the hotel guests it was an enjoyable novelty, for the locals and regular visitors the only novelty was the lassie from the castle. In her limp black dress she stuck out as she had stuck out in the Grahams' loft, but as always she seemed unconscious of her oddness and, as always, she got away with it. Davina, thought Clunie when she saw her arrive with Keith carrying her guitar, was odd and to wear the same sort of clothes as other people would not suit her.

She was in better spirits than she had been the night before owing to Miss Bethune's failure to contact her mother. "She'll keep trying of course," she said but added that she would very likely keep on failing. "It's too much to hope that my mum has passed out of my life but she's very sly."

There was no doubt, Harry and Alice Craig agreed later, that wherever it came from the girl had charm—when she liked to use it. In marked contrast to the Grahams' party where it was all focused on Malcolm, he was the only sufferer from the cold indifference which she used with equal skill. The Craigs themselves were charmed by her enjoyment of their party: she charmed Elspeth and Ross McAdam by eager interest in their Scottish songs and "us singers" friendliness. She was intrigued by Tosh's pipes, laughed heartily at Andy's monologue and everyone was delighted when she was danced through an eightsome reel, not by Keith but by Harry himself.

Her own group of songs, strategically placed just before the foursome reel which was to end what might be called the formal part of the entertainment, held the listeners spellbound. Taking up her position with her guitar she smiled at the audience and confided to them that until she came to Scotland for this, her first visit, she had no idea of its wonderful heritage of music; nor had she known that her grandfather and her great aunt were singers. She had been going through a lot of their songs, she said and added, "But don't worry. I'm not going to try to sing a Scotch song to this audience and after hearing Elspeth and Ross."

The little speech was well received and Clunie thought she had never heard her sing so well. Her voice had a new richness, due, perhaps, to the improvement in her health and she had been clever in choosing her songs.

But underneath the good humour of a successful party there were tensions and if Davina was at her best, others were at their worst. Jean was so glum that Alice thought it was a pity she had been persuaded to come, and in order to make sure that she didn't have to travel in the same car as Davina she had brought Hake who spent the evening glaring balefully at Clunie.

For Clunie herself the party was a mixture of high delight and irritation, culminating in fury. She loved dancing any dancing but most of all the Scottish dances, both for their elaborate elegance and their exhilarating element of romp. It was a long time since she had danced a reel and to some at least of the watchers the exhibition foursome was a revelation. Not only was she a natural dancer, graceful and neat-footed, enjoyment lit her normally understated beauty quite startlingly.

"Aye, you're a bonny dancer," said Pat as she formally took his arm to leave the floor. "And a bonny lassie. Why have we never danced together before?"

"You were too old—too superior," she retorted.

"Above your touch," he agreed affably.

"Clunie!" Davina put out a hand as they passed. "I'd no idea you were so—you look *gorgeous*."

"No, do I?" She laughed and put a hand to her cheek. "What I feel is hot."

"But you don't look it—you're glowing. And you're so *dancey*. Isn't she?" to Keith who was beside her.

"Yes," Keith said quietly. "She was always a dancey girl."

"There now," said Pat. "Make your curtsey," and smiling she curtsied and they passed on.

She danced an eightsome reel with Alan, dancing being one of the things they did together, the *Dashing White Sergeant* with Tom and a rollicking *Shottische* with one of the bothy boys. Then Alice at the piano and the boy with the accordion struck up the *Waltz Country Dance*. She smiled at Pat coming towards her, but Keith was there, holding out an imperious hand. There was nothing to be done except take it. Pat had not been quite quick enough.

The waltz country dance is one to dance with a special partner. You meet another couple, with them dance a gentle graceful movement and then waltz away till the music brings you to the next meeting. It was characteristic

202

of a stormy relationship that though the last encounter, at the reception desk, had been thoroughly unpleasant Keith had apparently forgotten it. But the pattern was not quite normal. Usually Keith was a lively, rather flamboyant partner: tonight he danced beautifully in silence. He was very little taller than Clunie and when they waltzed he held her tightly so that his cheek was close to hers and often touched it. There was no response from Clunie. Her body was rigid, her face expressionless. At the end he lingered for a moment before he let her go, then kissed her quickly and with a return to his flamboyant style led her off the floor. Then he went back to shoulder Malcolm out of the way and re-establish himself beside Davina.

Jean's forethought had been wasted, indeed unfortunate. Keith had driven Davina to the Brig, having first taken her to the Lodge to have a meal with him, so that the arrangement with Hake meant that Malcolm arrived at the ceilidh alone and for the first time openly resentful. In the foursome reel, though he looked magnificent in his kilt, he was stiff and unsmiling and danced badly, mortifying Elspeth who took dancing almost as seriously as singing. As the evening went on he was subjected to some ragging from Keith's young fans, which he was in no mood to take, while Keith himself soared to the top of his form.

He was convulsing his admirers with the unsuccessful sword dance which was one of his regular turns when Alan remarked dispassionately that the years did nothing to diminish Keith's bounce. "I've never met anybody with more," he said. "You can almost imagine him giving himself a start and rising to the top of Everest without further exertion."

The sword dance was not amusing Clunie, who was no longer in the mood to be amused by anything, but this surprised her into an involuntary laugh. Alan went on to speak of Davina's singing.

"I must say she's damn good. And Keith himself isn't a better showman. Is the charm part of her image?"

Clunie said she didn't think so. "In London she's aloof, take it or leave it, but she probably felt an unsophisticated audience like this needs charm."

"She laid it on thick enough," said Alan. "Surprising she thought it worthwhile."

It was not very surprising, Clunie thought. Though she had given no sign even of remembering them she had simply taken her, Clunie's, words to heart and projected the appropriate image. But she was not really interested in Davina. She was furious with Keith. She was almost more furious with Pat. Men, she thought bitterly, are extraordinarily dense. It was to be expected of Keith that feeling, as he obviously had, one of his upsurges of emotion about her he yielded to it without a thought. The interested eyes watching them, the speculation—even sniggers—his manner and that kiss sparked off, meant nothing to Keith. But Pat . . . She had expected better of Pat. The exhibition foursome had not only been a revelation to the spectators. If she looked radiant it was because she felt happier than she had ever been in her life, not because of the pleasure dancing gave her but because she was dancing with Pat. Reels are not romantic. They are strenuous, they can be sweaty, there is no prolonged contact and broad grins are more appropriate than languishing smiles, but if the hand that clasps yours and the arm that swings you are right, not to mention the grin, nothing more need be said. Or so she had thought till Keith came barging in.

"What on earth has come over Malcolm?" Alan murmured in her ear. "Has he gone mad? Look."

Clunie wrested her thoughts from Pat, who was near but withdrawn, and obediently looked. Malcolm had seized the opportunity offered by the sword dance to take Keith's place beside Davina again and was talking urgently, his head close to hers, his face desperate. She was looking straight in front of her, saying nothing but expressing negation in every line.

The sword dance ended. Keith, flushed and laughing, was uproariously acclaimed by the boys and girls, and Davina turned and spoke a few words to Malcolm. She got up and leaving him staring after her, sheet-white and rigid, threaded her way through the crowd to Clunie. She was nearly as pale as Malcolm.

"Clunie, I want to go home," she said. "Could—"

"Are you ill?" Clunie asked. "Keith's driving you, isn't he? Tell him, Alan—but get some water first."

Davina shook her head. "No, I'm all right. It's hot in here, that's all. I don't want to wait for Keith. He's tight, I think."

"I'll take you home," said Alan.

She looked at him. "Oh—would you . . ?"

Clunie took her arm. "Hold up," she said. "We'll slide

out as though heading modestly for the ladies. Front door, Alan."

"My guitar—"

"We'll take care of it," said Pat's voice.

In a moment or two he strolled over to the piano and took Davina's guitar from the top of it. Two other kilted figures converged upon him.

"Where's Davina ?"

"Gone home, I believe."

Keith"s eyebrows rose. "Has she indeed? I wonder why. She came with me. Has she actually gone, McKechnie?"

"That I couldn't say," said Pat, looking dubiously at the guitar and its case. "Hey, Ross! How the hell does this thing go in?"

Ross McAdam bustled forward helpfully and pointed out that both instrument and case had a wide end and a narrow end. "You put the wide bit—"

"I can see that, you fool, but does it lie on its back or its front?"

"Like this," said Ross taking the guitar from him. "Davina gone off without it? That was great singing we had from her tonight."

"Damn good," Pat agreed. "She felt a bit knocked up apparently. Not long out of hospital."

"So I heard." Ross looked solemn and sympathetic. "I hope it hasn't been too much—"

"Who took her home?" Malcolm interrupted hoarsely. Ross, after a startled glance, became very busy with the guitar case. Keith laughed.

"Well, it wasn't me, mate," he said. "I say, Malcolm.

What about Stronachie tomorrow? If Alf and Bill did the—"

Malcolm turned on him. "You go to hell. I'm finished. You can find somebody else for your bloody expedition and kill yourself for all I care."

"Now look, boy," Keith began angrily but he got no further.

"If you boys want a punch-up," said Harry in the voice which never failed to quell the most boisterous or quarrelsome customer, "get outside. I'll have no disturbance in my bar." He addressed the company with a cordial landlord's smile. "Time, ladies and gentlemen, please! We hope you've all enjoyed . . ."

Malcolm flung out of the room. Keith, shrugging off his anger, looked resigned and rather amused. Under cover of Harry's speech and the following applause Pat said, "Go after him, man. You've tried him high enough. What are you *doing*, fooling about like this with an expedition in front of you?"

"He's such a fool! The girl doesn't care tuppence for either of us but he won't believe it. Who did take her home?"

"Alan. She really was knocked up. Go on, now. You know you'll never find a better partner and you don't care about Davina any more than she does for you."

"The all-seeing eye of McKechnie, huh? I'm not so sure about never finding a better partner, but I'll see what I can do. I hope there's no violence, that's all."

"Away wi' you," said Pat. "What for would you get violent?"

Keith was already moving off. "Oh, *I* wouldn't," he said over his shoulder. "He's bigger than me. But he might be a trifle impetuous."

Having seen Alan take charge of Davina, Clunie was on her way back to take charge of Davina's guitar when she met Hake who, not being a frequenter of the Brig, was heading with stately tread for the front door.

"Hallo, Hake," she said. "Have you enjoyed the ceilidh? Jean getting her coat?"

Hake replied stiffly that it had been a very pleasant evening and added with unmistakable huffiness that Jean had told him not to wait for her. She would go home with Malcolm. "Well—g'night," he said and stalked on, leaving Clunie reflecting that at the present rate she soon would have no friends left in the glen. But how like Jean to ditch poor Hake, without a thought for his pride, in order to go home with Malcolm . . .

As she went along the passage Jean herself emerged from the ladies' cloakroom, carrying her coat as if she had snatched it up, and rushed to the side door. At the same moment Pat came out of the bar with Davina's guitar now safely encased.

"To you," he said holding it out.

Clunie took it. "What's sent Jean off like a rocket? Is the place on fire?"

"Oh lord! Is she out already?"

"Well? What's happened? Hake's gone off by himself and—"

"Och, Jean's away to protect her wee brother," Pat said and explained briefly. "Keith went after him to make it up and no doubt he'll do it if she doesn't throw herself between them."

"She's got no sense at all," said Clunie. "Should I go and haul her off?"

From the car park came the sounds of engines starting and doors slamming and Pat shook his head. "Too much of a crowd already," he said. "I'll look after Jean."

Harry's office was the place for the guitar and Clunie put it there and then went back to the bar to give a hand with the clearing up. It had been a good party and that being so there was enough spirit left in the staff and their friends to deal with the aftermath at once. Feet might ache but they would ache just as badly in the morning and the bothy boys, weighing in so cheerfully now, would not be available when elation had passed. There were bursts of song, bursts of laughter and impromptu dances which looked dangerous for glass and china but in fact did no damage.

Into the pandemonium—in which work was going on with surprising efficiency—presently strolled three gentlemen, unruffled and apparently sharing a joke: Keith Finlay, who immediately collected the attention of Alf Page and Bill Carter; Alan Ritchie and Pat McKechnie. Pat joined the strong-arm gang to manhandle the piano down from the movable dais and into its everyday corner and Alan carried a tray of glasses to the bar where Tom had a team of washers-up, observing hopefully that there didn't seem to be room for any more willing hands.

"No," said Tom. "You get away to your bed. Davina's not the only one who's been in hospital recently. She

209

didn't pass out on you, I hope?"

Alan laughed. "Not her. She was fine as soon as she was clear of her admirers. You might tell Clunie I've gone to bed if she's looking for me."

Tom gave Clunie the message along with the report on Davina and advised her to follow Alan's example. "We're overstaffed if anything and you've done plenty today."

She felt she had done more than enough, she had never been so tired, but she didn't want to go before she heard what had happened in the car park and she was not going to run after Pat. Meanwhile there was no avoiding the questions and comments of the girls, who had not failed to observe Davina's departure and the scene between Malcolm and Keith. They did not believe that Davina had been overcome by the heat and tiredness. It had looked to them like she'd run into difficulties with her two-timing game: Malcolm looking like death and then him and Keith having a blazing row—though that hadn't come to much seemingly. Rather disappointed glances were cast at Keith in businesslike conference with Page and Carter, but excitement was revived by somebody who had heard from one of the boys that Malcolm had told Keith he could find somebody else for his expedition and he hoped he'd kill himself.

Clunie, feeling rather sick, was detaching herself when she was stopped by Bessie. Bessie was one of the more sensible girls and a keen climber. Malcolm, Bessie was sure, would never say he hoped Keith would kill himself: no climber would say that to another. And she couldn't believe he'd pull out of the team—not when he thought it over. All the same, that Davina was a right troublemaker. "You didn't say anything about her subbing for me in the bar, did you?"

"No, I didn't," said Clunie. "She's going back to London any day."

Bessie looked relieved. "Oh well, that's all right. Wendy you know, Wendy Carter—she's going to do it." She grinned happily. "They're letting Mike go home tomorrow and I'm having a week off."

"Marvellous!" Clunie responded. She added that with Wendy as a sub Bessie could be quite easy in her mind and moved away as she saw Pat approaching.

In the car park Pat had found Jean running about like nothing so much, he told her frankly, as a flustered hen. It was unlit apart from the confusion of headlights and she had no idea where Malcolm and Keith had parked their vehicles.

"Just as well," said Pat, taking a firm grip of her arm. "Where's Hake's car?"

"Over there, but he'll have gone. I told him I'd go with Malcolm."

Pat glanced at the corner where Hake had parked. Characteristically he had chosen a spot which more wily drivers avoided. "It'll take him another ten minutes to get out," he said. "Come on."

"No! Let me go. I must find Malcolm . . ." She struggled angrily but the hand grasping her arm was large and relentless.

"It's no use losing your temper with me, Jean my lass," said Pat. "You're going with Hake if I have to carry you

211

and push you into his car by force."

"Pat, you don't understand. It's—"

"Yes, I do. You don't. This is between men and it's high time you admitted that Malcolm's a man and let him manage his own affairs. C'mon now like a sensible woman." He was so authoritative, so unlike the easygoing Pat McKechnie she knew that Jean stopped struggling and looked up at him doubtfully. He led her on towards Hake's traffic jam, saying, "I think Davina gave Malcolm the final brush-off tonight. Leave him and Keith alone and you'll find they've been planning a training climb. Malcolm'll be sore but he'll be back on course—*provided* you let him alone."

There was no hurry about Hake who was still firmly wedged and Jean paused. "Do you think that?" she said. "I thought she'd said something awful to Malcolm, but then Keith's in love with her too ..."

"Not him," Pat said rather grimly. "If you ask me the only girl Keith's ever loved is Clunie."

"But . . . well, I mean I know he was keen on her at one time and she was terribly gone on him, but I thought . . . Do you mean you think they still . . ?"

Gone on! Pat cursed himself. Why the devil had he brought Clunie in? "I don't know any more than you do," he said curtly and for the third time he urged her on and passed her to the now totally baffled Hake.

"Nothing happened," he told Clunie in the bar. "I packed Jean off with Hake."

"Hake? I thought he'd gone."

"Couldn't get his car out."

212

Of course, thought Clunie, Hake would get his car boxed in. "Well, that's a good thing," she said. "Though she's probably waiting up for Malcolm with hot milk. What about him and Keith?"

"Oh," said Pat, "by the time I saw them they were planning to go up to Stronachie tomorrow."

Stronachie was a great complex lump of mountain beyond the Torran range and comparatively unexplored because of its inaccessibility. No vehicle could get nearer than eight miles and for this reason a tough and determined mountaineering club, to which Keith belonged, had built a hut with the object of, so to speak, conquering Stronachie.

"I've never been up there," Clunie said doubtfully. "Have you?"

Pat said he had been once in his ambitious days. "It did more than anything to cool my ardour. The hut wasn't there then though. It'll help."

"They're staying, are they?"

"At least one night, I gather. More if it's going well."

A pretty severe test for strained relations, Clunie thought, boxed up in a small, comfortless hut in the middle of nowhere. "Did Malcolm seem all right?" she asked.

"Well, he wasn't exactly jolly," said Pat, "but he never says much. He seemed willing enough to follow the leader." He glanced at her. "Keith knows pretty well what he's doing."

In view of his success it must be assumed that Keith knew what he was doing as a climber and a leader. No doubt Pat knew what he was doing in matters of estate management. Those, in Clunie's opinion, were their respective limits. "Well, goodnight," she said.

The Stronachie party assembled at the Brig next morning just as the early breakfasts began. "They should have been away two hours ago," Harry said irritably.

"Och well, they haven't that far to go," said Tosh who had strolled over from his cottage. "And maybe they'll take an easy day after the night they had."

Harry said, "They won't," and lowered his voice. "The only thing to do with Malcolm is to drive straight at it. Keith knows that."

"Pity he didna think what he was about last night," was Tosh's muttered response. He added that so far as he was concerned, if Keith liked to make a fool of himself he was welcome. "But ye'd think whiles he's fair daft, that laddie, for all he's cool enough on the hills. He was downright mischievous last night. I was kinda hoping that if Malcolm didn't give him what he was asking for Pat would."

It was felt that this was the real start of the Finlay Expedition to the Hindu Kush and in spite of the comparatively early hour quite a number of people had turned out to help load Keith's Land Rover and Malcolm's van and cheer the take-off. Bothy boys, randomly clad in the first garments that came to hand, carried equipment and stores, maintaining an irreverent flow of comment. Wendy Carter was checking gear in partnership with her husband and in the background stood Maureen, gazing tearfully at Alf, and Jean who had brought her bike up in Malcolm's van.

Clunie, coming out with a list of stores supplied by the hotel which Harry had thrust at her, was dismayed. As a wife Maureen had some right to be there but Jean would have done better to stay at home, preferably in bed. Alf Page took no more notice of his drooping wife than he usually did, but if Malcolm was as unhappy and strained as he looked she thought Jean's anxious face must be almost more than he could stand.

As she checked the list of stores with Keith it struck her that he was not far wrong in refusing to become involved. He was quick-moving, alert and above all free to give his whole attention to the job in hand: strong enough to subdue passion and emotion in himself, ruthless enough to be indifferent to the feelings of others. The stores checked, he scribbled his initials at the foot of the list and was off to the next thing without an unnecessary word.

Withdrawing from the front line Clunie remarked to Wendy Carter whose checking was also finished that she was glad she wouldn't be taking part in the loading up for the expedition itself.

"You may well be glad," said Wendy. "Mind, you can't be too careful—you know that as well as I do: you've got to check and re-check and check again, but I'll admit it's a strain on wifely devotion." They joined Maureen and Jean and she added cheerfully, "Shouldn't be long now."

Judging by the litter still strewn on the ground, Clunie thought she was optimistic. "Well, I'm going to have breakfast," she said. "If you'll forgive me for saying so, Wendy and Maureen, this spectacle lacks audience appeal."

Wendy agreed. "But take note, you spinsters, husbands like the little woman there to admire and wave."

"Anyway," said Maureen, whose husband seemed unlikely to notice if she waved or not, "what I feel, you *never know*. I mean, climbing *is* dangerous."

"What isn't?" asked Wendy. "A tiddlywink in the eye could be very nasty."

"And they say the mortality rate on bowling greens is terrible," Clunie added. "Come and have breakfast, Jean. Be my guest."

Jean hesitated. "Well . . they'll be expecting me at home."

"Ring up."

"And I'd really rather wait and see—"

Suddenly doors slammed. Unbelievably, everything was in. Engines came to life and a derisive cheer arose as the two vehicles moved off. Bill Carter winked at Wendy, Keith turned his head and catching Clunie's eye raised a hand with a curious little smile. Malcolm and Alf looked straight ahead.

"At last!" said Wendy and with a speaking look at Clunie led the weeping Maureen away.

"Come on," Clunie said to Jean. "Remember I'm a wage slave. We'll have to eat fast."

Jean still hung back. "I was going to ask you if we could have a walk. Wouldn't that be better? I'd bring lunch or whatever."

"A walk! God forbid! I'm so stiff the very thought of walking makes me shudder. No, it's now or never for today."

216

"Oh. Well, I don't want anything to eat but I'll have some coffee."

The dining-room was not busy. Those who had a climbing programme had already breakfasted and the less energetic were not yet down. Clunie steered Jean to a corner in the extension and ordered a substantial meal for herself and coffee for both of them.

"I thought," said Jean, "that you had quite a lot of free time on Sundays."

Jean's habit, dating from childhood holidays, of expecting each of them to know what the other was doing at any given moment irritated Clunie intensely. She began by saying shortly that she was going out and then since Jean waited expectantly and there was no secret about it added that she and Alan were going to take a picnic lunch and dawdle about in his car.

"Oh," Jean said, surprised. "I didn't think you and Alan ever did things like that."

"We don't often get the chance, Alan's life style being nomadic," Clunie replied, "but we enjoy it when we do. It'll be nice and peaceful."

Jean said tartly that she was glad somebody could be peaceful and then repented. "I'm sorry, Clunie, but I'm *so worried*. Did you know Malcolm had a row with Keith last night? He even said he wouldn't go to the Hindu Kush."

"If so, they evidently made it up again," said Clunie, busy with bacon and eggs.

"Well . . . they did. Malcolm took it back about the Hindu Kush. But—oh I *wish* they weren't climbing

217

Stronachie today. And there's that awful hut . . ."

Clunie jeered. "My good girl, what *are* you imagining? Do you see them pushing each other off ledges or dropping bits of rock on each other? You're a climber— not a very good one but you know better than that."

"Of course I do," snapped Jean. "Don't be so dense. You've done nothing but laugh at Malcolm ever since that awful girl got her hooks in him." She paused and then added, "I sometimes wonder if you're putting on an act to save your pride."

"Another crack like that, Miss G. and I'll forget I'm a lady and punch you on the nose," said Clunie. "You needn't worry about my pride—*or* my heart. And if you'd stop fussing you might see you're doing Malcolm more harm than Davina ever did."

"What do you mean?"

"Well, if you hadn't taken it so big he probably wouldn't either. Incidentally, it's doing Davina harm too, though I don't suppose that bothers you."

There was quite a long pause. Clunie ate toast and marmalade and wished she had kept her mouth shut. "Drink up that coffee and have some hot," she said. "I shouldn't have let fly. It's not my business."

"Oh, that's all right," said Jean. She drank her coffee but refused to have more. "I don't see what harm it's doing Davina. If you mean her visit to the castle being cut short that's because of Molly."

"It's mostly Molly," Clunie agreed.

As if this admission had restored her confidence Jean turned again to attack. She thought it only natural that

218

she and her parents should be concerned about Malcolm. "You never seem to think what might happen to Alan in those wild places he goes to but—"

"Alan's looked after himself in wild places for years. It —it's so diminishing for a man to have women flapping about him."

There was another pause and then Jean said in a voice which was no longer aggressive, "Pat said something like that last night, but . . . Stronachie's such a brute and you know what Keith is. He'll be looking for something new, not just another Very Severe. Well, I don't think Malcolm's fit for a climb like that. Do you know what Davina said to him last night?"

"No," said Clunie. "She was a bit upset but she didn't say anything to me."

"Well, Malcolm didn't say much," said Jean, "—except that it's all over and he hopes he'll never see her again." She sighed and then looked at Ginnie curiously and went on, "Pat thinks Keith's never cared for Davina at all. He thinks you're the only girl he's ever cared for. I thought that was all over years ago but last night I did wonder —"

Clunie had had enough. "You go home," she said.

CHAPTER TWELVE

THERE WAS quite a lot to do in the office but soon after eleven o'clock the last packed lunch had been collected, all the departing guests had paid their bills and Clunie was free to change into old clothes, pick up their own lunch and search for Alan who was finally discovered drinking coffee in the kitchen.

They had a very satisfactory day. Though they were perfectly content to spend most of their lives apart they were, perhaps, better friends because being together was comparatively rare. As Alan remarked, custom had no chance to stale their far from infinite variety. It was at times like this, dawdling along in the old car which Clunie was free to use when he didn't want it himself, that Alan became communicative. Absorbing without comment the refreshment of familiar and well loved mountains, moors and glens, he talked and she learned about the strange life he led, his hopes and aspirations. She had no difficulty in understanding and accepting them: her father, a classical scholar, was more at home in the past than in the present and, as she had said, she rather envied the maniacs who were governed by an absorbing passion.

But Alan was not too obsessed to be interested in her when he thought about her and she had her innings when they topped for lunch. It was very pleasant lounging on a sunny, heathery hillside, letting the talk drift where it would and giving her thoughts and ideas a good airing. On the whole Alan approved of her decision to leave London: "No good getting stuck in a groove before you're sure it's the right one." The Edinburgh idea he regarded as rather unenterprising but in a spirit of live and let live he forgave her for being what he called a settler.

"I'm not so settled as all that," Clunie protested and enumerated the countries she had visited and worked in. "We don't all want to spent our lives scuttling about the globe."

"What I'm saying," said Alan.

"Even you may get tired of it. Mrs Graham is sure that one of these days you'll want to get married and then you'll settle down and be a respectable citizen."

"She didn't say I'm not respectable?"

"Not quite. It was implied. She did say 'east, west, home's best'!"

"God, what an original mind that woman has!" Alan, having finished his lunch, lay back and closed his eyes. "I read somewhere about an explorer who came home every two years or so, begot—begat?—another child and went off again. I wouldn't mind that sort of marriage."

Clunie looked at him with laughing eyes. "What about Davina? Another maniac with a career to keep her busy. But I doubt if she'd be good with the children. Grannie and Aunt Clunie would have to cope, I fancy."

"And would do it very well," he said handsomely. "My mind would be perfectly easy. The trouble is that I might get fond of the brats and be unwilling to leave them." He reverted to Edinburgh. "There's nothing wrong with it. Might be a bit slow till you picked up some buddies, old

221

friends and new, but you've already picked up Pat for a start. You don't seem to fight nowadays. Grown out of it?"

"Well, I wouldn't say that," said Clunie dubiously. "Sometimes we get on all right—very well in fact, but then . . . Oh, I don't know. He can be pretty dense."

Alan was lying flat on his back, his hands behind his head. By moving it very slightly he was able to see her profile which even a brother could recognize as pleasing. Regarding it with some amusement he remarked that he thought a lot of Pat.

"You always did," she said, her tone acid.

"True and you needn't sniff. It just shows how sound my judgment was even at an early age. But now I know why I think a lot of him."

"Oh?" She looked round. "And why do you?"

"All sorts of reasons, but it would be too much like work to go through them. The main thing is he's a whole, mature man." Two pairs of very similar eyes met and in reply to the question in hers Alan went on, "The longer I live the more I hand it to the chaps who grapple with the world as it is. It's pretty hellish and damned worrying to put it mildly, but there are plenty of them; doing their jobs, bringing up families, making a good thing of life in spite of it. Pat's like that. Nothing'll get him down. People like me—and Keith—are just escapists. Divine's another. Chronic adolescents."

Clunie had seldom been more surprised. She had thought that in Alan's book, as in the books of most breakaways, the men who stayed at home, doing more or less mundane jobs and bringing up families rated as dull:

unenterprising and certainly not in any way heroic. After a moment she said, "Aren't you a bit carried away? You and Keith and Davina—you're all mad of course, but isn't it a good thing? I've often wished I had something I was mad about—a mania. I wouldn't call it adolescent to know what you want to do, and you've all—all three of you—got the courage to do it instead of just conforming."

"Maniacs don't need all that much courage," said Alan. "I don't. I've got to know how to avoid natural hazards and it's not worthwhile for the most savage savage—of whom there are few—to attack a solitary tramp. Keith's moments of danger are enjoyable, he being what he is, and Davina has no imagination so she's not bothered. Chaps like Pat have the courage, the enduring courage. As for conforming, Pat isn't a conformist. He won't break the law—much—but he doesn't give a damn for the conventions. Which, let me point out, are just as numerous as in the days of Queen Victoria. They're different but quite as silly—more so in many cases."

"A most interesting dissertation," Clunie observed politely. "There is clearly much to be said for looking at our civilization from a distance."

"Likewise an unprejudiced mind and time to think," added Alan. "Shouldn't we be getting back? When's your next engagement?"

They had lingered on the hillside for longer than they realized and didn't dawdle on the way back. But the road they were on was the one which passed Stronachie and they stopped and had a look through the powerful binoculars which accompanied Alan wherever he went.

"No climbers in sight," he said, handing them to Clunie, "but there's a devil of a lot of Stronachie. You'll see a herd of deer about a third of the way up—on the greenish bit to your left."

Sections of the mountain rushed at Clunie as she got it into focus. The south-east face at which they were looking was now in shadow and it was formidable: sheer rock and, it seemed, acres of boulders and loose scree. "Glory!" she exclaimed. "I'll never try my boots on Stronachie, that's for sure."

"Found the deer?"

"Yes, and they can have it. No wonder Jean's in a state. I'd forgotten what a brute it is."

"It's not all so savage," Alan said as he put the car into gear. "Does Jean think Malcolm will start brooding about his broken heart at the wrong moment and peel? Or drop a boulder on Keith?"

"Well, not the boulder because of his conscience, but she's worried about his concentration. He's not happy, poor Malcolm."

Alan said, "He'd have done better to stick to you," and grinned when she turned and stuck her tongue out at him. "His heart would have been broken anyway—it's that kind of heart—but you wouldn't have dropped him with such a crash."

"I might even have married him. You can't deny he'd be a kind and faithful husband and think of his looks."

"Think of his conversation," said Alan. "And his sad puzzled face when you wanted a good rousing quarrel . . . No, no, Clunie. I was a bit anxious that summer after your

224

spin with Keith, but you know better now."

"Brothers," Clunie said bitterly. "They know everything."

"But you'll admit I let you alone. You get no helpful advice from me."

"Oh, I admit it freely," she said. "You're an adept at minding your own business."

Alan said he reckoned that minding your own business, letting people alone, was the prime virtue. Clunie agreed that it came high but thought that like all virtues it could be carried too far, citing Divine's mother as an example. "Poor Davina! She was in *despair* when I nearly ran over her in Kintorran."

"Well, if her mother hadn't interfered she wouldn't have come," Alan pointed out. The Welfare State would have sent her to a convalescent place and Miss Bethune and Molly, not to mention Malcolm, would have been spared a lot of misery. Not that there's any vice in Davina—or not much. She's just a born nuisance: a lot of appeal and no sense. I'm going to supper at the castle tonight, by the way."

"No!" Clunie stared at him. "Don't tell me you've succumbed to the appeal?"

"Not succumbed, but appeal is enjoyable so long as you keep your head."

"Who asked you? Does Miss B. know of the treat in store?"

"She asked me. She came down in a red flannel dressing-gown to let Davina in. She wants to hear about primitive peoples, so she says, but my guess is that the cordiality was because I'm not Malcolm or Keith and Davina undiluted is more than she can take."

"Well, have a good time," said Clunie, reaching for the picnic things in the back of the car. "I expect you'll feast on tinned soup and fish fingers. You can take the guitar with you."

Pulling up in the Brig car park Alan said placidly that he had feasted on worse than tinned soup and fish fingers. He was, in fact, partial to a fish finger. And he would take the guitar if Clunie remembered to remind him.

But Clunie was not called upon to remind him about Divine's guitar. When she went to fetch it from Harry's office so that it should be under her eye it was not there. What she did find, prominently placed on her desk, was a telephone message for Alan. Miss Bethune, with many apologies, was obliged to cancel the evening's engagement. She hoped that he would go and have tea or a glass of sherry before leaving the glen.

Clunie felt vaguely troubled: Miss Bethune would never cancel an engagement lightly, however trivial it might be. Had Molly taken a turn for the worse? Or even died . . ? Nobody could tell her anything. The message had been taken by one of the junior staff who merely wrote it down as it was given and she sent it on to Alan and turned to her work.

She was kept very busy. Climbers who had been staying in the hotel came to pay their shot before setting out in cars for Glasgow, Edinburgh, Aberdeen or farther field to be ready for work in the morning, and boys and girls from the bothies settled their very modest bills. "See you next

226

weekend," they said and went out to kick motorcycles to life or pedal silently away on pushbikes. Clunie felt very fond of them. They were tough, some of them very tough indeed, but they were good-humoured and friendly and she admired their zest for a form of sport which demanded so much of them: skill, courage and the sheer effort of getting to the hills and back again to their jobs. And she liked too the contentment in their eyes when they grinned at her. The hills gave them more than exercise and adventure, whether they knew it or not.

When at last she was free to go for dinner the dining-room was nearly empty but Alice and Alan were drinking coffee together and she joined them.

"Bad luck you missed your fish fingers," she said to Alan and asked Alice if she had heard of anything wrong at the castle.

Alice had heard nothing. "I wondered if you had. I half thought of ringing up but then I thought what a nuisance I'd be if Molly's having another turn or something."

"They probably found there were only two fish fingers," said Alan who never subscribed to gloomy speculations.

"Or they couldn't face the prospect of Ritchie on primitive peoples after all," said Clunie. "Alan, have you any money? I *would* like a drink."

Alan went off to the bar and Bennie arrived with soup. "There's no very much left," he said. "What would you say to a steak? Stan says seeing it's you . . ."

Clunie said, "Marvellous!" and as he hurried away Alice remarked that there was no doubt the staff—some of them fed better than the guests *or* the manager in this hotel.

"They're harder to get," said Clunie taking up her soupspoon. Her thoughts were still on the castle and she asked, "Who took Divine's guitar? Do you know?"

"It was Pat," Alice replied with some reluctance. "He was out climbing but they came in about tea-time and he said he'd take it. He hasn't come back."

Clunie swallowed some soup. "Well, well," she said, and to Alan who arrived with her sherry, "Did you hear that? The mystery's solved. Pat's eaten your fish fingers."

"He has, has he?" said Alan. "Hell! Who'd have thought Miss Bethune would be so fickle? I hope they choked him, that's all."

He strolled away and Alice said, "You know Davina's likable in a way and I felt very sorry for her being pushed between her mother and Miss Bethune, but Harry says the sooner she goes the better and he's right."

"Oh, did Harry say that?" Clunie asked with wide eyes. "I thought he was rather taken with her."

Alice sniffed. "So he was. They all are. Alan and now . . . Not that it means anything, but what's Pat *doing* all this time?"

"Well, that I can't tell you," said Clunie and was thankful when Alice, after brooding for a few minutes, got up and went away. Overwhelming boredom had suddenly descended on her. She wondered how soon Morag would be fit for work. It couldn't be too soon.

She was just finishing her dinner when Pat walked into the dining-room. "Good," he said. "I was afraid you'd have gone to bed. I've something to tell you."

"Won't it keep?" she asked discouragingly.

"Oh it would *keep*. It doesn't call for action. But it's hot news and you'll be sorry if you don't get it fresh just because you're cross."

Clunie thought of sweeping out but after a short struggle curiosity overcame dignity. "Oh all right," she said. "I'm not in the least cross; tired, that's all. Have you fed?"

"Yes." He waved reassurance at Bennie who was looking daggers at him. "Had supper at the castle."

"Fish fingers?"

"What? No—bacon and eggs. Miss Bethune's masterpiece though she can cook sausages too. Look— you go into the lounge and I'll bring coffee."

There were not many people in the lounge and Clunie made her way to a couch under the picture window through which Torran Mhor could be seen against the darkening sky. She was very tired, but the oppression had lifted a little and it would be nice to know why Pat had eaten the supper that was rightfully Alan's. He came in carrying the coffee tray and heaved a long sigh as he sank down beside her.

"Don't say you're tired," she said. "I thought you were tireless."

"Not *tireless*," he admitted, "although I used to think I was."

"Feeling your years, I expect."

"Very likely." He took out his pipe and as an afterthought a packet of cigarettes, inviting her to indulge. She took one and he lit it for her and sat back. "One thing

I *am* too old for," he said conversationally, "is feeling so mad it's all I can do not to grab a man and choke the life out of him." Clunie looked up with startled eyes but he went straight on. "Another thing is getting mixed up in a female stramash which is no concern of mine."

"Stramash?"

"Stramash. A confused and highly charged scene, the outcome of which, I'm happy to say, is that I'm driving Davina to Inverness tomorrow morning and pushing her off on the London train."

"Begin at the beginning," said Clunie, "and don't leave anything out."

Pat did not quite begin at the beginning. After a short unrestful night he had found himself that morning in a state of fidgets, which was not a thing he was used to, and of doubt. If Keith had appeared as an honest and success-ful rival he would have known what to do: he would have taken himself off. But Keith did not appear as a rival. Though he was probably as much in love with Clunie as it was in him to love any girl he had no intention of burdening himself with a wife. Pat regarded him therefore as a threat, not only to his own hopes but to Clunie's happiness, and it seemed to him that the best thing for both of them was that he should stick around, pursuing a policy of unequivocal but unembarrassing courtship. It was, he thought, working pretty well till that damned Waltz Country Dance shattered him. Clunie's delight in dancing reels again made her so lovely, so radiant, that it was no wonder she set Keith ablaze he was not the only one—but his love-making as they waltzed had none of his usual flamboyance. He held her and at the end of it kissed her as if he could not help himself and his face was more serious than Pat had ever seen it. True he had reverted immediately to flamboyance but it could be that he had, as it were, acknowledged defeat: that he had realized that she meant more to him than his freedom. There was no telling what Clunie was feeling. The only thing her face revealed was determination to reveal nothing, but afterwards she had been strangely remote, all her sparkle gone.

Making no attempt to see her in the morning he joined the two tough undergraduates in a punishing climb. He did not enjoy it but its effect was salutary. By the time he had had his bath and some tea he could see that he might have made too much of that bloody waltz, mishandled the whole thing. He went along to the office.

It was empty but Harry was in his own room. "Clunie?" he said. "She went off with Alan."

Pat was startled. "You mean—you don't mean they've gone home or something?"

"Lord no! At least I hope not. She's due on shift at six," said Harry and swore at Davina's guitar which was still cluttering the place up.

"I'll take it," Pat said. "Pay my respects at the same time."

Since it was a condition of sale of the Glen Torran estate that Miss Bethune retained occupancy of Castle Tornay for her lifetime it was not, strictly speaking, part of what Pat called his parish. Sir James Finlay, however, had informed him when he was appointed that for all her gruffness and family pride the last of the Bethunes needed

231

looking after. "It needs tact, mind you," he added warningly. "She's touchy. But just keep an eye on things." So Pat called at the castle fairly regularly and contrived to smooth the ladies' path in various ways without giving offence.

On this Sunday evening he saw nothing wrong with the outside of the castle—no blocked gutters, no missing slates—but he ran into trouble as soon as he went in. After some delay the door was opened by Davina, still rather pale and wearing her scowl.

"Oh—thanks," she said taking the guitar. "I thought it must have got lost. Come in, will you."

It was a command rather than an invitation but Davina was seldom gracious and he suspected nothing till he was inside and heard sounds of hysterical sobbing somewhere upstairs.

"What's the matter?" he asked sharply. "Is Miss Tullis —"

"There's nothing the matter," said Davina. "She's putting on an act." She shut the door and shouted, "It's Pat. Brought my guitar. Come down, Aunt Charlotte."

Pat's only desire was to get out fast. This, he felt, was not a case for his sympathetic eye or any man's except possibly the doctor's. "Look here," he said, "it'll be better if I don't stay now. Miss Bethune —"

"No, it won't," Davina said flatly. "Somebody's got to sort us out and it may as well be you as you're here. It's far better to leave Molly alone anyway. She'll soon stop yelling if there's nobody there."

The sobs had in fact abated and Pat, reluctant but

curious, followed her to the living-room where Hamish was occupying the best armchair. Dog and girl exchanged looks of dislike.

"I knew Miss Tullis was ill," said Pat, "but what's the crisis?"

"Oh . . ." Davina hunched an impatient shoulder. "It's all nonsense. I want to go back to London but I've got no money and Aunt Charlotte won't give it to me till she gets the say-so from my mother. She's got the money—Mum sent it to her—and Mum couldn't care less what I do but she won't believe that. She's phoned *and* written but—"

"Good evening, Pat," said Miss Bethune coming in to the room. "How kind of you to bring Davina's guitar."

He shook her outstretched hand saying that it was no trouble at all. "But I'm afraid it's an inconvenient time for a caller, Miss Bethune. I'm so sorry Miss Tullis is ill. If there's anything I can do . . ."

"Thank you," said Miss Bethune. "Get down." She swept the offended Hamish off the chair and sat down. Miss Tullis, she said, was very poorly. Very poorly indeed. "I confess I am anxious about her. She eats nothing, the sedatives Dr Graham has prescribed have no effect and these hysterical turns leave her quite exhausted. I am hoping she may fall asleep."

"She'd be as fit as a flea in five minutes if I were out of the place," said Davina. "She's playing you up."

"Davina, I must ask you—"

"Well, you know it's true. She—" A bell shrilled in the distance and she got up looking hopeful. "I'll go."

"*No,*" said Miss Bethune very firmly indeed and

233

marched out of the room and along the stone passage to the cubbyhole which inconveniently housed the telephone.

Davina said sourly that it was probably a wrong number and then an idea occurred to her and she turned urgently to Pat. "Look—will *you* give me the money? She'll—"

"No." Pat was as firm as Miss Bethune.

"Well, but why not? She'll pay you back. And after all it's *my* money. She's got no right to—"

"You can save your breath," said Pat. "I won't do it. Why can't you shut up? Your mother's bound to get in touch in a day or two—if she isn't on the line now. Why the flap?"

"It's not a flap," she said angrily. "It's—oh, what's the good of trying to tell you? Everything's absolutely bloody but you won't see it. How'd *you* like to be treated like a criminal?" Pat laughed heartlessly and she glared at him. "Molly's more of a criminal than I am. All this moaning and groaning and fading away—it's sheer blackmail."

Tyranny by weakness was something with which Pat was not familiar but recalling Miss Dulles's pleading eyes, soft mouth and drooping form he saw that it could be a formidable weapon and felt sorry for Miss Bethune.

"I'm not surprised my grandfather ran for it," Davina was saying. "The only mistake he made was not strangling Molly before he went. She's even got me down though I know it's phoney and I never see her. And then there's Malcolm. He's got so crazy it's a toss-up whether he'll kill himself or Keith—or both."

"Well," said Pat. "we won't go into whose fault that

234

might be, but if it sets your mind at rest Malcolm and Keith are even now climbing a mountain called Stronachie—or more probably coming down—in preparation for the Hindu Kush expedition."

"Malcolm and Keith?" she cried and somewhat to Pat's surprise the defiance left her face and she looked genuinely concerned. "But that's—that's terrible. Why didn't somebody stop them?"

Pat was beginning to assure her that there had been no need to stop them, that Malcolm, though unhappy, was perfectly sane, but he was interrupted.

"Davina," said Miss Bethune, opening the door, "a man wants to speak to you on the telephone. He says he is your husband."

CHAPTER THIRTEEN

CLUNIE GASPED. *"Her husband?"* It was so startling that she felt her exclamation must have made everybody in the lounge jump. A glance round showed her that no one had even looked up and after a moment she said, "*That's* what knocked Malcolm out last night. She must have told him she's married."

"She did," said Pat. He looked rather grimly amused. "As we know, dear Davina is only clever within narrow limits. The Malcolm affair had got beyond a joke. She wanted to put an end to it so she broke the husband to him and after that she could think of nothing but getting clear before the body was found and the suicide letter which revealed all. Not that it's illegal, so far as I know, to drive a man to suicide, but she may think it is. And she's a bit scared of Miss Bethune."

Not without cause, Clunie thought. "Well, and so what happened?" she said. "Go on."

Pat went on. Miss Bethune, a good deal shaken, sat down and told him where to find the whisky. Crossing the hall to the kitchen he could hear Davina's voice talking excitedly. When he returned Miss Bethune had lit a cigarette and though her hand trembled she was collected. It was something, she remarked sardonically, that Davina and the young man, whoever he was, were married, but she could not imagine why she and her deplorable mother had kept it secret.

"Why had they?" Clunie asked. "Oh—part of

pressurizing Miss B. to have Davina at the castle?"

"Partly," said Pat, "and partly because Davina wasn't sure if she was still married or not. For over a year she had neither seen nor heard of her Denis."

She had returned to the living-room after quite a brief conversation in a state of mingled nervousness and euphoria but ready to explain everything, beginning with the fact that they couldn't talk any longer because Denis was in a call box and had no money. As Clunie could imagine, Pat said, it had all been highly confused and repetitious, but what it boiled down to was that Davina had been married for over three years, since she and Denis were nineteen. Part of the time they lived together in a room or a flat, part of the time they didn't, owing to frequent quarrels and fluctuating fortunes. Denis was a musician too. He played the trumpet. But it was hard to get started in show business and they had had all sorts of jobs. Something over a year ago, however, about the time Clunie first met Davina, two things happened: Davina's mother married again, a horrible business type who thought of nothing but money, and Denis disappeared. Up till then, Pat presumed, it had been possible, though never easy, to touch Mum when they were hard pressed but the horrible business type had put an end to that.

"Davina doesn't know where he's been or what he's been doing, but now he's got a proper job with a real orchestra and a basement flat in Earls Court and she's going to join him. She's really very gratified," said Pat. "It's impressive that Denis actually took the trouble to go to her mother and ask about her. But she says that though

237

they often fight they like each other quite a lot." He glanced round. "Do you think you should be giggling?"

Clunie's elbow was on the table and her head on her hand but after a moment she sat up and dabbed her eyes, saying in a voice that was still a little unsteady that she wished the young couple all happiness and success. "It's one kind of marriage, after all, and I dare say it suits both of them better than the more orthodox kind. Is Miss Bethune resigned?"

"Well, I wouldn't say she approves," said Pat, "but it solves a major problem. She can get rid of Davina with a clear conscience and incidentally without having any dealings with Davina's mother. That cheered her up, so she invited me to stay for supper and went off to cook the bacon and eggs while I checked the train. I'll collect Davina," he added, "in ample time tomorrow morning. We don't want any last minute hitch. Hallo, what does Tom want?"

Tom in his neat white jacket was coming across the room towards them, smiling to the knitters as he passed. He stopped to pick up the coffee tray and, still smiling, murmured, "You're wanted in the office. Both of you."

It was a rule well understood at the Brig that except for old and tried friends who could help, guests were not disturbed by the Rescue Service. Two experienced climbers saw Tom enter the lounge and Clunie and Pat make an unhurried exit. In a few moments they closed their books, knocked their pipes out and followed, yawning. The other readers continued to read and the knitters knitted, some of them remarking that it was getting on for bedtime.

The word had gone round and with a sinking heart Clunie saw people making for call-out action stations: Tom for the equipment store, Stanley the cook for the kitchen with Bennie hurrying after him. The window at the reception desk was closed and in his office Harry was talking on the telephone and Andy and Tosh conferring in a low rapid mutter.

"There you are," Andy said when Clunie and Pat went in. "Glad you weren't in your bed, Clunie. Here's the story . . ."

Ten minutes ago, at 9.45, a radio message had come from Stronachie that Finlay and Graham had not returned to the hut. Alf Page made the call and anyone who wondered why such a disagreeable character had been chosen for the expedition might now know the answer. Without wasting a word he had given a perfectly clear description and a good assessment of the situation. Leaving Carter and himself to climb the Devil's Elbow, a known route which was a good introduction to Stronachie conditions, Finlay had gone on with Graham. "We reckoned they were going for a first," said Page laconically. He had no idea where it was. Neither he nor Carter had been on Stronachie before.

"Have you any clue?" Pat asked Andy. "You probably know Stronachie better than anybody."

"It's a big area," was the reply. "I can think of plenty of climbs nobody's done yet, but the trouble is there's too many of them."

"There's jest the one thing," Tosh put in. By the time

they got to the but wi' all that gear it would be gey late to start a big climb. If they've any sense they'll no be that far away." But for all anybody knew, he added, they might have forgotten about sense, or else miscalculated distance and difficulty and had to bivouac for the night.

It was not an unfamiliar dilemma for the Mountain Rescue Service. Two men missing but no accident reported: the men experienced, supremely competent and well able to withstand a night on the mountain, provided the weather stayed reasonable and they were unhurt. But there was nobody who could have reported an accident. If one of them was injured, or both, it was a matter of urgency.

Andy had decided to call out the full Glen Torran team with capable volunteers as search and carry men. Most of the team had already been given their instructions: Clunie was left to finish the job, alert police and ambulance and ask other teams—Fort William, Glencoe and the RAF—to stand by.

"What about the Grahams?" she asked. "And the Finlays . . ?"

Sir James and Lady Finlay were abroad and might for the present be left in peace—it would in any case be difficult to contact them. "Have to tell the Grahams," said Harry. He glanced at Clunie. "I'll do it if you like."

"Oh—please do it," she said.

Andy, Tosh and Pat had already hurried away. Harry spoke to Dr Graham and went after them and she was left alone, lonelier than she had ever felt in her life and with vital work to do. This was the call-out that the almost forgotten mug-hunt and even Mike and Willie's accident had been leading up to, when the lives, not of strangers but of Keith and Malcolm and later perhaps of other men she knew well, might depend on her keeping a cool head and her wits about her. She looked at the list and rang the next number . . .

A few minutes later the door opened and Pat came in, already wearing climbing gear.

"You'll be all right," he said, putting a hand on her shoulder. "Alan had gone to bed but he'll be along in a few minutes. And—keep your heart up. Keith's a bit like a cat, you know. He always lands right way up and he's got nine lives at least."

"You have to go?" she said.

He looked at her. "Of course. You know we're all needed and glad to go."

"Yes, I know. Pat—" She got up from her chair and held out a hand, "—I just want to—to tell you he—Keith—*is* out of my system . . ."

Pat took the hand. "Are you sure?" he asked. "I thought last night . . . Are you sure?"

"Yes, I'm sure. He knew it too. This morning he—he sort of said goodbye."

She was very near tears and he kicked the door shut and took her in his arms. "My wee girl . . ." He lifted her face, smiled into her eyes and kissed her. "Lord, Clunie! What a moment!" he said as he let her go. "I'll be back, love . . . Oh hell! Davina."

"Alan will take her," said Clunie.

"Harry'll have to cash a cheque for her."

"He will. I'll see to it."

He came back and kissed her quickly and then the door closed and she was alone again with her job to do. She took a deep breath and picked up the telephone.

To every one of her calls the reaction was the same. "Stronachie? *Who* did you say? Finlay and Graham—*Finlay?*—Good God!"

"Christ!" said Harry when he came back. "This is going to be murder. Press—TV—cameras by the hundred . . ."

"The RAF say they'll have a chopper ready to take off at first light if it's wanted."

"It will be, I reckon. They could have miscalculated, as Tosh said, but it isn't likely."

"Will the Press and TV come here?"

"Oh, that's for sure. We'll send them on to the hut but they'll come here first."

"Will you cope with them?" begged Clunie, her limbs turning to jelly.

Harry, looking more bothered than she had ever seen him, said he would do his best. "But if you get caught just give them the facts. Be as brief as you can, but don't let them think you're holding out on them."

As he spoke Alice came in followed by Alan. "Press?" she said, looking from one worried face to the other. "What bothers me is that scene last night. How many people know they had a row? The girls were all agog."

"Oh God! Trust them not to miss anything," said Harry. "We'll have to take a line. Just—"

"Yes, but we can't guarantee that everybody will stick to it. There's Davina for instance."

242

Clunie exclaimed. "Oh—you don't know about that yet. She's going back to London tomorrow and—hold on to your hats—she's going to join her husband."

"She's *married?*" They all stared and Alice began, *"Well!* Of all the —"

"We've no time now," Harry broke in. "Gasp later."

"There's just one thing," said Clunie. "Pat was to drive her to Inverness in the morning but I said you'd do it, Alan."

"A pleasure," Alan responded gloomily.

"You'll never do a more valuable job," Alice told him. "That clears *her* out of the way." She cast her mind round weaknesses in the discretion line. "Wendy'll be all right, but that drip Maureen will want watching. The Grahams won't talk but Jean will *look*—"

"You're wasting your breath," said Harry. "All we can do is play it by ear and hope for the best. Clunie, you'd better go to bed."

"Oh no! I couldn't possibly sleep."

"Don't argue. Nothing'll happen for hours yet. It's just a matter of watch-keeping now. Away you go. You too, Alice."

A few minutes later Alan used the same argument to Harry. "Take a rest while you can. I'm the one that hasn't a job to do—apart from driving Davina to Inverness—and I'm quite reliable."

"Oh, I know that," Harry said. "I wish to God Keith Finlay was as level-headed."

Alan was surprised. "I'd have said he's about as cool as they come."

"Well, he is and he isn't. He's the kind that knows it'll never happen to him, though he's helped to get plenty of good chaps off the hills. And," added Harry, "he's such a damned good climber it never has, whatever risks he's taken. Andy's often said he'd be the better of a lesson, but that's not a thing you can think of now." He sighed and looked at his watch. "They should get to the hut before long."

It was not a dark night. The sky was not clear but the clouds were moving and a half moon helped by torches made the rough eight-mile hike from the road comparatively easy though it was far from enjoyable.

Andy and Tosh, with the men who were most familiar with the ground, made a preliminary search in the hope that, as Tosh had suggested, Keith and Malcolm would not have gone far from the hut: hoping too that their lights, flares and radios might raise some response. But there was a limit to the usefulness of what they could do without wasting strength that would be needed later and they returned to the hut with only negative news. From all directions men had been gathered and there was little comfort in the overcrowded hut. Little comfort too in the shepherds' forecast of "Dirty weather gin mornin'."

"Aye," said Andy heavily. "I doubt it's going to be a tough one this."

Though it was just getting light when Clunie heard the RAF helicopter go over she got up at once. She didn't think she had slept at all. Not only were Keith and Malcolm missing on Stronachie, she was engaged to Pat.

At least she thought she was. It had all been so quick. She really hadn't thought—not *thought*—about it at all. Pat was going off on what might prove a very dangerous rescue and she could not let him go without telling him that he was wrong in thinking that, she was still infatuated with Keith. But—engaged . . .

Rather ruefully she remembered laughing at Tina when she was first engaged. Tina's entire system had been thrown out: she could neither eat nor sleep; she felt sick; she fidgeted and stared into space . . . "Just glands, dear," Clunie had said callously, but suffering much the same symptoms now she wished she had been more sympathetic. After all, getting engaged is one of the major upheavals in anybody's life, especially when it happens suddenly. For a panicky moment she wondered if she knew Pat well enough; he had been in her grown-up life for so short a time. Then she remembered how he had looked at her and had no more doubts.

Harry was in the office when she went down. "Got the fidgets?" he asked. "Well, it's better to keep busy. Did you hear the chopper?"

"Yes, so I suppose there's no news?"

"Nothing yet, Harry said. Andy was pinning a lot of hope on the helicopter, but it wasn't easy country and the weather was closing in. They both turned to the window. "Raining already," he said. "The chap will fly as long as he can, but I'm afraid it won't be long. Go and get some tea. And you can bring me some."

Alice, wearing her dressing-gown, was in the kitchen and so was the cook, fully dressed in his whites. Stanley was always bad-tempered in such crises as this and expressed himself blasphemously about the folly of climbers, but nobody minded. Hot food would be ready at any time for anybody who needed it.

He told Clunie sharply that she would eat her breakfast before she did anything else. "Harry can wait for his tea."

"I'll take it," said Alice and gave Clunie a resigned glance as she passed. With Stan in this mood you couldn't win. If she didn't appear appreciative and eager to help, he was offended: when she did he made no secret of his opinion that irregulars hanging about were nothing but a hindrance. He set Clunie down at a kitchen table and kept an eye on her. She might think she wasn't hungry but she would damn well eat what was put before her.

It was a struggle but there was no resisting Stan's authority and she did feel the better for her meal when she went back to the office to relieve Harry. While she was taking his instructions Wendy Carter came in looking as if she hadn't slept much either. She had come to say she was a trained nurse and felt she ought to be at Stronachie.

"I don't know who they've got but I can climb, you see, and I've been on rescues before. The only thing is, what about the bar? And there's poor Maureen . . ."

In the circumstances the bar didn"t sound very important and Maureen was merely a nuisance. The hotel, however, was not overstaffed and with both Tom and Bessie absent and the prospect of Press and Television men, not to mention sightseers, crowding the bar, dining-room and reception, Harry himself would be hard put to it to cope. And above all there were the communications to be maintained.

It was almost a pity Davina was going, Clunie thought. She had been good the night Mike and Willie came off Trochy. "Alan will help," she said, "but he has to take Davina to Inverness."

Harry sighed. "We'll manage somehow. I think you should go, Wendy, but it's no good going just to sit in the hut. Wait a bit and we'll see what Andy thinks."

She nodded. "All right. Let me know. I'm sorry about Maureen. She gets in such a state, poor girl."

"We'll look after her," Harry said and added as Wendy closed the door that Alice might think of a foolproof job for her.

"Washing glasses shouldn't be beyond her," Clunie suggested. She wondered what sort of state poor Maureen would get into when Alf went off to the Hindu Kush and remembered with a jolt that at best it was questionable if there would be a Finlay expedition to the Hindu Kush.

By eight o'clock the weather had worsened. There was driving rain which at any time of year could turn to snow on the high ground, the tops were in heavy cloud and the helicopter arrived at the Brig and put down very precisely in the overflow car park. With Andy and a couple of keen-eyed shepherds as observers it had flown for over an hour, but visibility was now so bad that it could do no more. The men on the ground had taken over and the pilot's orders were to stand by in the hope of an improvement in the weather. And he had one piece of good news: there was a level patch near the hut on which he could land—if, he said, he could see at all. For stretcher

247

cases and weary men to be spared the eight-mile carry from the hut to the road would be of the greatest value.

The purpose of this flight was to fetch some extra equipment and as Harry took Andy's list he remarked that the pilot could probably do with some breakfast. "Take him along, Clunie," he said.

"The name's Dave," said the pilot. He was a cheerful young man and Clunie liked both his undramatic attitude to the rescue operation and the way he had instantly become one of the team, though he had not, he told her, met any of them before.

"You're Clunie?" he said as they went along to the dining-room. "I have a message for you. A private message. Pat sent his love and said tell you not to panic. What would you panic about ?"

Clunie was somewhat startled and her newly engaged feelings surged up. Blushing she stammered, "Oh well I'm not. At least—no. No, I'm not panicking."

Dave, who looked about eighteen, gave her a fatherly beam. She was a smashing girl and he liked the blush and the tell-tale expression of guilt. "I asked if I'd give you a kiss for him, but he said he'd attend to that himself. Sudden, was it?"

"Yes," she said and laughed, feeling better. "Very sudden. I hardly know if I'm on my head or my heels. Is Pat in a panic?"

"No, I guess Pat doesn't panic," said Dave. "Not sobs you'd notice. He's pretty pleased with life."

On his return flight he took Clunie's love to Pat, the equipment and supplies Andy wanted and Wendy. Andy had suggested that Dr Graham should be given the chance to go but the Grahams had the qualities of their defects and met anxiety with iron self-control. The doctor said that as he could be of no use at present, being no climber, he would be better employed looking after his patients, but he would stay within reach of the telephone.

Jean too displayed the Graham stoicism. Soon after the helicopter left she walked in and said she had come to see if she could help. "I won't fuss," she added looking bleakly at Clunie.

"I know you won't," said Clunie. "And you could help, but what about your mother?"

"She's all right. Got the washing-machine going. It's really easier *not* supporting each other."

Clunie could believe it. "What would you like to do?" she asked. "The bar's a problem. Bessie's away and Tom and Wendy Carter are with the team. It's sure to be busy."

"I don't know enough about drink."

"Well, could you cope with reception? We'll see what Harry says but I'll be next door and I can tell you things."

Yes, Jean thought she could do that.

"There's just one thing," Clunie said. "This'll be headline news. Think you can stand the sensation-mongers?"

"They won't know I'm involved," was the reply. "Sympathy's what I can't take." Jean paused and then said, "And in case you're too delicate to mention it, I know—we all do—that there's bound to be a lot of talk about—that girl, but probing won't get anything from me."

"Look here, Jean," said Clunie warmly, "whatever's

happened on Stronachie nobody who knows Malcolm or Keith would connect it with Davina, so forget it. Incidentally, she's going back to London today Alan's gone to drive her to Inverness."

"Oh? Sudden, isn't it? And why Alan?"

On the verge of telling her of Davina's married state Clunie stopped. At this stage it wouldn't help. Instead she said that Pat had called at the castle yesterday and found them dithering about which day Davina should go. "So he said he'd take her to Inverness this morning and now Alan's gone instead."

"I see." Jean turned away and began taking off her wet outdoor things. "Well, I won't pretend I'm sorry. Pity she ever came. Where'll I put these?"

Traffic in the glen was already thickening up. Neighbouring rescue teams, RAF vehicles and police cars rolled over the bridge. Press and recording vans would follow and these, Harry knew from experience, would stop, looking for a story and human interest and hoping for refreshments. He sent Clunie along with the keys of the bar for Bennie, who was to open up with help from Alice and, if necessary, one of his juniors. Poor Maureen, he had decided, would be safer in the kitchen. One look at her would show even a moderately keen reporter that she would dribble out any kind of human interest he cared to suggest. Meanwhile Jean, with a deadpan face, bent her very able mind to the duties of receptionist and Harry himself was poised for emergency action wherever it might arise.

As Clunie left the bar after handing over the keys the

250

side door swung open and Davina came in with Alan, wearing an expression which disclaimed responsibility, behind her.

"What on earth—" Clunie began.

Davina clutched her arm. "Oh, Clunie! I *had* to come. I couldn't go away not knowing . . . I mean it's my fault, though how was I to know they'd get so steamed up?"

It was like holding a live bomb. At any moment a pressman would be on them and it would go off. Why on earth had Alan not driven straight past? Clunie gave him a furious glance but it bounced off.

"Davina," she said with all possible emphasis, "it has nothing to do with you. Malcolm and Keith—"

"But it has! You don't know! Malcolm was in such a state last night I had to tell him—Alan says Pat's told you about Denis? I thought he was going to kill me—Malcolm, I mean—or else kill himself."

There was a good deal Clunie would have liked to say about a married girl who came into a community pretending she was free but time pressed. She said brusquely, Well, I can tell you that I saw them off yesterday and neither Malcolm nor Keith was thinking about you. They were thinking about the expedition. That's true, Alan, isn't it?" This time her glance was one of appeal and Alan responded.

He said accurately that he hadn't actually seen them off. "But I've told Davina that they were hard at work on the Stronachie plan when I got back after taking her home on Saturday night. I think myself they're probably okay." On expeditions it was commonplace for climbers to be over

-taken by darkness or bad weather and bivouac till they could go on, he explained, and it was Keith all over to be tough in practice climbs. "That makes sense, but it's also typical of him not to warn the other chaps he's going to do it."

Davina listened wanly. As she had no idea at all of the dangers of mountaineering—or anything connected with it—the words meant nothing to her, but she felt some genuine guilt and she was reluctant to give it up. "Isn't there anything I can do?" she asked.

It sounded so pathetic that Clunie felt a pang of compunction but she was firm. "No, Davina," she said. "It's nice of you to offer, but the place is swarming with helpers. You stick to your arrangements and don't miss your train. I hope—" She broke off.

Jean was running towards them along the passage. The shock of seeing Davina showed in her face but she came on.

"They've seen them," she said to Clunie. "They're on their way up to them now. Harry says get back to the R/T and listen like hell. There are some press men here and he's got to cope. Hurry up—"

Clunie began, "Are they—" and stopped. "Bye, Davina. See you some time and good luck," she said and went racing after Jean.

CHAPTER FOURTEEN

IT WAS NOT YET KNOWN if the two men were alive. Both were wearing cagoules of vivid scarlet and one of the shepherds whose eyesight, like that of seamen, was trained by experience had caught a glimpse through the murk of a tiny red spot high on the mountain. Tosh and Pat were with him and while Tosh radioed the hut and Pat sent up a flare the shepherd kept his range, straining to fix the first cagoule and find the second.

"I think I've got him," he said. "I'm no sure, but can ye see the one?" Pat's eyes, skilfully directed, did see it. "Well now, down mebbe a hunder and fifty feet and a bittie to your right there's a muckle great jag. Could a' stopped him Aye! Look! There was a wee movement . . ."

"We'll go straight up," said Tosh. "Or as straight as we can get." He peered at the rock face confronting them and swore. "Can ye see any marks, Jock?"

The shepherd cast about for signs of boots or of pitons hammered in. Tosh scrutinized the face for a feasible route and Pat, the least experienced of the three, stared with him. He thought he had never seen rock so hostile—bitter. It was nearly black and glistening with moisture and he felt a stab of fear. Fear was nothing new. No climber, unless it might be Keith Finlay, was a stranger to it, which was a good thing provided it didn't lead to panic. But this was a new kind of fear. Clunie . . . He had held her in his arms for less than half a minute. And she loved him.

253

"Here's where they started," shouted Jock away to the left. They joined him and the three of them roped up, dismissing from their minds every distraction.

"Away we go then," said Tosh.

Tosh was highly skilled and there was no surer man on the hills but he was slow. Pat, on the end of the rope and with a much greater reach than either of the others, presently saw Page and Carter out-pacing them on their left, making directly for the higher of the two red cagoules, but it was a nightmare climb and he controlled his impatience. Tosh was the leader and rightly. It would help nobody if he, Pat, used his height and failed through his comparative inexperience. And, as it happened, it was Tosh who reached Malcolm, wedged behind the "muckle great jag" of rock and waved the other team on.

Malcolm was conscious though, as Tosh said, off and on; one of the "on" moments having coincided with the flare and enabled him to make the movement which the shepherd saw. His face was covered with blood and one arm was injured, but the worst injury, so far as they could see, was to his right leg which, as the muckle jag stopped his fall took the whole of his weight and impetus. Obviously it was seriously damaged but the greatest problem for the rescuers was that his foot was immovably trapped in a crevice. In his restless near-delirium the other leg moved which meant that there was no serious spinal injury, but that was only partially reassuring. It was difficult to see how the foot could be saved.

"What a long time you've been," he gabbled. "Keith—where's Keith? Is he—he's not—he's not dead? It was my fault—all my fault—I—"

"All right, laddie, all right," said Tosh. "Dinna fash yerself. We've got you safe and here's a wee jab . . ." As he pushed in the needle, Pat was talking on the R/T. There was a sudden shout. "Keith—cramp!" Tosh paused for a moment then Malcolm was mercifully unconscious and with the greatest care he examined the leg and tried tentatively to move the trapped foot. "Aye," he said heavily. "I dinna jist see . . . But we'll jist need to wait. One thing—we know what went wrong. Did it get through?"

"Yes," said Pat. "The hut and the Brig both got it."

Bill Carter's voice came through. They had reached Keith who was alive but unconscious. "Not too good," he said. "We're not far from the top. Could one of you come up? We'll let down a rope and we'll go on. It looks bloody awful, but Andy should be up by now and the RAF doctor . . ."

The rope came down, some thirty perilous feet to the left.

"Will you go?" Tosh said to Pat. "It'll need your reach. Take care now . . ."

Harry Craig was hard-pressed. More and more people kept pouring in and the first whiff of rumour reached him. A zealous young representative of a scandal-sheet had heard in Kintorran that Finlay and Graham had had a row.

Highly amused Harry told him, "We had a ceilidh here Saturday night and it got a bit noisy at the end. I wouldn't care to say how many rows blew up. But if Finlay and

Graham had one it was soon over. There was no sign of it when we saw the team off yesterday morning."

"I heard there was a girl in it."

"There usually is a girl in it," said Harry. "We had a very attractive visitor here." He heaved a comic sigh. "Gone now, alas!"

It was at this moment that the shout came through on the R/T, a desperate but confused noise to those in the reception area. Harry said, "Just a minute," and went through to his office.

"That was Malcolm," Clunie said shakily. "He thought he was falling again . . ." She pushed the note pad along to him.

"Keith! Cramp—" Harry read. "How did you get it?"

"Pat was talking. He said Malcolm was sort of half-conscious and then Tosh gave him an injection and he gave this yell . . . He's right out now."

"Well," said Harry, "it solves one problem," and he took the paper and read it to a white-faced Jean and a greatly sobered group of reporters, who for the first time, perhaps, understood the reality of the accident. They went quietly off to the bar.

Almost immediately came the first sightseers and Jean took the impact.

"Hallo, there!" the leader of a quartet, two men and two women, greeted her. He was a jovial man—all four were jovial types and pleasantly excited. "Where's the bar?"

"Along the passage." She pointed. "You'll see the notice."

"Trust me," said the leader. "Ta, dear. Having a spot of

drama, aren't you? We heard on the news that Finlay's one of the two missing. Have they found them yet?"

Jean said they had. She understood that rescuers had reached them and both were alive.

"Isn't the other one the local doctor's son or something?"

"That's right."

"Goodness! What his mother must be feeling!" sighed one of the women. "I wonder how long it'll take to get them down. Because if it's going to be long we might as well lunch here, mightn't we, Geoff?"

"Could do," said Geoff. "Any idea how long it'll be, dear?"

"No, I'm afraid—"

"I wish we had," Harry coming along from the bar chipped in. "Lunch? Perhaps you'd like to book a table. You'll get any news there is. That way . . ."

"Ta, dear," quoted Clunie from the inner office. "Well done, Jean."

"Really—" burst from Jean, "— how can people be such ghouls? Can't they be stopped?"

"No, but the police will keep them out of the way." Harry gave her a friendly nod. "Stick to it and just think what a godsend it is for them on a wet day."

She gave a reluctant laugh. "It is exciting of course," she admitted. "Any mountain rescue is."

"That's the spirit," said Harry as he hurried away.

A few minutes later Clunie appeared and reported that Pat had climbed safely up to Keith. "And Tosh says Malcolm's had a hot drink and a good shot of dope and is a lot more comfortable. His pulse is okay so that's good news, isn't it? Will you ring your mother? Oh Jean . . ." Jean's head had gone down and she put an arm round her shaking shoulders. "It's all right, love. He's going to be all right." The porch door opened. "Oh blast! Go in there . . ."

"Don't fuss," Jean said angrily. She gave her nose a ferocious blowing and faced the newcomers.

When Alan returned from Inverness he brought Bessie with him. He had found her waiting to thumb a lift just outside the town. They had heard about Keith and Malcolm on the news, she said, and Mike had sent her back. "Though I knew as soon as I heard that I'd have to come. It's just one of these times when you wish you could be in two places at once."

"Perhaps you won't have to stay long," said Clunie, "—but Harry will be jolly glad to see you."

Bessie went off to change and Alan stayed to hear the latest reports. At that stage Clunie, listening on the Glen Torran frequency, had a clearer picture of the rescue operation than any of those actively engaged in it with the exception of Andy who was in command. He was racing to the summit by the easiest route with the RAF doctor, Wendy Carter and a number of strong, experienced climbers loaded with equipment.

Harry had drawn a rough sketch or diagram and Clunie had it before her as she recorded the messages coming in. Alan, with one hand on the table, studied it over her shoulder. Pat, she said, was now with Keith—"Here"—she pointed. Page and Carter were on their way to the summit. "It's never been done this way and they say it

258

looks bloody awful." Tosh had tied on with Tom and a lanky police sergeant and they were going up by a slightly different route, leaving the shepherd with Malcolm.

"What's the latest on the casualties?"

"Keith's unconscious. There's no serious injury visible but they can't tell. Pulse and respiration not bad. Tosh is terribly anxious about Malcolm's foot. It's so jammed that he's afraid it may have to be taken off before they can move him." Clunie's voice shook and she gestured with her pencil towards the outer office. "We're not passing that on."

"No," said Alan. "Time enough if it has to happen. God! Malcolm of all people . . ." He straightened up without taking his eyes from the sketch. "They're not so far from the top, but if it's as bad as they say and they can't take them up it'll be a hell of a distance to bring them down. It's probably impossible but it would be convenient if the helicopter could sit down on or near the summit."

"Harry thought of that. He's been up and there's a sort of plateau. It's very small though and the weather's so bad . . . Did you get Davina off all right? I felt bad about pushing her out so fast but there just wasn't time for her."

There was a short, not very mirthful laugh from Alan. "Don't worry. She was in London before we got to Inverness. I'm not saying she isn't sorry about Keith and Malcolm but only one thing concerns Davina for long." He met his sister's eyes briefly. "Us maniacs are like that."

"Not you."

"Well, not far off. And I've got a family I mind about. She has a husband, as we now know, but I'd say the matrimonial tie's pretty loose. Where's Harry?"

"Everywhere. The place is bursting at the seams."

"Gapers?"

"By the score. He says what a godsend this is for them on a wet day."

The laugh this time was more amused. "I'll go and find him. See if there's a job for me," said Alan.

Clunie hoped that in allocating him a job all parties would remember that he was still officially a convalescent. To say anything, however, would be worse than useless.

The hours passed very slowly. There were times when the R/T was silent for so long that Clunie's hands clenched and she wanted to yell, "What are you *doing?* Get on with it!" though she knew that the rescuers were working with all possible speed and that success depended on meticulous planning and preparation. For her and for many others it was a day of waiting, and curiously lonely. Harry came in and out, Alice brought coffee for her elevenses and sandwiches prescribed by Stanley who remembered how early she had breakfasted, but visits were hurried and in the outer office Jean dealt stolidly with routine business and gapers and didn't want talk, which was understandable. What, after all, was there to say?

When the pressure in the bar and dining-room eased, Alan, who had been helping Bessie, came to take Clunie's place while she went to lunch.

"Harry says to take Jean with you," he said. "The office can be closed for a bit."

Jean, however, preferred to go home to see how her mother was getting on and Clunie sat with Bessie and Maureen. It was a trying meal which she thought Jean had been well advised to skip. When they weren't talking about Mike's wonderful progress and splendid constitution she and Bessie were doing their best to encourage poor Maureen.

Alf would be quite safe, they assured her. "Andy's ever so careful you know," said Bessie. "He doesn't let people take any risks."

"And Alf's a first-class climber," said Clunie.

"That's just it," said Maureen who unfortunately knew a little too much. She turned doleful eyes from one to the other. "Rescue work is always dangerous and he'll be the best climber there, so he'll be in more danger than anybody." Slowly she rose to her feet. "I don't think I want anything more. I think I'll go to the Dormobile and lie down for a while."

Good idea, they said cordially. Why not take a couple of aspirin and get some sleep?

"Well . . . I might. I'm not sure I've got any." She sighed. "It's the waiting."

"How right she is," said Bessie looking after the limp figure. "But my gosh, what a drip! If it was her precious Alf they were trying to bring down, she'd really have something to worry about."

Clunie remarked that neither Maureen nor Alf seemed to be very good choosers; it was hard to imagine a worse matched couple; but privately she thought Bessie might be worried if Mike was on Stronachie with the team instead

261

of nursing his broken bones in comfort, and then was slightly shocked at herself. She was actually competing in the anxiety stakes not only with Bessie but with Maureen of all people.

Looking back after hours of strain her newly-engaged emotions appeared strangely remote. They were immature—naive. She was more than just "in love" with Pat. She had been in love with Keith and had felt that there was nothing she didn't know about love but she was wrong. That had been an affair only of the senses, all fevers and chills and without any kind of fusion. What they felt for each other, they felt separately, and it struck her that she had never worried about Keith being in danger; never carried about with her a sickening picture of him on a bloody awful mountain in the rain . . .

Alan had news to report when she went back to the office. The weather was showing signs of clearing, or at least of a break, and it had been decided to take Keith up to the summit. There was hope that the helicopter might be able to pick him up: the RAF men thought it feasible, provided the weather gave the pilot a chance, and the hundred and fifty or so feet which separated the two injured men was the most difficult part of the whole climb and well-nigh impossible for a stretcher.

"So," said Alan, "it looks as if Keith will have a comparatively short lift and then a nice ride in the chopper while poor old Malcolm has to be manhandled all the way. Wouldn't you know it would be that way round?"

"Where's Pat?" asked Clunie.

"Pat? Still with Keith I think. Wait . . ."

Andy's voice came through. He was with Keith but the RAF team was taking over his rescue and he, Andy, was going down to Malcolm with Pat. They were taking Wendy Carter with them. "Malcolm doesn't sound so good," said Andy. "We can't afford to waste any time. The doc says get Dr Graham to arrange for a transfusion—he'll know the blood group." He added that the RAF doctor would see Keith on to the stretcher and up to the summit and then follow them down to Malcolm. He had told Wendy what to do.

The chopper, said another voice, would pick Dr Graham up and take him to the hut.

"Roger," said Alan and picked up the phone. When he had given Dr Graham the message he got up.

"Alan," said Clunie.

"What?" he said on his way to the door.

"Alan," she repeated a little desperately, "I—I think I'm engaged to Pat."

He turned and came back. "You *think* you're engaged to Pat?"

"Well—it was just as he was going out last night, you see."

For a moment he stared at her and then grinned. "What a time to choose! Dye mean to tell me it took a call-out to get Pat off the ground?"

"Well no. It was me, really."

Alan said everything was now perfectly clear. He gave her a quick hug and a kiss. "I couldn't be more pleased," he said. "I had high hopes you were heading that way but on Saturday night I was afraid Keith was going to wreck it." Clunie wondered how many other people had thought the same, but he was going on, "Well, that's *you* settled. What a relief."

"Were you afraid you'd have to provide for my old age?"

Naturally it had been an anxiety, he said. He looked at her again. "Are you worrying about him? You needn't. Old Andy—"

"Don't bother to go on," said Clunie. "Bessie and I spent the whole of lunch trying to sell that to poor Maureen."

"Oh. Well, I still think you needn't. I think that tonight—maybe pretty late but tonight—we'll be able to drink your healths."

"Alan—don't tell anybody, will you?"

"No, better not," he said solemnly. "You never know. He might repent it when the pressure's off."

While they talked, Pat was on the way down from Keith to Malcolm with Andy and Wendy. It was, and it remained, the worst bit of climbing in his experience. Going up had been hard enough and harder for Tosh, able though he was, because of his shorter reach. Getting Wendy down was a nightmare. She was a sturdy little girl, an adequate climber, but she had neither the reach nor the strength demanded and in spite of the safety harness she was wearing there were moments so dangerous that he wondered if anything justified exposing her to them. What Wendy did have, however, was courage and a level head. She did exactly what Andy told her to do without hesitation and when finally they reached Malcolm she gave him all her attention as if she had done no more than walk from one ward to another.

Malcolm was perceptibly weaker. Wendy's face as she looked at him and took his pulse was grave, and Pat had an untimely memory of Mistress Quickly describing the death of Falstaff: "His nose was as sharp as a pen . . ." He and Andy, with corroboration from the RAF doctor, afterwards maintained that Malcolm owed not only his foot but his life to Bill Carter's apparently unremarkable young wife.

The position could hardly have been more difficult as it was only the jutting rock, not a ledge, which had broken the fall and now stood between them and a sheer drop, Jock the shepherd managed to get himself out of the way to make it possible for Wendy to work with Andy's help and Pat acting as anchor man. With perfectly steady hands she gave the injection supplied by the doctor and then as Malcolm's colour and pulse improved a little she crept down to the trapped foot. It was clear why his condition had deteriorated. Though Tosh had succeeded in stopping the worst of the bleeding there had been a steady, though mercifully slow, minor seepage.

"Well, there's one good thing," said Wendy. The boot's sopping—quite soft. I think we'll be able to free it."

Lying flat on her stomach, head down, she got her small capable hand into the crevice where no man's hand could go and with infinite care and delicacy began to scrape . . .

Clunie was not alone in feeling relieved that Jean decided to knock off when the message came through summoning her father to the hut. Her stoicism was almost more of a strain than Maureen's lack of it.

"You've done a good job," said Harry. "I don't know how we'd have managed without you, but I've felt guilty about your mother being alone."

"Oh well, I wanted to be in touch," Jean replied. "And Mother hasn't been alone. Elspeth's been with her." She added that her mother was very fond of Elspeth who went often to see her when she and Malcolm were away. "But we'll want to be at the hospital as—as soon as it's time." She looked at Clunie. "Will you keep us posted?"

Clunie said, "Of course."

"Don't start for the hospital till we tell you," said Harry. "It'll be a long time yet and you'll be better at home than hanging about there. We'll give you plenty of time."

"Thanks," said Jean and pedalled away.

It was some hours before Clunie was able to tell her that Malcolm was down. The stretcher still had to be carried over two or three miles of rough going but Harry thought that she and her mother should now start for the hospital. Malcolm had stood the descent well, though it had been extremely difficult and slow, and the RAF doctor was satisfied with his condition.

"The usual 'as well as can be expected', I suppose," said Jean. "But when they get him to the hut there's still the eight miles to the road and the ambulance journey."

"No," Clunie assured her. "The chopper took Keith off and it's back at the hut with hospital people to take over."

"But it's dark!"

"They've rigged lights for it. VIP treatment all the way."

"Oh." There was a little pause and a slight sniff and then Jean said, "That'll be a sight for the gapers—if they can walk that far."

"I wouldn't mind seeing it myself," said Clunie. "I don't know about gapers, but I bet there'll be cameras. Now you get along to the hospital and see them land. And mind how you drive. Would you like Alan to take you?"

"No, thanks all the same," said Jean. "Elspeth's coming with us. I say, Clunie . . ."

"What?"

"I—I can't talk about it but we're grateful for all you've done. Everybody's been so—"

"Och, get away," cried Clunie. "Don't be soft."

More than twenty-six hours after the call-out a lot of weary men and one exhausted girl assembled at the Brig, their mission completed. It had been successful. Both casualties were in hospital; medical skill had taken over and the rescue teams could relax and feel the satisfaction they were entitled to feel. But it was a sober satisfaction. Many of them knew both men well, everybody knew Keith Finlay by reputation and had at least heard of Malcolm Graham as the man chosen to partner him in the Hindu Kush expedition. From the reports already received from the hospital, to which he had been smoothly transported by helicopter from the summit of Stronachie, it seemed there was every reason to hope that Keith would make a complete recovery, even, conceivably, in time to lead the expedition as planned; but there was no such hope for Malcolm. His condition was more serious and even if the surgeons could save his foot, it was so badly injured that his climbing career was clearly finished.

Drinks and a hot meal were provided for the rescuers and the bar, dining-room and kitchen were busy with all the resident staff on voluntary duty and more guests eager to help than could be used. In the prevailing atmosphere of excitement it was not to be expected that the non-helpers would be content to go to bed or immure themselves in the lounge. The bar was crowded and as the first of the rescuers appeared Clunie suddenly realized that Pat would come in at any moment and she could not meet him in the presence of such an audience.

Their exchange the night before, though it felt conclusive at the time, had been so brief and seemed so long ago that she almost thought she must have dreamt it. And of one thing she was sure. Even if it was real this was no time to make it public. Pat by himself would be bad enough. Resisting an impulse to rush to her room and crawl under the bed Clunie rushed instead to her office and went feverishly to work tidying up the records of the Stronachie accident.

A few minutes later Pat came quietly in and closed the door behind him. "I thought I might find you here," he said. They looked at each other and he smiled. "Did you come over shy?"

She nodded. "I—I couldn't believe I didn't dream it."

"I know," said Pat. "It's had to be pushed into the background. My poor wee girl, what a start to your engagement! Never mind. Tell me—are you happy?"

The mists cleared from Clunie's mind. Nobody had ever looked at her like this. Keith's eyes could be ardent—off and on; Malcolm's had held doggy devotion; in others she had seen admiration and desire. In Pat's was the complete love of a man—what was it Alan called him?—a whole man for the one woman.

"Yes, I'm happy," she said and went into his arms.

"But we'll have to be canny about this," he said holding her. "I don't want to take the skin off your face. Feel . . ."

She felt the stubble. "Well, I'm not unduly sensitive but—not too impassioned, perhaps? Later on. For now just pretend I've been your wife for ten years."

"I doubt if I'm up to passion at the moment anyway," Pat said frankly. "Later on, as you say."

His kisses, though they were gentle, did not lack conviction and Clunie thought afterwards that nothing could have brought them closer, bound them more securely than those moments of quiet after strain and exhaustion.

"My darling Pat," she said, "you're so tired. Come now and have a drink and then food. Stan's made gallons of strengthening soup and after that I think it's bacon and eggs."

Pat said that already he felt greatly refreshed. "I thought I was past being hungry, but soup and bacon and eggs after a dram—and accompanied by another dram—yes. Come on."

"Stan has an unfailing instinct for the right food," said Clunie. "Do I look scraped?"

She lifted her face and he examined it solemnly. "No.

269

You have a kind of glow but I dare say nobody'll notice. It's not blatant."

In the bar they became part of the crowd of tired, unshaven men and those who waited on them. Only Alan, seeing them together, caught their eyes and unobtrusively raised his glass.

The Stronachie rescue was the climax of Clunie's time at the Brig and, it proved, nearly the end of it: a week later Morag was pronounced fit and returned to be affable about how well her stand-in had done, considering. She was glad to get away. The Brighouse Hotel episode, an eventful, fateful episode complete in itself, was over. And she was going to marry Pat—soon, before Alan disappeared again.

It gave an extra sense of finality that the answers to other questions besides that of her own future were known before she left. Nobody had heard anything about Davina and her Denis and probably never would, but Keith was recovering fast and already considering candidates to replace Malcolm in the Hindu Kush party, though the expedition would have to be postponed for a while, and Malcolm was going to keep his foot. It would never be a good one, he would always walk with a limp but, said the surgeons, it would serve him well, provided he didn't expect it to dance reels or climb Everest.

And, to the great relief of Harry Craig and other friends, the rumour of a flaming row between Finlay and Graham came to nothing. There had been talk. The police had asked Andy about it and reporters had nosed about, but with the evidence of Malcolm's delirious shout and Keith's subsequent corroboration the police question was a formality and the media soon forgot it as a bigger, better sensation was revealed. Wendy Carter was a most unwilling sacrifice on the altar of Human Interest. She was photographed, a filthy, rather tearful little object clinging to her husband in the glare of the lights rigged for the helicopter. She had a fan mail, which she ignored, and talk of the George Cross upset her terribly. Anybody, she said angrily, would have done as much—that was, any nurse who was also a climber.

"Well," said Andy, "seeing it makes her so miserable we'll say no more about it. A lot of folk might get medals for Mountain Rescue Service that nobody ever hears about. But I'll never forget that wee crater lying on her tummy saving Malcolm's foot for him."

"Do you think," Clunie asked Pat as they drove away from the Brig, "that Davina had anything to do with the accident? Jean was scared stiff about Malcolm going on that Stronachie climb."

"We'll never know that," said Pat. "Malcolm may not have been at his best. Emotion's so bloody tiring and if you're suffering from one kind of tension it can lead to others—cramp for one. But Keith can be over-confident and that climb was sheer hell."

Clunie shuddered. "I suppose it would be too much to ask you to promise never to climb another hill without me to look after you?"

Pat said his manly pride wouldn't dream of it. I don't ask you to promise never to climb another hill without me

271

to look after *you.*"

"That's different," said Clunie. She sighed. "Poor Malcolm. Dad called him the magnificent young animal and he really hasn't *got* anything else. He'll be lost without his climbing."

"Well, he couldn't go on being a magnificent young animal for ever," Pat said realistically. "I'm not saying this isn't a sore blow. Of course it is, poor chap. But you know, Clunie, he's not climbing mad as Keith is. Environment—and Keith—made a climber of him. If he'd lived at Wimbledon it would have been tennis and now he'll concentrate on golf."

"He's not a maniac, in fact," murmured Clunie. "I expect he'll marry Elspeth and settle down to a nice humdrum family life."

"That's right," said Pat. "Like us."

Also published by
Greyladies

THE GLENVARROCH GATHERING
by Susan Pleydell

The advertisement in *The Times*

"Glenvarroch. Scottish family with large house on West Highland sea loch welcomes paying guests for summer holidays"

attracted an oddly assorted group: a schoolboy, an American couple, a schoolmistress from the Midlands, a young man writing a novel and an exotic brother and sister from London. But after a while the charm of the visitors begins to pall, and the C.I.D. warn Professor McKechnie that his daughter Fiona may be in danger.

Originally published in 1960

A YOUNG MAN'S FANCY
by Susan Pleydell

The spring term is always disaster-prone, but this one at Ledenham School surpasses itself. The Headmaster's invaluable secretary collapses with appendicitis and has to be replaced by Oonagh – 'Swooner' to the boys; a young master's fancy, lightly turning to thoughts of love, causes a major crisis at Governors' level; the Headmaster's daughter Alison's romance is all but blighted by avid public scrutiny and comment.

We meet several of the same characters from *Summer Term,* decent chaps and the right sort of girls, plus a few outright cads to give added spice.

Originally published in 1962

PETER WEST
by D. E. Stevenson

This turbulent love story, echoing through the generations, is set in the beautiful Highland village of Kintoul, with its tumbling river, ruined castle and pine-clad hills. It follows the mingled fortunes of the crofters, the minister and doctor, and those at Kintoul House – Peter West and the shades of his mother. This is a world where integrity and honour stand firm against the easy path, and despite many a wrong turning, are the only sure way to lasting happiness.

Peter West was originally published in 1923, both as a serial in *Chambers Magazine* and in book form.

THE DAY OF SMALL THINGS
by O. Douglas

"To you and to me this is the day of small things – Who said that? Someone in the Bible, wasn't it? And the small things keep you going wonderfully: the kindness of friends; the fact of being needed; nice meals; books; interesting plays; the funny people in the world; the sea and the space and the wind – not very small, are they, after all?"

Old friends and new in the Borders and Fife: Nicole and her mother, Lady Jane Rutherfurd; Mrs. Heggie; Mrs. Jackson; and Barbara Burt, now Mrs. Andrew Jackson, of Rutherfurd.

Originally published in 1930

LEADON HILL
by Richmal Crompton

Marcia Faversham, having despatched her husband John on a four-month fishing trip, is looking forward to the peace and tranquillity of the house without him. But not only does she have her young family – Hugo, a sturdy, golden child, slightly ashamed of his younger brother Tim, struggling to keep up in a surgical boot and irons after polio, and Moyna, gentle and kind but adoring Hugo – but there's Miss Mitcham causing difficulties.

Miss Mitcham, small and sharp, is a power to be feared in Leadon Hill, watching, watching, from behind the lace curtains of the drawing-room of Ivy Cottage, and dissecting reputations at her select little tea parties. Marcia suffers from their gossiping tongues, but now they have a new victim, for 'The Chestnuts' has at last been let, to Miss West, young, single – and from Italy.

Originally published in 1927.

MATTY AND THE DEARINGROYDES
by Richmal Crompton

Matty, even in her sixties, is game for any adventure. She has found in the second-hand clothes business a life of colour and excitement, and when Matthew Dearingroyde comes searching for his long-lost cousin to restore her to the bosom of her family, she is quite willing to bring her buccaneering spirit to the task of being a 'poor relation', shedding the tawdry finery she loves in favour of the subdued and genteel garments of Miss Matilda Dearingroyde.

In this warm and delightful novel, Richmal Crompton tells the story of Matty's impact on the different Dearingroyde homes at which she stays; of how she instinctively guesses at the drama which lies beneath the surface in each household; of how she shamelessly interferes and how, in the end she is gloriously triumphant.

Matty is a magnificent character.

Originally published in 1956

LITTLE G
by E. M. Channon

The story of how a crusty young Cambridge mathematician, prematurely set in his ways, is sent to the country for six months by his doctor and gradually learns that there is much more to life than mathematics.

A light-hearted witty soufflé of pretty women, roses, cats, tennis, and a most unexpected use for mathematics.

Originally published in 1936.